were looking for. They were both men with long experience in the Borderlands. This kind of action was second nature now. They moved laterally apart from each other, as if by signal but simply by instinct, yet still angling toward the target . . .

Which boiled up out of the sand with startling suddenness—and it was something Roland hadn't seen before. "What the hell is that?"

"It's a varkid!" Mordecai shouted, popping his gunstock to his shoulder and sighting in.

Roland was aiming too, as his mind came to grips with the varkid—a giant insectile red and black creature about the size of a skag, it seemed almost all jagged chiton, enormous barbed jaws, six clawed feet, no visible vulnerable parts. It was one of the most armored creatures he'd ever seen. And like pretty much any creature of Pandora, it was vicious and aggressive. It came at them, quick and scuttling, clacking its jaws open and shut hungrily. Those jaws were big enough to sever a man's head from his neck with one snip.

Roland only had time to fire from the hip, almost point-blank—a moment after Mordecai fired, hitting the cluster of three eyes behind its jaw parts. There was barely any head to aim at. Roland's shotgun spread caught the creature in its thorax, the blast knocking off chunks of its craggy natural armor plates.

The varkid squealed and retreated, shaking its foreparts in pain, just as Roland was taking aim again—and he assumed the thing was going to back off.

He was wrong. It leapt into the air, coming down on Mordecai before he could get a bead to fire again . . .

ALSO AVAILABLE FROM THE WORLD OF
BORDERLANDS

The Fallen

BORDERLANDS® UNCONQUERED

JOHN SHIRLEY

Based on the Gearbox
Borderlands games

POCKET BOOKS
New York   London   Toronto   Sydney   New Delhi

Pocket Books
A Division of Simon & Schuster, Inc.
1230 Avenue of the Americas
New York, NY 10020

This book is a work of fiction. Names, characters, places, and incidents either are products of the author's imagination or are used fictitiously. Any resemblance to actual events or locales or persons, living or dead, is entirely coincidental.

Written by John Shirley

First Pocket Books paperback edition October 2012

POCKET and colophon are registered trademarks of Simon & Schuster, Inc.

For information about special discounts for bulk purchases, please contact Simon & Schuster Special Sales at 1-866-506-1949 or business@simonandschuster.com.

The Simon & Schuster Speakers Bureau can bring authors to your live event. For more information or to book an event contact the Simon & Schuster Speakers Bureau at 1-866-248-3049 or visit our website at www.simonspeakers.com.

Manufactured in the United States of America

10 9 8 7 6 5 4 3 2 1

ISBN 978-1-4391-9848-3
ISBN 978-1-4391-9852-0 (ebook)

Dedicated to the fans of all Borderlands games

PROLOGUE

Marcus Tells a Tale

"Lady, I'll be getting you to ol' Fyrestone as quick as I can," Marcus said, looking in the bus rearview at the woman sitting a few rows behind him. He tapped his fingers on the steering wheel, pondering the situation. They were sitting on the tarmac of the spaceport, about half an hour before sunset, as he waited for a report on the bandits. There was a Claptrap robot sitting in a rear seat, muttering and clicking to itself; so far, he had no other passengers besides the robot and the lady. "I got an alert about a crew of particularly vicious Psycho bandits," Marcus went on. "A new bunch, just wandered into the Fyrestone region. Interlopers from the far side of the Arid Lands. We haven't had a hard bunch like this so close in a while. There're missions on the board to take 'em out, but no one's had the nerve yet. I'd do it myself, but I'm getting on in years, and . . ." He tapped his heavy belly. "I don't move so fast anymore. So I drive the bus, and I sell guns to other people so they can do it."

"That's all quite . . . *fascinating,*" the woman said, with undisguised sarcasm. "But when do we *go?* It'll be dark soon. I'd like to get to Fyrestone."

"Soon as I hear the coast is clear, we go. We've got to drive sharp, quick as we can, get through that territory."

Marcus checked his wrist communicator; there were still no missed calls, no texts, no report on those bandits. Maybe the ECHO link was down. He ran a quick link test on it, tapping the test icon, and . . . yep. It appeared the damn thing was down. Again. Bandits might've dismantled the transmission tower for scrap metal.

"I wonder why you don't have hoppers at the spaceport," said the woman. "Instead of this bus."

Her voice was silky, but there was a keen edge of warning in it, whatever she said. Something subtle in her tone conveyed, *Don't mess with me.* There was a stillness about her, too, a relaxed readiness, that suggested a professional warrior, someone who could handle herself. And he'd seen her take a high-quality pistol out of her luggage, sticking it in a holster just before she got onto the bus.

Her slim face and magenta hair were partly masked in purple dust goggles and helmet. What he could see of her looked kind of familiar, anyway, but she was sitting in shadow, and he couldn't view enough to place her. What with the helmet and goggles, worn from the moment she'd stepped off the shuttle from orbit, Marcus figured she didn't want to be recognized. Which hinted that maybe she wasn't a complete stranger to the planet Pandora. She was coming from deep space, but he suspected she might also be coming home. Only she didn't want people to know *who* was coming home . . .

The spaceport authorities would know whatever name she'd given them, and he had those guys on his payroll. But fake identities were easy to come by. Hell, he sold them himself sometimes.

That thought made Marcus wonder what he could sell to this woman. He could tell by her luggage and that gun, she had money, all right. Likely he could sell her some more weapons. He was going to have to try to draw her out, get a fix on who she was—could be that information itself might be worth money.

"Or *is* there a hopper that I haven't seen?" the woman went on, glancing out the window.

"Nah, no hoppers, lady. See, I arranged that . . . I mean, the only hopper service 'tween here and Fyrestone was shot down, right outta the sky. Bones of the riders picked clean. Not *safe,* those hoppers."

"So we're stuck with this old rattletrap bus," the woman murmured. Louder, she said, "I really have to get to Fyrestone. If you can check to see if you have any *balls,* we could just go. Any bandits bother us, we can take care of them between the two of us."

Marcus chuckled, still watching her in the rearview. "You're a salty one, you are. So you're a fighter, eh? We've had some tough women fighters on this planet—the only kind that survive."

"One way or another, all women are tough."

"And of course, General Goddess, that Gynella. Whew, that one!"

"Gynella?" She seemed to perk up at that, looking back at him—at his eyes in the mirror. "How's that panning out?"

"Oh, well, what's happened with that—well, that's a whole story. Be glad to tell you. Got the inside word on it from a lot of sources. I'm working up a history of Pandora, see, and I—"

"Suppose you tell me about it on the way to Fyrestone."

Marcus sighed, controlling his temper. "Now, look, lady—"

"This bus goin' anywhere?" asked a gruff male voice.

Marcus assessed the man climbing the steps into the bus. Big galoot with a swag belly, wide shoulders, small piggish eyes, a lantern jaw. But he was young, not long out of his teens. He had a lot of fresh-looking tattoos, and his mercenary costume looked secondhand. Cheap gems glittered in his gold front teeth; he had a rifle in one hand, duffel in the other, brand-new goggles pushed back on his close-shaved head.

Marcus knew the type. Likely a kid who'd failed at everything else—kicked out of some homeworld college, looking for a fresh start where the quick money was. Only most people looking for quick money in the Borderlands of Pandora found quick burials instead.

"Take a seat, kid, if you're going to Fyrestone," Marcus growled. "We're about to leave."

"Hey, pal, I ain't a kid, okay? You got that?" The young adventurer, standing in the aisle, put on his best angry-bull look.

Marcus snorted. "Could be you'll get the chance to prove it, you ride with us. We're about to run through some nasty bandit territory. And I haven't got the all-clear."

The adventurer licked his thin lips. "Yeah, well, if you think it's . . . you know . . ." Then he noticed the woman, sitting quietly in her seat. His vantage point from the door gave him a good view of the parts of her he was most interested in. She was voluptuous, and her battle-ready clothes were tight-fitting. Real tight-fitting.

The young man stared at her, and his mouth

dropped open. "I, uh . . . I can handle bandits. Um, who's . . . I mean, hi, lady. We going to be traveling together to Fyrestone? My name's Jakus." He pronounced it "Jake-us," with a long *a,* and he did it emphatically.

"Jakus. Naturally." They couldn't see her eyes, but her voice suggested she was rolling them.

"You haven't told me your name," Jakus said, trying to charm her with a grin that would have made a skag shudder.

"No," she said. "I haven't. Are we leaving or not, Marcus?"

"Sure, sure, get on the bus if you're coming, Jack-us."

"It's *Jake*-us." Frowning, the adventurer got into the seat across the aisle from the woman.

Who is *she?* Marcus wondered again, as he closed the doors and started up the bullet-scarred old bus. Clearly, he wasn't going to find that out easily.

She was interested in Gynella's story, it seemed. And he knew a hell of a lot about it—and about the other side of the equation: Roland, Mordecai, Brick, and Daphne. Yes, that was the way he'd do it. Tell the mystery lady the story, win her trust, then draw her out.

They were soon rumbling along the dusty, pocked highway toward Fyrestone, Marcus glancing nervously at his wrist communicator—still no word on the bandits—and scanning the horizon.

It was typical rugged gray-brown Pandora wasteland terrain, flat for long stretches but gouged with sudden ravines, shadowed by rocky buttes and stony hillocks, which often stood alone, like weathered fortresses in the dusty mist. It was hot out there, the pale blue, cloudless sky looking sun-faded. Desert plants flecked the landscape, casting long shadows as the sun slipped toward the serrated horizon; in the distance he could see small packs of skags wandering near their burrows, forever hungry for prey, and vulturine rakks turned kitelike in the sky. The bus thumped over the remains of some large yellow scythids, their carapaces crushed; he'd smashed them into roadkill on the way to the spaceport.

On some of the higher buttes, in the distance, he could see the tops turning pink and dull scarlet— sunset was coming. It'd be dark soon . . .

When he could, Marcus kept an eye on the two humans in back, tilting the rearview mirror for a better look—the interior mirror wasn't good for anything but looking at the passengers—and he wasn't surprised when Jakus set his rifle aside and moved across the aisle to the seat beside the mystery woman. Jakus put his arm across the back of her seat and leaned toward her, trying to look suave.

"So, pretty lady, when we get to Fyrestone, we could have a drink, whatya say? I'm buying, of course, and then maybe we could find us a cozy little—ow!"

She'd shoved her pistol's muzzle hard against his jaw. "Get back in your seat, or I'm gonna have to splatter your brains on the ceiling. If there *are* any in there to splatter."

Jakus gulped and hurried back to his seat.

"Hey, she's a pistol, ain't she, kid?" Marcus laughed. "Ha, get it, a—"

"Shut up, you old—! Wait, who's that on the road up there?"

The kid pointed, and Marcus returned his attention to the road just in time to slam on the brakes. The dust plume following the bus kept going when the bus stopped, shrouding the windows. But he saw them, clear enough, about twenty meters ahead: four Psycho bandits, and towering over them a Bruiser, all of them masked and bare-chested, blocking the road side by side, all with powerful weapons in their hands.

"By the Angel!" Marcus swore.

"They do not look like paying passengers," the Claptrap robot called tremulously from the back. "I do not advise letting them on board."

Marcus's expert eye automatically evaluated the Psychos' weapons. The Bruiser, on the right, had an Eridian blaster rifle, alien tech that fired energy balls; the other four, right to left, respectively carried a GPR330 Painful Death shotgun, a Dahl

Punishing Pounder combat rifle, a Tediore Genocide Guardian, and a Hyperion Sentinel combat rifle. He made the mental catalogue in a few seconds. "Shit! Just the bastards I was planning to not run into."

"You *oughta* run into them!" the woman snapped. "Run 'em over, and let's get on down the road!"

Marcus had been considering doing just that, but her contemptuous tone almost made him put the bus in reverse instead. Then he saw the Bruiser raise his blaster and point it his way—no way he could let that murderous lunatic get a bead on him while he was backing up.

He slammed his boot hard down on the accelerator.

The bus roared forward right at the Psychos, and almost instantly a big piece of his windshield vanished from its frame to his right, the glass and broken louvers coming into the bus in spinning fragments, some of them cutting Marcus's cheek, nicking an earlobe. Other rounds slammed into the engine, and then the Psychos scattered, all of them getting out of the way in time except for the smallest one in the middle.

The bus's front wheels crunched over the littlest Psycho, squeezing one long and piteous scream from him.

Psycho roadkill for the trash feeders, Marcus thought, grinning to himself.

Smoke was rising from the engine, and it was making a *chucka-chucka* sound it had never made before. But they kept moving—

—until the bus shuddered as an Eridian blaster impact struck it, and he heard a back tire blow. The hulking vehicle swerved sickeningly as he struggled with the wheel; then a hummock of shrubs and rock seemed to rush up at him till they came to a jolting stop, Marcus clutching at the wheel to keep from going through the windshield.

Dust and smoke billowed around them, swirled chokingly through the shattered windshield.

Grimacing with pain in his back, Marcus straightened up and looked at the engine lights, then out the windshield.

The engine was dead, steaming, smoking, the front end dented. But the engine didn't look totaled from there.

He tried restarting. It said *chucka-chucka-chuck* and nothing else.

He got up, grabbed the weapon he kept racked to the left of the driver's seat. It was a Vladof ZX10/V3 Detonating Hammer assault shotgun. He'd thought of bringing a rocket launcher along, but they made some of the temporary visitors to Fyrestone nervous. What the hell did they expect? This planet had the rep of being the most dangerous world with breathable atmosphere in the galaxy. He should have brought the big guns—and an extra shield. The only energy shield he had on the bus had burned out on the way to the spaceport. Cheap off-brand gear . . .

Marcus opened the door, glancing over to see if his passengers were dead.

Good, they were shaken but alive. He hated swabbing blood and guts from his bus. But he rarely had to do it. No more than a few times a year.

The Claptrap robot in back was jumping up and down in excitement. "This is not part of the itinerary, hellooooooo!"

The young tattooed adventurer was licking his lips, looking nervously out the dusty windows, peering between the metal louvers. "Where— where are they? You killed one, maybe, but . . ."

"They're out there, and they're not far behind," Marcus said, climbing out of the bus.

"Then you oughta close that door!"

"How am I gonna figure out if we can drive outta here otherwise, ya dumb son of a mama skag?" Marcus called out as he stepped onto the stony ground.

Checking the shotgun's readiness as he went, Marcus hurried, coughing in the dust and smoke, to the engine. He could see sparks crackling, but it looked more or less intact. Salvageable once he got it to a shop. But he was going to need help getting it there.

Shotgun at the ready, Marcus scanned the area,

looking down the highway, which was about ten meters from the back of the bus. He didn't see the Psychos. He knew damn well they were out there, and they'd be back soon, when they'd worked out their tactics. Smarter than some Psychos—a lot of them would run at you screaming. The Bruiser knew there'd be weapons on the bus, and they'd be coming, soon enough, probably at a flanking angle.

Marcus checked his ECHO communicator. Still no response from Fyrestone. Not that anyone there was reliable at the best of times.

Swearing to himself, Marcus climbed back up onto the bus, closed the door, and sat in the driver's seat, hurriedly flipping on the bus's transmitter. It had a little more reach than his ECHO comm. He tapped it and, wincing with pain, leaned over to speak into the grid. "Anybody there? Fyrestone?"

The only response was a crackle from the speakers.

He shifted the bus's transmitter to aim at T-Bone Junction. Last he'd heard, Scooter was working out there. He was the best man on the planet for automotive emergencies. When he was sober.

"Scooter! This is Marcus, you picking up? You out there?"

Another crackle. Then, "Hey, Marcus, you old gut humper!" came Scooter's voice on the ECHO, thick with an unplaceable bumpkin accent. "You done got your bus in a skizz hole again?"

"Ran into some Psychos. Squished one, but there's four of 'em left, and I can't raise anybody from Fyrestone. Link's down. You're the only one I can raise!"

"Well, catch a ride, boy!"

"I'm nowhere near none of your ride stations, dammit! We can't walk to one without getting my passengers killed. Spaceport frowns on that!"

"Well, hellfire in a honey box! I'm a gonna have to get you some help. See what I can scare up. Take me some time, now. You're gonna have to hunker down and kill you some Psychos and whatnot. And probably some skags, could be some of them fire skags out there between the town and that spaceport. And maybe some tarantellas, then ag'in, now, could be some skrappies, maybe a nice 'n' smelly rakk or two, not to mention them hungry ol' crabworms—"

"They're coming!" the kid shouted, his voice hoarse with fear. "The Psychos! They're out to the left side of the bus there!"

"Scooter!" Marcus said. "Listen up! You got to send help and a repair crew!"

"Like I said, I'll do 'er, but it's going to take a while to get 'em there, pardner. We'll make it quick as we can, quick as a greased-up—"

A rifle round sped between armor louvers and shattered a side window.

"Scooter! Can you trace my coordinates from this signal?"

"Yep, I got your location, just hold 'em off there,

old son—we'll see what we can do. Won't be real quick, but if you can hold out, why, I'm gonna charge you a big stack of cash for this'n—"

Marcus switched off the transmitter and ducked down, not a split second too quickly.

The window next to the driver's seat exploded inward, blasted by an energy ball that singed the top of his head as it went past to detonate on his right. Shrapnel from a shattered window louver zinged past.

"Anybody dead yet?" he yelled, looking over the back of his seat at his passengers.

"We *will* be if we don't take the fight to the enemy!" the woman yelled fiercely. "I say we get out and rush 'em! With me around, you might actually get somewhere!" She was hunched between seats, but he saw her goggled face bob up long enough to fire her pistol four times out a shattered window. "Crap! I think I missed the bastard . . . No! I got him! I got that Bruiser . . . Oh, wait, he's up. I just wounded him." She ducked back down as half a dozen bullets slammed into the armored side of the bus.

"You got any shields, lady?" Marcus asked her.

"Naw, I was gonna buy one from you!"

"And I got plenty for you to buy, but they're over in Fyrestone. Only one I had on the bus crapped out on me when I drove out to the spaceport."

Jakus was flattened on the floor as three more

energized bullets sizzled screaming into the bus. Another tire blew. "What we gonna *do*?" Jakus called. "Driver? Yo! You got any ideas?"

"Listen, amateur—" the woman began, turning to Jakus.

"I'm not an amateur!"

"Okay, prove it! Get out there and head 'em off! If you're going to survive on this planet, you've got to be able to take out a handful of Psycho bandits on your own! You've got the rifle! All I have with me's a pistol!"

"Yeah, well, uh . . . How about sending the robot out first?"

"That would *not* be a recommended use of my hardware!" the robot protested shrilly. "My guarantee has expired! Hellloooooooo!"

Marcus shook his head impatiently. "The robots, they aren't fighters, kid. That's not what they're for."

"Look, *Jakus*," the woman went on, "you want to give me the rifle, *I'll* do it. But you better head back to the spaceport after. You're not going to survive out here without the guts to fight!"

Marcus looked at Jakus, saw him chewing his lower lip. Then the amateur nodded, prepped his rifle, got up, and headed to the door. His voice was hoarse as he said, "I'm *goin'*."

"Might do just as well to fight from the bus, kid," Marcus pointed out.

"I . . . I'm gonna see if I can sneak up on them, maybe if I nail the big one . . ."

Marcus shrugged and opened the door. It would keep the Psychos busy, anyway.

Jakus stepped outside the bus, looking around, face twitching. Then he headed off around the hummock, hunched over, rifle at the ready to fire from the hip.

Marcus lost sight of him. A few seconds passed. Then he heard a thud, saw a flash of light . . . and something flew over the hummock, falling like a soggy cannonball on the hood of the bus.

It was Jakus's head, blasted from his neck, rolling to stare sightlessly right at Marcus.

"That's not what I meant by 'head them off,'" the woman said dryly. "Damn amateurs."

Marcus sighed. "Dumb kid! Well, anyhow, we know where some of 'em are."

"Dammit, I should've taken his rifle," the woman grumbled, shaking her head in disgust. "How about giving me that shotgun? I'll trade you the pistol. Give you the Vladof back later."

So she knew her weapons. Who the hell *was* she? "And if you get killed? The Psychos gonna give it back to me later? I don't think so, lady. Not a chance."

"Okay, fine. But if we just sit around in here, they're gonna blow this bus up with us in it." She started for the door. "I'm not waiting to be fried in this hunk of junk. While you're enjoying your break, I'm gonna see if I can take a couple out, discourage the scum from getting too close."

"Wait a minute, dammit! We'll go together and stick close to the bus. Come on."

Hefting the shotgun, Marcus went out the door first; she followed behind, pistol ready.

"I'll stay here and keep an eye on things in the bus!" the Claptrap called after them. "Ah-ha, yes. This seat needs cleaning, by the way. I'll make a note of it."

Marcus looked around, but the Psychos were keeping their heads down. He pointed to a spot where she could hunker behind a low boulder, on the right side of the hummock, and she nodded, moved quickly to station herself there.

He climbed over the still-steaming front bumper of the truck to get to the other, stepped onto the ground, and saw a Psycho bandit coming around the hummock, bent from the waist and surprised to see him waiting there.

He fired the shotgun almost point-blank and exploded the bandit's head from his shoulders.

"A head for a head," Marcus muttered as the bandit flopped dead at his feet.

He heard a noise and looked up to see another bandit, this one with a scar slashed across his bare chest in an X shape.

The bandit fired spasmodically, the round going

over Marcus's shoulder, and jumped back as Marcus fired. Marcus's shot missed him, but then he heard the *crack-crack* of the woman's pistol. Just as he'd hoped, the bandit had backed into her firing line.

Marcus didn't bother to check. That woman knew what she was doing.

He grabbed the first bandit's weapon, then turned to look at the bus—and swore. The shot that missed him had smashed into the severed head on the bus's hood, blasted it to pieces, scattered them all over what was left of the windshield and inside.

"Gonna be cleaning up messes till sunrise," he said. He climbed back over the bumper and went to look for the woman.

On the other side of the hummock, he glimpsed a flash of light, a blinking outline of a woman that was there and gone—and a Psycho staggering back, lightly wounded. The Psycho dived behind an outcropping of blue stone.

Where was the woman? It'd looked as if she'd gone invisible for a moment . . .

No, he must've been wrong. It was dusk, starting to get dim and shadowy. He must have been seeing things.

Then she was there, behind, tapping him on the shoulder. "We'd better get in the bus."

He opened his mouth to ask her about what he'd seen, but she turned away from him in a way that suggested she didn't want any questions. He mutely followed her back to the bus.

What was going on? Had he really seen her vanish? How had she reappeared behind him?

They climbed into the bus and closed the door.

"Am I . . . am I safe now?" the Claptrap asked.

Marcus ignored the robot. He checked the ECHO—no new messages had come through. But Scooter had been clear that he was sending help, and despite his eccentricities, Scooter was usually dependable.

He carried his shotgun to a seat a few rows back and settled in where he had the best cover. Keeping his head low, he peered through the louvered windows, seeing no movement. "I don't see anybody. If you wounded that Bruiser, as you figured earlier . . . and wounded that Psycho . . ."

The woman nodded as she sat across the aisle from him. "Yeah—I figure they'll be licking their wounds."

"That's disgusting!" the Claptrap called out.

"It's only an expression," she said absently. Adding to Marcus, "They'll be patching themselves up, thinking about how to go at us. Probably be near dawn before they make a move."

Marcus nodded. "That's my instinct. With luck, Scooter'll get someone here to help us by then."

Time passed—maybe not much. A minute felt like an hour as they waited for another attack.

Finally, the woman said, "Well . . . I don't think I can sleep. Know any stories?"

"Yes, *do* tell a story!" the Claptrap shrilled. "Do you know the story about the Brave Little Claptrap?"

The woman rolled her eyes. "Anyway, you were mentioning Gynella . . . and Roland. I'm curious about that."

"Are you?" What was her interest in Gynella and Roland? "Okay. I've got a few supplies in the bus. We can have something to eat, a drink, and I'll tell you a story. A true story. As far as I know. It's about Roland and what happened when he and Mordecai and Brick got together and . . . ah! This happened a ways back but then again, not so very long ago. It started, as so many stories do, in Fyrestone. On a certain day, when Roland showed up there, looking for someone in particular . . ."

ONE

Squinting against the noon light glancing off scrap metal, Roland jumped out of his scratched, dented, blast-blackened outrunner. He looked down Fyrestone's sunbaked, dusty main street with a certain feeling of disbelief.

He could hardly believe he was back *here* again.

A lot of Fyrestone looked like an aboriginal camp, with circular huts and lodges, but made out of rust-streaked metal, many of them with gatelike steel doors and big numbers painted on the side. Some appeared to be made from parts of old surplus spacecraft and assorted junk, welded together in the vague shapes of shops and impromptu dwellings; others looked prefab, probably brought there by prospectors and Vault Hunters, kits assembled by robots. Nobody'd made any effort at decoration; there were more graves than there were people.

What a hole.

But somehow, he thought as he strolled down the street, hand on his shotgun stock holding the gun barrel casually on his shoulder, *everything seems to start here.*

And it was here, he'd heard, that he'd find Skelton Dabbits, the mining engineer who'd gotten hold of the orbital scans, if Roland's source in New Haven was to be believed. Energy signatures on the engineer's purported scans indicated crystalisks, out past the Eridian Promontory.

Roland was crystalisk hunting. They were part of his retirement plan. He was thinking of making a bundle on Eridium crystals, using the moolah to get to Xanthus—a watery world, as different a planet from this one as he could imagine. He wanted to look up some old friends. Maybe start a sport-fishing business. He used to like to go sport fishing for the big ones, back on the homeworld. And he'd had a bellyful of Pandora.

But that kind of lifestyle change was going to take money. Crystalisks might just provide the scratch he needed.

Asking around, Roland was directed to a small, hemispherical, metal-mesh hut on a side trail— you couldn't really call it a street—off the main drag of Fyrestone.

He found Skelton Dabbits sitting out front in the sunshine, using a large skag skull as a stool.

Dabbits was a spindly little man in mining togs that were too large for him; they hung on him as if he were a coat rack. The hair on his bald, freckled head was wispy, and so was his beard. He was alternately drinking from a flask and chewing smoked Primal testicles. He looked up at Roland through his green-tinted goggles, seeming unsurprised to see him—must have gotten the message Roland had sent through Scooter.

Dabbits asked, "You *him*?"

"I'm Roland, if that's the him you mean."

"That's the him! Roland!"

"You Skelton Dabbits?"

"If that's the me you mean. Skelton Dabbits is me all over! You care for some of this?" He offered the flask. "Got some real sweet little narco oil mixed in it. Might make you nod a bit."

"No thanks. How much for the scans?"

Dabbits cringed a little and looked up and down the side street. Almost whispering, he said, "Keep your voice down about that, mister! I had to steal those babies from my last employer. As for how much, that is a matter for consideration, and I'm still considering it." He saluted Roland with his flask, took another pull on it, and his head drooped a little. He seemed to stare off into the sky, as if he could see through the atmosphere to another planet entirely . . .

"Dabbits!" Roland said sharply.

His head jerked up. "What? Where?"

"*The scans*, man. How much?"

"I told you . . . I'm considering on that. They won't go cheap. Took a big risk. I don't know if they found out I broke into that mainframe and printed 'em out. If they did, the bastards at Dahl will come after me. But see, they fired me, and that wasn't fair, no justice in it, so I stole those scans to get my own back."

Roland wondered how reliable Dabbits could be. "What you get fired for, exactly?"

"Oh, they said I was a narco head. Just because I nodded off while I was flying the prospecting hopper and it crashed into a . . . well, we don't need to talk about that."

Roland shrugged. "I'll give you three hundred for the scans, sight unseen."

"Three hundred! No screekin' way, bucko! I took a big chance, putting the word out down here, about those crystalisk readings. There's big money in it, you'll get rich off 'em, and you'll be laughing that you got the scans off an old fool for a pittance and a penny."

"If there're such big riches in it, why don't you go claim it yourself?"

"Because it's dangerous territory! For one thing, General Goddess is right in the way. And she's shooting down anything that flies over. Orbital shuttles won't take you there, nor hoppers. Too dangerous. You got to go overland. I look like I could make that trip? I'm an engineer, not a fighter. Soon's I sell these scans, I'm getting off this hellhole of a world, and I know a nice, quiet planet where they got some righteous narcoweed growing wild. Why, you can pick it like posies—"

"Dabbits? I'll make it five hundred."

"Five hundred? Why, that's not half enough to pay my way!"

Another five minutes of haggling, and they settled on a thousand. Roland paid him, declined the bag of Primal testicles Dabbits wanted to throw in on the deal, and took his scans back to the outrunner.

Back on the sunny main drag, Roland sat in the driver's seat—the outrunner was a two-seater, apart from the support for the turret gunner behind—and spread the semitransparent scan sheets out on his lap, holding them below the line of sight of anyone who might be looking his way. He squinted at the scan map and nodded to himself. The crystalisk den—biggest concentration of the creatures yet found on the planet—was marked in Dabbits's shaky handwriting. Roland knew enough about energy signatures to recognize the flare lines Dabbits had circled. It sure looked authentic—Eridium that moved around, seemingly migrated. That meant crystalisks.

Trouble was, the entrance to the den complex

was southwest of the Eridian Promontory, the other side of a lot of desert and a big mountain range. And it was true there weren't any hoppers going out that way. Dabbits was right—he was going to have to go overland by outrunner. That'd put him right up to his neck in bandits, and maybe the army of General Goddess. Bandits he could handle. But armies? He'd need a couple of solid fighters along to help him with that.

Last he knew, Brick was over in the settlement on Jawbone Ridge, acting as a bodyguard to some mining agent. That'd be a start. Hell, Brick was a couple of guys all in one.

If Roland brought Brick in, he'd have to split his profits with him, but judging by the flare-line strength, there should be plenty of Eridium crystals to go around.

Smartun was waiting for his Goddess.

A man of medium height, intense black eyes, and otherwise unremarkable features, Smartun leaned against a wall in the shade of the Devil's Footstool coliseum. Gynella had converted the rickety coliseum atop the Footstool to a kind of temporary fortress.

Heart thudding with anticipation, Smartun waited for Gynella, outwardly calm, arms folded across his metal breastplate. Rakks wheeled and wended, not far above the narrow windswept butte of naked stone. He looked off to his right, past the edge of the cliff and across the burning white desert far below the top of the Devil's Footstool—the Salt Flats.

Heat shimmered up off the flatlands, a long way below the high, columnar, chop-top pinnacle of the Footstool; the far horizon was blurred by heat, dust, and, perhaps, an unknown murk given off by sheer desperation.

Smartun heard a muffled shout and looked across the parade ground at the barracks. They were getting restless in there. The barracks was a fairly new construction, a big Quonset-shaped metal building, housing Gynella's core militia of two hundred soldiers.

The wind sighed and lifted skirls of dust from the parade ground—and then the metal door of the new First Division quarters banged open, and the Psycho bandits and other thugs who'd joined the Division began to troop noisily out, hooting and muttering standard imprecations.

Smartun snorted to himself. For better or worse, they were his people now. Mostly for the worse. Or it would be for the worse if *she* weren't around.

He was a relative newcomer to the planet. Wanted for cat burglary, pocket vacuuming, and human trafficking on Red Ferrous Three and for Egregious Sneaking and Corrosive Treachery on the Mudball Colonies, he'd fled to the one planet law enforcement had given up on. Unlike the Psychos and the Bruisers and the other demented thugs of the Pandoran backcountry, he had not been there long, hadn't been damaged and mutated by the curious radiation of the Headstone Mine, the subtle emanation of Eridium-based devices, or the warping effect of Vault obsession. In consequence, Smartun's brain worked fairly well, despite his sociopathy, and he was usually able to think things through. Hence his fellow expatriates—abandoned criminals who'd become the various Psychos of Pandora—knew him as Smartun, for "the smart one," and he had almost forgotten the name he'd been given at birth: Albatoir Anzlesnass. Forgetting that name was a development to his liking.

Smartun nodded a polite greeting to Flugg, the much-scarred Bruiser whom Gynella had made into a sergeant, as Flugg swaggered out to inspect the troops. The sergeant only glowered back and, waving his rusty hatchet, snarled instructions at the Psychos and the other bandits, the human debris that General Goddess had gathered up into her First Division army. They were a ragtag bunch, and like most of the wild bandits on Pandora, they wore no shirts; they were muscularly ripped, randomly deformed, foul-smelling, some wearing goggles and masks.

But there was one concession to military

uniformity. On each man's chest was an image, tattooed or worn in a crude banner in place of a shirt, of the letter G, in scarlet, somehow made to resemble a skull viewed in profile, under which were the silhouettes of rifles crossed like crossbones.

It took several minutes, but Flugg managed to get the troops lined up in five almost orderly rows facing the entrance to the coliseum fortress. Not a moment too soon, for then the double doors of the fortress creaked open, and out strode Gynella herself, the "General Goddess" of the Army of Pandora. Gynella was at least a head taller than Smartun and more broad-shouldered, muscular, physically powerful—but she was perfectly proportioned, a beautiful golden-skinned woman with flowing flaxen hair, glinting almond-shaped emerald eyes, full red lips that needed no cosmetic in an oval, strong-boned face that seemed perfectly shaped for a man to cup in his hands. She wore a silken red cape and a tight, plunging, lightly armored bodice of black and silver, emblazoned in red with her skullish G and crossed-rifles symbol. Her powerful tanned thighs—he had to avert his eyes from those, as the sight made him feel faint with desire—were set off by knee-high scarlet and black boots and the black edges of a metallic blue microskirt. Holstered on her right hip was an Eridian pistol; on her left was a short sword in a silver scabbard. Her long-fingered hands were gauntleted in black and leather, exposing only her bloodred fingernails. She clicked those nails now on the metal of her skirt, as she stood with her hands on her full hips, gazing at the core cadre of her army.

Gods above and devils below, he thought. *I adore her.*

At her side was the cadaverous Dr. Vialle, dressed in a white smock and rubber gloves and dingy bloodstained white trousers. Close behind them came her hulking bodyguard, Runch Menzes, whom Smartun believed to be a creation of Dr. Vialle. There were clues to Runch's laboratory origins in the facts that his bulging eyes were set so wide they were nearly on the side of his head, his mouth was but a wide slit that almost bisected his great, thick, scaly head, and his right arm ended in something like a crustacean's pincer instead of a hand. More to the point, Runch's mouth, when opened wide enough, could extrude acid-dripping insectile mandibles. As if to make up for his physical hodgepodge, Runch wore an elaborate uniform, designed by General Goddess herself, made of shiny dark blue leather and gun-metal links. On his chest was the ever-present symbol, stenciled across the links. Vialle wore Gynella's symbol, too, in the form of a pendant. Smartun himself wore the insignia stenciled across his chest, in red, on the bullet-resistant breastplate he'd brought along from Red Ferrous Three.

Smartun took a respectful step toward Gynella, carefully not coming too close, aware of Runch's bulging eyes watching his every move.

Saluting crisply, Smartun said, "First Division is present and accounted for, my General."

He barely managed not to stammer as he said "my General," trembling with the phrase's implication of her being *his*. As if she could be his, in any sense at all. He lived for Gynella, his General Goddess . . .

She nodded to him. "Very good, Lieutenant."

He adored her imperiousness, the sense of entitlement that she wore as flaringly as the red cape, the way the delicacy of her flaxen eyelashes contrasted with the hard slice of her gaze as she inspected her charges.

He would die for her, of course. But he had other hopes. Foolish dreams they were, perhaps, since she hadn't given him much reason to hope. But if he served her one way, could he not serve her another?

She took one graceful but decisive step toward the men, into the sunlight, so that the metal highlights of her armored décolletage shot out glints. Her troops ogled her shamelessly, gazing at her as if hypnotized, their reeking collective breath rolling out from their gaping mouths as they waited in pent-up expectation. Slowly she raised her right hand to the medallion she wore around her neck—a mere circle of platinum on a silver chain, with a grid in its center, but an object of great significance. And when she touched it, the men all groaned softly, in concert.

The medallion contained the ActiTone, the locus of her control over them. But she merely tapped it, as if absentmindedly, with the nail of her index finger as she spoke, her deep, sensuously resonant voice carrying easily across the parade ground.

"Men of the First Division! You have chosen to leave the chaos and misery of your former lives, for a life of meaning, a life of order—and of power!"

The word *power* elicited a roar of approval from them.

"Quiet, you scum!" bellowed Sergeant Flugg.

Gynella, their General Goddess, went on. "And so, to bring order and lawfulness and profit for those of us who bring it, to make this planet peaceful and ourselves rich . . ."

Another roar of approval at the word *rich*.

"We shall expand our numbers. We shall move onward! We shall take more territory! Today, prepare yourselves for the attack we shall carry out tonight, on a prosperous . . ." She hesitated, knowing that many of them didn't know what that word meant. "A rich new settlement that will give us more troops, more resources, more weapons, more land . . . and some women to entertain the very bravest of my soldiers!"

Oh, Lord, but she's ruthless, Smartun thought approvingly, as her men roared lustily. *Truly a goddess.*

"And now," Gynella boomed. "Will you follow me into battle?"

As usual, the First Division shouted in unison, "We will!"

"And will you fight to the death for the banner of a new world?"

"WE WILL!"

"Then . . ." She grinned sharkishly, her fingers going to the circle of metal around the grid on her medallion. The men moaned in anticipation. They knew what was coming. *"THEN FEEL MY LOVE!"*

And with that, she pointed a finger at the men, while with the other hand she twisted the dial on the device, and the ActiTone chimed like a bell made of thin diamond. The sound seemed to gather strength, to amplify across the Devil's Footstool; the very air quivered visibly with it. She made her arm quiver, giving the impression that the impulse was traveling from her pointing finger.

All of the men standing before her, including the sergeant, fell to their knees, groaning with pleasure, hips bucking, eyes rolling, saliva dripping from their open mouths, as the ActiTone activated the pleasure centers of their brains.

Smartun, however, felt nothing from the ActiTone. He had not been treated with the susceptibility drug the way the others had. Gynella and Dr. Vialle, who had come together from Kali Four half a galaxy away, had brought the Acti-Tone and thousands of doses of the SusDrug, as Vialle called it, stolen from the Dahl Corporation's chemicals research lab. Homeworld Security had pursued them and lost the trail.

Smartun had taken up with Gynella the moment he saw her; he adored her already. He didn't need a drug with a vibratory trigger. It had worked on the Psychos they'd captured. It had allowed her, bit by bit, to build up a small army. It might allow her to take over the planet.

Gynella switched off the ActiTone, and the men fell on their faces, gasping and spent, murmuring her name. "Gynella . . ."

One of them surprised Smartun. The biggest Psycho brute of the bunch, a one-eyed, noseless murderer called Splonk, got up and staggered toward Gynella. "More!" he said. "Want you! Want . . . your . . ."

The other men looked up with a mix of horror and fascination as the big brute stalked swayingly toward their General Goddess.

The sergeant and her bodyguard and Smartun— all three at once—started to block the oncoming Splonk. But Gynella made an imperious gesture with a slash of her hand. "No! Let him approach if he dares!"

The men gasped and murmured at that. Was it really possible she would let him touch her? And...?

She waited calmly until Splonk was in reach. She smiled. He reached for her. Her right hand flashed, drawing her short sword. Her body spun in place as she drew it, and as she came back around, the blade slashed lightning fast through Splonk's midsection, right through his waist.

The Psycho Bruiser stopped, gaping, gagging, staring... then looked down as she drew out the sword with an expression of contempt. He watched as his entrails slopped onto the ground at his feet.

Splonk sagged to his knees, then fell forward onto his own entrails with a sickening *squish*. The smell of blood and excrement rose richly from the corpse.

Gynella yawned, then bent, delicately wiped the blade on the Psycho Bruiser's back, and resheathed it as she straightened up. "You others—back to your barracks. Rest! We fight tonight!"

She flicked a hand at them, and they backed away, then turned and went mutteringly, sated and exhausted, into the barracks. Smartun called to Sergeant Flugg, who turned from the barracks door with a look of resentment that was so plain it could've been a hand-painted sign. Flugg passionately hated taking orders from Smartun. "Yes, Lieutenant?"

Smartun pointed at the reeking cadaver of Splonk. "Clean up that mess, Sergeant. Feed it to the skags in pen three."

Flugg looked as if he wanted to snarl a refusal, but he glanced at Gynella, saw the look in her eye, and gave Smartun a sloppy salute. "Sure thing, Lieutenant."

Gynella turned to Smartun. "I have a mission for you. Come inside."

Licking his lips, Smartun nodded and followed her into the entranceway to the old coliseum. Vialle followed them; Runch stationed himself in the shade, outside the door, to keep an eye on the barracks.

As the door closed behind them, the metal latch echoing in the bare rusty-steel hallway, she turned first to Vialle. "Doctor, for the first time, the drug failed! Perhaps we're not giving it to them often enough."

"Failed?" He shook his head. "It worked!" he declared in his piping, oily voice. "Even on that oaf you killed. But human behavior—or, in this case, semihuman behavior—is not entirely predictable. There are always a few variables and oddities, with genetically random degrees of resistance. But you handled it perfectly! The occasional thug with a bit of self-will will be winnowed out, exactly as you did it. I salute your efficiency!" His mouth twisted in a mocking smile as he bowed to her.

"Better increase the dose anyway," she said. "Go on, back to your lab. I want to talk to my special operative."

Special operative. He loved it when she called him that.

"Listen, Smartun," she said, taking a small computer memory tab from a pocket of her skirt. "Take this, put it in your palmer, study the files. Selina cracked Dahl's threat-assessment program for Pandora. We've found a group of people who have to either be recruited or eliminated. First on the list . . . one Lilith." She grimaced and shook her head. "Too powerful, and she'll never submit to my rule. I knew her off-planet. If Lilith comes back to this dirtball, have her assassinated. Immediately! And using every resource at your command! And *don't try to do it yourself*. Get someone expert to shoot her in the back. She's too dangerous to take on headfirst. The second one on the list is a certain Mordecai. He's a crack shot. Might be of use . . . and might be recruitable. Third, there's a Bruiser called Brick."

"I've heard of him."

"Brick would definitely be useful to me—on several levels, I suspect. But if he can't be recruited, see that he's eliminated as well. Still, we'll try the Sus-Drug on him first. And the last one—you ever hear of a mercenary, former military, name of Roland?"

"Big black guy?"

Her nostrils flared. "*Oh* yes. That's him."

Smartun grunted. "I saw him in action once, from a distance, just outside of New Haven. Bunch of raiders jumped him, tried to take his outrunner. Kind of surprising how little time it took him to deal with it. He killed four men in three seconds."

"Exactly! Good-looking galoot, too. I've got surveillance vid of him in action. He really caught my eye."

Smartun didn't like the sound of that. But he kept his expression neutral and said only, "Not my type."

She smiled icily at his feeble joke. "He's *our* type—a deadly soldier. If we can recruit him, he'd make a great subcommander. His military experience would be quite useful."

"And suppose he can't be recruited? Suppose he resists the SusDrug—and anything else you might offer."

"Oh," she said, shrugging airily as she turned to walk toward the door of her headquarters. "If Roland refuses us, if he truly resists . . . then see that he's killed. But kill him with respect. A nice clean head shot."

This town, Roland thought, striding down the rubbishy street, *makes Fyrestone look like an urban paradise.*

Jawbone Ridge was a crusty, dusty, trash-strewn settlement of shacks, humplike cement bunkers, retrofitted mining trailers, and tents on a long, wide ledge of rock just under a toothy, jawbone-like ridgetop of dull red stone. Come to think of it, Roland figured, you couldn't really say it was a settlement. More like one of those vacant lots where debris piles up, just gets blown there by the wind. The gritty wind of the desert had brought the town mostly shady con men, out-of-work thugs, failed miners, itinerant drunks—Jawbone Ridge was known for its numerous liquor stills—and a few shopkeepers. The shopkeepers, Roland saw, had slammed their steel shutters down to coincide with sunset. It seemed they were afraid of something. The sun wasn't quite down completely, but already the place was shut up tight—except for the Steel Incisor Saloon down at the end of the road. The boozing dive was made of pieces of old mining machines, trucks, earthmovers, and robots, all cobbled together, welded into the boxy shape of a building like a wrongly made jigsaw puzzle.

Roland put a hand on the Hyperion Invader automatic pistol holstered to his right hip and headed down the street to where light spilled out the open front door of the saloon and someone giggled madly from within.

So far, asking around the area, he hadn't been able to find Brick. He'd seen a wanted poster of him, put up by Atlas—the Atlas Corp. was mad at him for something or other. He'd spotted a place where a wall looked as if it had been punched right through—Brick liked to punch through wanted posters. But no Brick himself, not in person.

If Brick worked as a bodyguard for a mining boss, where was the mine? The only mining concern left in the area might not be in the town itself. So where was it—and where was Brick?

Instead of Brick, he found Mordecai. Roland stumbled right across him, literally, as he walked in through the door of the Steel Incisor Saloon. He tripped over the groaning, prostrate figure of the legendary Pandora gunman.

"Ow!" Mordecai said.

"Sorry," said Roland, leaning over to help him stand—which wasn't hard, since Mordecai was a lean little guy. Lean but wiry, and dangerous. He had a pointed black beard, a leather helmet, and goggles; unruly black hair thrust like a rooster tail out the back of the helmet. "Didn't see you there, Mordecai."

"Not you with the ow. *Them!* They smashed two bottles over my head. At once. One each."

Mordecai pointed at two women standing at the bar across the room—like everything else in the saloon, it was made of random rusty metal parts. One of the women was short and stocky, with 'roided, heavily tattooed bare arms; she wore a sleeveless camo-patterned paramilitary outfit with a red *G* stenciled on it; under the *G* was the outline of crossed rifles. She was shaved bald, and her eyes were hidden in dark wraparound sunglasses; her broad face was tattooed with two blue lightning bolts. Her teeth gleamed with gold, and she was toying with a big serrated knife as she looked Roland over. Towering over her was a big, gangly, awkward-looking woman, the tallest woman Roland had ever seen. She had leanly muscled arms that seemed too long for her body, her big hands ending in curved implanted steel talons; her hair was spiky gray, and her face was long, too long, her eyes like blots of darkness, her mouth froggish and crookedly outlined in lipstick; she wore a low-cut armored top showing pendulous breasts that hung to her waist.

She also looked Roland over and made a contortion of her mouth, a twisting that was probably intended as a smile, baring filed yellow teeth. "Hey, sweet thing," the big woman said.

"Uh . . . hi," Roland said.

"That's Broomy," Mordecai muttered.

Roland gulped. He'd heard of Broomy. "Why they call her Broomy, anyway?" he asked in a whisper.

"You don't wanna know. Her pal there, her name's Cess."

Broomy turned around and ordered a drink from someone Roland couldn't see. "Gimme a KK!" she snarled, her voice grating. When she turned her back, he saw she wore a crude, badly stitched cape, with a skullish *G* and crossed guns on it.

"Yuh, yuh, a Kerosene Kooler, here ya go!" piped up the Claptrap robot bartender, reaching up from the other side of the bar to pass over a seething mug of green fluid. Broomy grabbed the drink, splashing half of it on the bar, and drank thirstily.

"Come on back and have another bottle on us, Mordecai!" called Cess, laughing, waving a bottle of yellow liquor. "This time I'll let you drink from it instead o' bathin' in it!"

Mordecai rubbed his head ruefully. "Good

thing I had my helmet on. Just stunned me. Then Broomy tossed me over here."

"What'd you do to piss her off?"

"It's what I *wouldn't* do." He looked at Roland's pistol. "Nice Invader autopistol. Modified with the scope and everything, huh? I had one, but a skag ate it. Almost took my arm with it."

"I don't see a weapon on you. You don't look natural without a gun."

"Got a static Cobra burstfire leaning over against that table right there. And a couple grenades. Anyway, Bloodwing's here. He's got my back—*usually*."

Mordecai looked up at the metal rafters and whistled. Something creaked and fluttered up there, then came flapping down to land on his shoulder. "Some use to me *you* were, pal," he told the creature, "letting them blindside me like that."

Bloodwing made a raspy sound and ducked its head, seeming to laugh. It was a vulturine, leather-winged animal, its head deathly white, its eyes lurid red-orange, its beak the color of steel and almost as tough; it had enormous talons, which Roland had seen put to good use tearing the face off a bandit.

"Yeah, very funny, Bloodwing," Mordecai said. Bloodwing took to preening itself on its master's shoulder. Mordecai took a medical vial from a pocket, drank the solution off in one gulp to erase the pain from the blows he'd taken on the head, and turned to Roland again. "What're you up to here?"

"Looking for Brick. Seen him?"

"Saw some broken walls and broken bodies that have his stamp on 'em, you might say. There's a mine out east of the settlement; that's where he hangs out, I'd guess. If he's still guarding the mine from bandits."

"East, huh? Due east?"

"Yeah, pretty much. But anything Brick can do I can do better—and I need a job."

"*Anything* he can do, Mordecai? Really? How about picking up an outrunner and throwing it at somebody?"

"Okay, not anything, but a lot. Did he really do that?"

"According to rumor. I guess you'd be a help on this mission. Come along, then. I'll give you the lowdown later. A good long-range shot might be more useful than—"

"Are you nutless wonders going to come over here and give us some action or *not*?" Broomy demanded, her voice so raucous it made Bloodwing's sound melodious.

"Or *not*, I'd say," Roland muttered, looking at Broomy and Cess.

"You guys are in my damn way," said a woman's voice behind him.

He turned to see a small but heavily armed

woman. She was black-eyed, pale, and unpretentiously pretty, with short, glossy jet-black hair. There was a combat rifle slung across one shoulder, two knives in a V of sheaths worked into her tight-fitting skag-leather jumpsuit, and on each hip was a pistol. Her bare arms were spiraled with tattoos of words in a language he didn't recognize. With her was a scar-faced, spiky-haired redhead in black leather, strapped with a dozen throwing knives plus a pistol on each side of her wide hips. The redhead returned him stare for stare.

Roland stepped out of their way with a mock bow, and the two women sauntered to the bar.

"I kinda like the look of that black-haired one," Mordecai murmured. "Never saw her before. The other one's part of Gynella's gang—her so-called army—like those two at the bar."

"Gynella, huh? I've heard something about her . . . but what I don't get is where all these women are coming from. Four women in one room—on *this* planet? Most I've ever seen in one place."

"Yeah, well, General Goddess has a cadre of fighting women, her special forces. Some of this bunch're on leave, they tell me."

Roland nodded. The way he'd heard it, the army of General Goddess was right in his way. It'd be good to find out more about them. "Come on. Let's suss this out."

He crossed to the bar, he and Mordecai both stepping over a dead man he hadn't seen before, half hidden in a pile of rubbish.

"Who's the stiff?" Roland asked, almost whispering.

"Some miner. He said no to Broomy too," Mordecai said out of the side of his mouth. "Only he wasn't as nice about it."

"Ladies, let's have a drink," Roland said as he stepped up to the bar. "This bottle's on me. But not the way you put one on Mordecai. I need my skull in one piece." Broomy cawed laughter at that, and he tossed a small stack of paper money onto the rusty metal countertop. The Claptrap, barely visible behind the counter, snatched the money and rolled away to make drinks. "I'll have whatever they're having," Roland added, although he didn't plan to actually drink any of the swill they sold here.

Broomy was already swaying—she closed her right eye as she peered at him with the left; then she closed her left eye and peered at him with the right. It was hot in the Steel Incisor, and the smell off Broomy, of rancid sweat, was hard to take. Roland edged away a little and glanced past her at the other two women, who were in close conversation with Cess.

"What makes you think you got what it takes to soldier up with General Goddess?" Cess demanded, looking at the pretty one with the short black hair with evident suspicion.

"Oh, Daphne's okay, Cess," the redhead said, eyeing Roland. "She's changing over to our side. Ain't working with that big lug at the mine anymore . . ."

"I didn't ask you, Khunsuela," Cess growled.

Khunsuela shrugged and swaggered over to Roland, who was pretending to drink his Kerosene Kooler.

So her name is Daphne, he thought, looking at the compact woman in the tight skag-leather outfit.

He suspected she might be the notorious Daphne Kuller. He'd never run across Kuller the Killer himself, but rumor in New Haven said she was a small woman, lithe and quick, a feared hired assassin used by intergalactic criminal gangs against other intergalactic criminal gangs. The Daphne he was thinking of had come to Pandora a couple of years back to hide out from some gangsters who'd taken it a little too personally when she killed their boss. If this was her, it seemed Daphne Kuller was looking to sign on with Gynella.

"I can handle myself, Cess," Daphne said, shrugging. She sipped her drink and made a face at the mug. "What the fuck *is* that? It'd gag a trash feeder." She put the mug down and pushed it away.

"Say, uh, big guy," Broomy said, sidling up to Roland, clacking her drink down on the bar. "Howzabout we—"

"Hey, Broomy, I was just about to make my move!" Khunsuela snapped, shoving herself in between Broomy and Roland. "Back off!" Khunsuela put her hand on Roland's arm and spoke purringly to him. "Come on, let's get in my outrider. I know a place where there's decent drinks, narcojuice, anything you want."

"Easy, ladies," Mordecai said, jeering. "There's enough of him to go around. How about if you both take him on at once? One of you could straddle him while the other—"

"Mordecai?" Roland said. "Shut up."

Khunsuela was running her fingers up Roland's arm. "Nice muscle sculpturing there, big fella—"

She broke off, gasping, as Broomy's enormous hands, coming from behind, closed around her throat, squeezing.

"Bitch!" Broomy snarled into her ear.

Then she bit Khunsuela's ear off and spat it out. Roland had to duck the bleeding ear as it flew by.

While he was ducked down, he noticed a mini-com almost coming out of Broomy's side pocket. The miniature computer and communicator might just have some data on Gynella's movements, since Broomy was in Gynella's inner cadre . . .

Khunsuela shrieked, clasping the bloody rags of

her ear with one hand and with the other she pulled a knife and stabbed it deep into Broomy's wrist.

Broomy roared, her back arching, her grip loosening so that Khunsuela was able to break free, gasping, spinning on her heel, and whipping out two throwing knives.

Distracted by pain, Broomy didn't feel it when Roland tugged the minicom from her pocket.

He got out of the way just in time to avoid being caught in the crossfire as Broomy pulled a small Maliwan Firehawk pistol from under a breast and opened up with it, firing repeatedly. A knife just missed Broomy's head; another chunked into her left shoulder and stuck, but she didn't seem to notice it—she was too busy shooting holes in Khunsuela's throat. One of the shots glanced off Khunsuela's shield, making it sparkle with the impact, but the shield ended at her collarbone. Above that she was unprotected.

Khunsuela staggered back, choking on her own blood, and fell over a steel spool that was being used as a table. She thrashed on the floor, spitting out bloody phlegm.

Roland looked the dying redhead over, wondered if he could maybe get her some Dr. Zed, help her out, but it was too late; her eyes were already glazing.

"Broomy, that's gonna piss Gynella off," Cess observed. "She just got that girl trained!"

"I don't give a dirty damn!" Broomy hissed, jerking the knife out of her shoulder. She threw the knife at the spasming Khunsuela. Grunting with pain, Broomy pocketed her pistol and poured green liquor over the wound in her shoulder. "Ouch, shit! Anyway, I *had* to shoot 'er. She was tryin' to knife me when all I was doing was givin' her a little warning choke. I wouldn't've *killed* her. Prob'ly."

"What about *her*?" Cess asked, nodding toward Daphne, who'd been coolly watching the fight.

Roland noticed that Mordecai was staring hungrily at Daphne.

"You know what?" Daphne said. "Forget it. I don't join up with people who sneak up behind their own crew, start in choking them over a *man*."

She started for the door, walking casually, unhurried. Mordecai hurried after her, so quickly Bloodwing was startled into the air, to flap around over them in ragged circles.

"Daphne!" She turned to Mordecai, frowning, as he said, "Wait! How about if, uh, we offer you another job? Me and Roland. I mean, if you can use all those guns. We could do some target practice, maybe have a little competition. See if you can shoot."

But Broomy was seething, glaring at Daphne and Mordecai. "You, Mordecai! You don't go near her! I decided I want both you and your big pal. And I don't want that slick female around here talking about how I'm sneaking up behind people."

Daphne looked at Broomy, pretending mild surprise. "Grabbing somebody around the neck from behind's not sneaking? Looked kinda like tunnel rat bullshit to me."

"Tunnel rat!" Broomy howled. "You're going down, you skuzzy, bad-mouthin' little—"

Mordecai stepped between Broomy and Daphne, raising his hands palms outward toward the big woman. "Easy, Broomy, don't make me have to—" He reached for the gun on his hip—and then realized he didn't have one there. "Don't make me . . . uhhh . . ."

Broomy started toward him, and so did Roland, taking bigger steps, passing her, just as Mordecai turned to Daphne, saying something about how maybe they should get out of there into the fresh air.

Broomy was jerking her pistol out again, aiming at Mordecai because he was in her way. Then Bloodwing dipped down and slashed at her face. Blood spattered. Broomy screeched and fired at Bloodwing, missing. It hovered, jabbed at her, pecking a hole in her cheek, then lofted to fly into the shadows of the rafters.

Roland cracked Mordecai on the back of the head with his sidearm—and he did it expertly. Mordecai went down, out cold. Roland figured that was the surest way, in the circumstances, to save Mordecai's life—just get him out of the melee.

"I took him out for ya, Broomy!" Roland shouted, reaching down and grabbing Mordecai by the collar. Following Daphne, he dragged Mordecai outside as Broomy swiped at Bloodwing, shouting imprecations.

A few moments later, relieved to be out in cleaner air, Roland eased Mordecai to the ground in the middle of the street. Bloodwing swooped out the open door and began flying around in tight, low circles overhead. Daphne looked up at the creature in amusement.

"Is that thing his pet, or is he *its* pet?" she asked wryly. "Nasty-looking buzzardy object. Feathers around its neck but leather wings. Can't make up its mind what it is."

"A lot of us suffer from that," Roland said distractedly, slapping Mordecai's cheek. "Hey, man, enough loafing. Wake up!"

Then Broomy burst out the door, waving Mordecai's rifle but blinded by blood. Bloodwing had torn the flesh of her forehead, doing only superficial damage but releasing considerable blood flow.

"Where's that bird thing? I'm gonna kill it!" She tried to swipe blood from her eye with one hand.

Bloodwing swooped past and shrieked mockingly at her. She fired in that direction, and a grazing round knocked a few feathers off the creature but did no real harm. It dived at her, raked her hand. She yelped, dropping the gun, and staggered back into the saloon, undone by her temporary blindness. She shouted over her shoulder, "When I get my eyes clear, I'll catch that critter and wring its dirty damn neck!"

Mordecai was sitting up, groaning. "She hit me from behind . . . really *is* sneaky . . ."

Roland decided not to disabuse Mordecai of the notion that Broomy had knocked him out. "Sure, sure, let's get outta here before she comes back. We gotta find Brick."

Mordecai got to his feet and picked up his rifle, then turned to Daphne. "You coming with us? I don't know how you are in a fight yet, but I'm guessing you can hold your own, if your skill comes anywhere near matching your nerve."

She smiled thinly. "No thanks. Got something else waiting."

If she had something else waiting, then why, Roland wondered, had she tried to sign on with General Goddess?

She turned and hurried off, ducking between two buildings, and Roland tugged Mordecai in the other direction. "Come on, goggle eyes, she's not into it. Let's see if we can find Brick."

THREE

The outrunner was jouncing through the badlands, with only the moonlight to fend off the deepening night. Roland was driving, Mordecai riding shotgun. Bloodwing was perched on the back of Mordecai's seat, hunched down against the wind of their passage.

Luckily the terrain was smooth around there, not too risky in the dark. But you never knew, Roland reflected. It was always possible to fall into a tunnel rat trap or blunder into an unexpected ravine.

Thinking about that, he slowed down, peering east, trying to make out anything like a mining camp against the gloomy horizon.

"I saw you swipe something from Broomy's pocket," Mordecai said, drinking another vial of Dr. Zed's best. "Anything I should know about?"

"I dunno yet," Roland said. "Just figured she might have some intel we could use."

"Yeah, about that—use doing what, now?"

"Hunting Eridium crystals—on the hoof."

"On the hoof! Oh, you mean crystalisks? I'm up for anything but what I've been getting, which is hammered on the noggin. Man, my head's killing me. First they smash bottles over it, and then she cracks me on the brainpan with her gun."

"Yeah, uh, you think that mining camp's around here?"

"We're there! Don't drive into that pit!"

Roland just managed to veer around a mining pit, the outrunner careening along the upper edge to the trestle-like structures of the mining camp.

"I don't see anybody around," Mordecai pointed out. "Could be bandits took the place down. You gotta shield on?"

"Yeah, but it's not switched on. You?"

"Nah, I'm short on gear. That's why I need work. I gotta replenish—whoa, look out!"

Brick was suddenly there in front of them, scowling—an enormous, muscle-bound, brick shithouse of a man, standing in the cone of light from an electric lantern hanging from a mining trestle. Roland hit the brakes; the outrunner skidded, but it ran into Brick—that is, into Brick's outstretched hands. The big berserker skidded back a little, then dug in his heels and stopped the outrunner cold. Then he dusted his hands and shook his head disapprovingly. "Roland, you're a, whatta they call it, a reckless driver."

Roland looked at the front of his outrunner. "You dent my vehicle up there? You *did*, didn't you!"

"I'll dent your fool head!" Brick said, his voice a volcanic rumble. "I nearly took you out with a rocket launcher. We've been under siege by the second division of that crazy goddess woman for two days."

"I didn't see any troops around here."

Brick rubbed his massive jaw thoughtfully. "Could be they got the word to go after easier pickings. I must've killed thirty of the bastards."

Roland shut off the outrunner and got out, Mordecai following. Bloodwing yawned and tucked its beak under a leathery wing for a snooze.

Brick looked the same as ever, with a face that seemed carved from stone, all heavy angles, just a crew-cut fuzz of hair on his close-shaven head, powerful bare arms. He wore an armored vest and fingerless gloves decked out with spikes and bolts—the same kind of bolts on his heavy boots. Around his neck was a chain, and the pendant on it was the mummified paw of a dog, Brick's beloved hound Priscilla, now gone to its maker. He had a length of pipe tucked through his belt; it seemed as if he'd been carrying that chunk of pipe around for years. How many heads had been stove in by it? Slanted across his broad back was a strapped-on rocket launcher. Brick loved explosives. And he could be an explosive himself, in a way—he had a berserker state of mind he went into, seemed to make him something both more and less than human. Roland had never faced it and never wanted to.

Brick looked Mordecai over. "You! I remember *you*." He said it as if remembering the time someone slipped skag droppings into his beer.

Roland smiled. "Mordecai's a pain in the ass sometimes, but he can shoot, Brick. He can take out the left nut of a Primal at thirty yards."

"Why'd anyone want to shoot off a nut when they can blow off a head?" Brick asked. "Makes no sense."

As was often the case, Roland wasn't sure if Brick was kidding. "He's also a good hunter. That's something I'm going to need. So Brick, I was thinking that—"

"You want me to shoot 'em, Brick?" came a familiar female voice behind him.

Roland turned his head very slowly, not wanting to startle anyone into shooting, and looked over his shoulder. Daphne was standing behind him, with a pistol in each hand, one pointed at the back of Roland's head, the other at Mordecai's.

"I knew she couldn't stay away from me," Mordecai said dryly.

"Why shoot us?" Roland asked.

"Because," she said, her arms unwavering as she pointed the pistols, "I don't trust you. Why take a chance?"

"I don't trust you either—you were gonna get a job with Gynella."

She chuckled. "Nah. I just wanted to hang around 'em, see what their plans were. I heard Cess say that General Goddess's Second Division would be pulling out of the area. So I came to tell Brick the good news. And what do I find . . ."

"You find the guy who tried to save your ass from Broomy," Mordecai said.

"I didn't need saving."

Roland could believe that. "Your arms are eventually gonna get tired. And my neck's already getting a crimp." He turned to Brick. "You've been working with her?"

"My partner in protecting the mine." Brick gestured for Daphne to lower the guns. "Mining engineers pulled out this morning. I don't think the bastards are gonna pay us our 'kill fee.'"

"We got a pretty good deposit," Daphne said, holstering the pistols.

Mordecai turned to look at her. "You and . . . *Brick*?"

"We both got hired the same time is all," she said. "Not that it's any of your business."

Roland didn't feel right about bringing Brick

into the mission if that meant bringing Daphne along. If she was who he thought she was, she was wanted by a lot of real sons of bitches, who wouldn't quit till they found her. He didn't want any distractions from the mission. And he had a feeling that if Brick went along, so would she.

"So what was it you wanted to talk tuh me for?" Brick asked.

Roland cleared his throat. "Oh, just wondering if you needed any more help here. I could use the work. But it looks like it's over with. We'll be moving on, then."

Brick shrugged. It looked like a mountainside in an earthquake. "Bah, I'm gonna go into town and drink a keg or two. Hey—what's that thing sittin' in the outrunner?"

"That's Bloodwing," said Mordecai.

"That stinky buzzard bat of yours? You call that thing a pet?" He put his hand to the mummified dog's paw. "That thing ain't no fitting pet for nobody. Not like Priscilla." Brick sniffled a couple of times and rubbed at his nose. He pointed off to the right, and Roland saw something stacked over there, almost like a lumpy log cabin, hard to make out in the darkness beyond their small cone of light. "What I found out is, if you lay out dead fellas real nice and straight and let 'em go stiff, why, you can stack 'em just like toy blocks. I was makin' a fort outta that bunch, the ones I killed outta Gynella's outfit. And Priscilla, when I was a kid, she used to watch me with my blocks, and then she'd smell 'em and knock 'em over, and we'd have a good laugh. Priscilla . . ."

Roland glanced at Daphne—she was rolling her eyes. He hoped Brick didn't notice that. He didn't countenance any disrespect to Priscilla's memory.

"Where exactly are you two going?" Daphne asked, quite casually, as Roland and Mordecai climbed back into the outrunner.

Roland frowned. On this planet, it wasn't done to be too inquisitive about where a man was going. Especially with the demanding tone she was using.

Mordecai glanced questioningly at Roland, and at last he said, "Ohhhh . . . out westerly. Check out that army. See if we can get Brick some more building blocks."

Roland started the outrunner, put it in reverse, backed it up, changed gears, and drove carefully but quickly out of the mining camp.

"You decide against recruiting Brick?" Mordecai asked when they'd gone out of earshot.

"We don't need the distraction of that woman along, not in any damn way, and I figured she'd horn her way into our mission. She seems attached to Brick. If she's who I think she is, she's dangerous—dangerous as all hell. And I mean dangerous to the wrong people. You feel?"

Mordecai said nothing. Bloodwing shifted on

its perch and made a soft squawking sound, then settled back to sleep.

"He's got something going," Daphne said. "Something he's keeping quiet. He was going to tell you about it. Then I showed up." Staring after the outrunner, she shook her head. "I don't like being aced out of anything. I don't know when we're gonna be able to collect the rest of our money from these Dahl bastards. They'll say we didn't do the job, just because the miners got scared and bugged out like a lotta pussies."

Brick grunted and scratched his head. "I dunno. Roland's okay. So what if he's got a mission. None of my business. I can always find something to smash. Or someone."

"Sure. But he's being secretive. Must be something big! Anyway, I haven't got anything else. I'd like to know what he's up to."

Brick grunted. "We could ask him."

"How we gonna do that?"

"I dunno. Find him."

She smiled. He seemed willing to tag along with her. She liked having him along—he was like a one-man army. Like having artillery. Only it was Brick.

"Okay. Let's grab our stuff and get in my outrunner. We're gonna follow and see what he's up to."

Brick looked at her with his head cocked, a sort

of craftiness flickering in his eyes. "I wonder if I should ask what *you're* up to. I don't know much about you."

She gave him a friendly shot with her fist to the arm—it hurt her knuckles. "I'm up to finding us a fortune. I've got an intuition Roland's gonna lead us to it."

He gave another one of his seismic shrugs. "Sure. Out westerly—plenty of heads to bash. I'm in. But first, I'm hungry. I could eat two or three skags. In fact, I think I will. Then we go."

"But we'll lose them!"

"Naw. Not a lotta traffic out here. We got the moon, we got headlights. Out here, easy to follow tire tracks. We can be right up on Roland's ass in no time."

"Broomy and Cess should've reported back by now," Smartun said, looking at the schedule. "We gave 'em two days, after the recall for the Second Division."

Gynella glanced up from the computer scan she was frowning over.

They were in her headquarters, a bunker with maps of Pandora all over the cement walls, tables with computers and communications equipment, glaring bulbs overhead, a chaise longue with a refreshment cabinet next to it for when she wanted to relax.

Smartun sometimes fantasized about stretching out on that chaise longue with her . . .

"What concerns me more," said Gynella, "is all those men we lost."

Smartun blinked and looked more closely at her. Was she really expressing compassion for lost soldiers?

"I mean," she went on, "it's a waste of resources. But . . ."

Ah, that made more sense.

"But, Smartun, it also demonstrates one thing. The man who killed most of them is a potentially valuable tool. He is a tool I wish to grip in my hand and use. A weapon I can take to war."

Smartun sniffed. "Oh, you mean Brick."

"Yes. I had a choice of losing another twenty troopers taking him down or pulling them back and finding a way to recruit him. With him and Roland leading the First and Second Divisions, we can rule this planet."

Smartun quivered inwardly. He liked it when she said *we*. "He had some help. That little woman with the tattoos."

"Yes. That woman. I know exactly who she is. She does not know me, but I know her."

"You reviewed the drone footage?"

"Yes." She rewarded him with a smile. "You're really quite clever with electronics. Your surveillance drones are . . . very responsive. And subtle. Daphne Kuller is alert, but she never spotted them."

He chuckled. "They're well camouflaged."

"I recognized her the second I saw the vid. She

once killed someone I was very close to. Of course, she was only doing her job, but I will punish her for it."

Broomy's face was nastily crisscrossed by crusting red slashes, the consequence of her encounter with Bloodwing. Still, Cess didn't think her face was much worse than it had been before—but she wasn't going to make that remark in front of Broomy.

They were climbing into Cess's outrider parked near the Steel Incisor, Broomy taking shotgun, sucking down Dr. Zed and painkillers, and snarling to herself, "Find 'em, make 'em pay. Find 'em, make 'em pay. Strangle that buzzard thing. Strangle it slow. *Real slow!* Maybe take one of 'em slave. Chain him up. Make him do what I want. The little one'd be easier. Mordecai. The big one, we shoot him dead. That's the plan. Yeah, that's the plan . . ."

"How we going to *find* them, Broomy?" Cess asked worriedly, starting the outrider and heading west. "Could take a long time, and we're supposed to get back to the Footstool. General Goddess—"

"Why, them tracks is clear. They headed off in the direction we got to go anyway. Westerly. We won't follow 'em direct—we'll take the trail up the ridge and over, then cut west, head 'em off, catch 'em unawares. We'll ambush 'em. We'll make 'em pay."

The geological formation that had lent its name to the half-dead settlement of Jawbone Ridge extended to the southwest some distance past the town, stabbing mile after mile into the wasteland. Roland and Mordecai drove along below the ridge, following it southwest. It wasn't yet midday, and they were still in the ridge's shadow.

A couple of large skags loomed up, their trisected jaws opening, tongues whirling. Roland sideswiped them just hard enough to break their necks and drove through the low depression of the skag den. The rest of the pack snarled in frustration as they left them behind.

Bloodwing straightened up, opening its wings as if thinking of taking to the air.

"Forget it, buddy!" Mordecai told the creature. "You're not going back there to feed on that skag roadkill. I need you here! We'll find you some food up ahead."

Grumbling to itself without words, squawking deep in its gullet, Bloodwing settled back into place.

"We got any food, Roland?" Mordecai asked, speaking loudly over the rumble of the engine and the hiss of the wind.

"Sure, I got a crate of canned food back there. Help yourself. Some of it's self-heating."

"When we stop. I could use a break."

"Yeah, okay, girls gotta have a pee stop."

"Fuck you, Roland." But Mordecai was smiling.

They stopped to pee and stretch their legs; they consumed a can of glutinously indeterminate food, and then Roland said, "We're burning daylight."

They headed ever westward, following the ridge as if the formation were a bony finger pointing their way.

It was getting dusky, the shadows from the shrubs and outcroppings lengthening, when they stopped on a low hilltop to make camp. "Really could go on a couple more hours," Roland remarked, pulling up, "but I want to go over Broomy's minicom, see what we can find out. If we could completely avoid the asshole army of General Goddess, that'd work for me big-time."

"Yeah, I'll take on an army if I have to." He grimaced, climbing out of the outrunner, stretching. "But I haven't got the ammo to kill 'em all."

Roland chuckled, arching his back to crick it straight after the hours of bouncing over the rough landscape. "You could take down an army if you had enough ammo, that what you're saying?"

"Well, sure, if I had the distance on them. I can pick 'em off, five or ten at once, move back, pick off a few more. I'm the best sniper on this planet. One shot, one kill."

Roland shook his head skeptically. "One shot, one kill is something you don't see often around here. Something about the radiation on this planet seems to make 'em resistant to a quick kill. Come on, let's make camp. I'm hungry."

They ate more canned food, and Mordecai shot a scythid for Bloodwing's dinner.

Then they did an inventory of their weaponry, poking through the back of the outrunner as Bloodwing, still perched on Mordecai's seatback, hunched over them with its head cocked, seeming to take inventory with them. Roland had his Scorpio turret but with limited ammo, and there was the outrunner's gun, which fired only small cannon shells, and he had precious few of those left. He had a Vladof Hammer, an orange-colored shotgun with a nine-shot magazine, deadly at close range. He had two crates of ammo for it. "I got twelve grenades . . . my sidearm, lotta ammo for that . . . I got this Eridian rifle, but it's been acting up. Not really reliable. I got the turret. You got your Cobra burstfire."

"We're kinda underweaponed, man. Not even a rocket launcher. I got badly depleted last mission. We should maybe take a side trip to a settlement, load up on some goods. I haven't got much money, but . . ."

"You know what, I can scrounge weapons almost as easily as I can buy them, Mordecai. Easier a lotta times. Of course, that usually means killing some Psychos and takin' their hardware, but I expect to do that anyway. We'll weapon up, don't you worry about it. Come on, let's look at my scan map—and Broomy's minicom."

He unrolled the scan map he'd bought from Skelton Dabbits. "You see that mark? See the readings? That marks the biggest den of crystalisks known on this planet."

"Long way to go. And a lot of hassle in between."

"Let's see just how much." Roland pulled out Broomy's minicom and activated it. "Now how do I get into this thing . . ."

It was Mordecai who figured out Broomy's password. He'd seen the tattoo on her: *Fuckemorkillem.* Lucky guess.

Some of the photos they found on the device made Roland's stomach churn. "Ugh—get outta that folder!"

They found what they wanted under *tactics*: a holographic image projected into the air from the minicom, displaying a map of the Salt Flats. It appeared in glowing yellow 3-D, with red and green lines for topographic and other markers.

Mordecai pointed at the Devil's Footstool on the map. "There, the Devil's Footstool! She's got it marked 'GG HQ.' That must be where they're centered."

"Squares with a rumor I heard. Those *X*'s—troop encampments?"

"Looks like every other klick across the Salt Flats, a lot of other places too. They've got it sewn up!"

"Well, maybe we can slip through." Roland shook his head. "But I figure they'll have people posted on high points looking for intruders in captured territory."

"Maybe we can go back to New Haven, see if we can get a hopper—or, if you can pay for it, even a trip to orbit. We can drop down behind their lines."

"Nah. She's shooting down anything that flies over. No one'll go there. And I can't afford the other method. Besides, I doubt we could get permission for an orbit drop back there. They don't care if we get killed, but loss of their shuttles or even pods . . . no way."

"So we got to go overland. We'll have to shoot our way through. Or find an easier mission."

Roland looked at him with his eyebrows raised. "That what you want to do? Wimp out?"

Mordecai grinned at him. "Are you kidding? This'll be the ultimate test of my sharpshooting, man. No way I'm missing this mission. I just wanted to give *you* the chance to blow it off."

"Very thoughtful. I'm after crystalisks and Eridium. So we head southwest."

They didn't see the varkids till sunset was melting into the night, and Roland was hunkering to build a campfire, thinking he should set up the Scorpio turret. There was still enough light for Mordecai to notice the ground trembling at the far edge of the hilltop.

"What the hell," Mordecai said, staring at the tremulous sand. He pointed. "Over there! We got spiderants coming up?"

Roland dropped the wood he was stacking and grabbed his Vladof Hammer, which was never out of reach when he was away from a settlement.

The two of them stalked slowly toward the place where Mordecai had spotted the sand movement, Mordecai with his Cobra burstfire in his hands.

They didn't have to discuss it any further, not then; Roland and Mordecai both knew the kind of things they were looking for. They were both men with long experience on Pandora. This kind of action was second nature now. They moved laterally apart from each other, as if by signal but simply by instinct, yet still angling toward the target . . .

Which boiled up out of the sand with startling suddenness—and it was something Roland hadn't seen before. "That's no spiderant! What the hell is that?"

"It's a varkid!" Mordecai shouted, popping his gunstock to his shoulder and sighting in.

Roland was aiming too, as his mind came to grips with the varkid—a giant insectile red and black creature about the size of a skag, it seemed almost all jagged chiton, enormous barbed jaws, six clawed feet, no visible vulnerable parts. It was one of the most armored creatures he'd ever seen. And like pretty much any creature of Pandora, it was vicious and aggressive. It came at them, quick and scuttling, clacking its jaws open and shut hungrily. Those jaws were big enough to sever a man's head from his neck with one snip.

Roland only had time to fire from the hip, almost point-blank—a moment after Mordecai fired, hitting the cluster of three eyes behind its jaw parts. There was barely any head to aim at. Roland's shotgun spread caught the creature in its thorax, the blast knocking off chunks of its craggy natural armor plates.

The varkid squealed and retreated, shaking its foreparts in pain, just as Roland was taking aim again—and he assumed the thing was going to back off.

He was wrong. It leapt into the air, coming down on Mordecai before he could get a bead to fire again—Mordecai was too meticulous a gunman to fire point-blank as a reflex. It knocked Mordecai onto his back, so that he dropped the burstfire rifle. He fell heavily, and the varkid was poised on his chest, snapping at his face with its barbed mandibles. Mordecai shouted in wordless horror.

Roland couldn't fire for fear of hitting Mordecai. He rushed toward the varkid, hoping to kick it off Mordecai, but Bloodwing got there first, the leather-winged raptor swooping down, screeching in fury. It struck the creature glancingly, before flapping up for another run, knocking the varkid to the side enough that Mordecai was able to tip the giant insect off him. It scrambled to get back onto its six legs, oozing green and red fluid from its damaged eye cluster.

Mordecai rolled over, grabbing his rifle as he rolled, coming up aiming, firing at the varkid, striking it just behind its heaviest armor sheath, where there was another cluster of sensors, just before the razor-sharp stinger on its hind parts.

The creature shrieked and flipped backward, then seemed to dive straight down into the sand. It was burrowing to escape, Roland assumed, firing at it—but most of his shot missed, as it vanished into the grit.

"Now what's it up to?" Mordecai muttered, checking his rifle. "Knocking my damn rifle out of my hands—did not expect it to—what the hell is that thing?"

They were both staring at it. It was as if a plant had been filmed and the film was running in fast action, the plant sprouting miraculously from the ground. Only it wasn't a plant. Its texture was grotesquely fleshy; it was like a bloated blossom of larval flesh.

"Uh-oh," Mordecai said. "A pod!"

"A what?" Roland said, aiming the shotgun.

"Just shoot it!"

They fired, and the fleshy excrescence blew apart, but more varkids were tunneling up, two small varkids that seemed to expand, to puff and crinkle up with armor that sprouted even as the things leapt at them. They were still metamorphosing as they came.

Roland wasn't going to give the things a chance to do any more growing. He rushed to meet one as it came at him in midair, shoved the shotgun into its maw, jamming his barrel between those seeking mandibles, and pulled the trigger.

It blew up from inside, a split-second disassembling in midair. Wiping bug ichor off his face, Roland turned at a warning screech from Bloodwing. It was clawing and pecking at a varkid that was bigger than a man, the chitonous horror gripping

Mordecai in an obscene clasp of all of its six legs. Only the barrel of Mordecai's rifle, vertical and between him and the creature's jaws, saved him from getting his head bitten off. He fell back, and Bloodwing flapped up to get another attack angle.

Roland ran to the melee, just in time to see the varkid flip about, changing position to drag Mordecai into a newly forming pit in the sand. It had hold of his collar and was dragging him down underground with it; it vanished into the sand, still gripping Mordecai, who shouted till his mouth was stuffed with dirt as his head was pulled underground, then his shoulders, his chest . . . And Bloodwing flapped and dipped and spiraled, shrieking in frustration.

Roland dropped his shotgun and grabbed Mordecai by the ankles and set his feet, pulling, backpedaling slowly, using all his strength, gritting his teeth so hard it felt as if they might crack.

Then there was a squelching sound and a release of pressure, as Roland went over backward, still gripping Mordecai's ankles.

He lay on his back gasping, horribly afraid he'd pulled Mordecai's legs from his body . . .

"Dammit, Roland, let go, you're crunching my ankles!"

Roland sat up and let go of Mordecai, who was brushing dirt off himself, spitting sand from his mouth between curses. He seemed embarrassed.

Roland stood, scooping up his shotgun, as Bloodwing landed on Mordecai's shoulder, affectionately butting his head with its knobby skull and squawking.

"Yeah, Bloodwing, I'm okay."

"You think they're gone for now?" Roland asked, looking around.

"I'm not gonna wait around here to see, are you?"

"Hell no."

"Hey, Roland? Thanks for pulling me outta that hole. I thought I was done for. Most guys would've given up on me."

Roland shrugged. "Let's find another place to camp."

"We still haven't heard from Cess or the rest of the female cadre, my General," Smartun said, coming into Gynella's headquarters.

She was staring at a 3-D holo map of the Salt Flats, which reticulated in the air between them. It tinted her yellowish gold and seemed to impose veins of red on her, as if she were radiating blood.

Gynella switched off the projected map and frowned at him. "Nothing from the women's cadre? What the fuck. You call them?"

"Broomy's not responding to a minicom signal. I'll try Cess."

She shook her head. "Probably got into trouble. I told them to back off Brick. He might've killed them. I've got some things to talk to Vialle about—and you may as well go with me. You've got to find out about all of this sooner or later."

"Find out exactly what, my General Goddess?" he asked gently.

She sighed and sat on the edge of the chaise longue, stretching out her long, powerful legs and pouring herself a drink. "We're on the run from Dahl. I am not sure they're going to chase us down here—they got kind of discouraged with this planet, from what I heard. But they just might."

"Something you can . . . clear up with them? Negotiate?"

Gynella shook her head. "We stole technology from them. Highly secret technology they really don't want out of their hands. Namely the Acti-Tone mind-control system. Not to mention a big supply of the best humanoid-effective knockout gas in this arm of the galaxy."

"Ah. I guessed as much. I saw the barrel he was taking the SusDrug from. Marked 'Dahl.'"

Smartun was doing his best to hide his excitement, but he couldn't help smiling. She was trusting him with a secret. That meant she'd decided he was important to her, really useful to her. He was a *keeper*.

"We didn't know it would work, when we first came here." Tense with nervous energy, Gynella crossed her legs, sipped her drink, and clicked her talonlike nails together with the other hand. "But we were confident we could knock them out."

"So you had it all planned before you came to Pandora?" He smiled. "When I met you, you didn't have an army."

She had taken up residence in New Haven, without the flamboyant appearance she wore now. Smartun had been a bandit back then, trying to resettle peacefully in New Haven. He'd hired on with her to scout the wilderness, finding bandit camps, nomads, Psychos, marking their positions, their numbers. He'd supposed she worked for one of the interstellar corporations, scouting the area for some mining project. Then she'd summoned him to this outpost. Where he'd found she already had a small army of thugs doing her bidding.

She seemed to like the fact that he didn't need the SusDrug to be loyal to her.

Gynella nodded. "It was all planned. It's time you had the full story. We did a computer model, Vialle and I, searching for the most lawless planet in the galaxy, the most social chaos, the most raw possibilities." She smiled ruefully. "Found more than we bargained for. There're big potential resources here and some more or less functioning settlements. But out there in the Borderlands, there's no one but savages, degenerates who used to be men. To me, they were an army of men who didn't know they were an army, just waiting to be recruited, if only they knew it. I wanted my own planet. And this one seems perfect."

He waited for her to go on, not wanting to interrupt her when she was in the mood to talk.

"We took your information, picked a camp of bandits," she said, "made sure they weren't wearing gas masks, circled it in a hopper—and fired three big knockout shells in. All but two went down. Those I killed, of course."

He nodded. *Of course.*

She clinked the ice in her drink against the sides of the glass. "Then we landed, shot them up with the SusDrug, and used a shocker to wake them up. That was fun—they twitched like they were dancing before they came out of it. Vialle gave me the ActiTone—*he* wanted to activate it, but no damn way I was ever going to let *him* do that. I want them fixated on *me.* They came at me. I activated it."

"Suppose it hadn't worked? They'd have overrun you."

"We were on the hopper, ready to take off. They never got that close. I hit the ActiTone, and the big smelly lugs turned into my happy little joyboys! They just fell to their knees and stared at me with their tongues hanging out and . . ." She snapped her fingers. "Now they follow me anywhere. Like lab animals reacting to wires in their brains. You know the score. What bothers me is, does that work over the long term? And what happens if they develop a resistance or when we . . ." Her voice trailed off.

"When you run out of SusDrug. Yes. I've wondered about that. What does Vialle say?"

"He says they'll be conditioned to respond to me anyway by then. We'll have them brainwashed—their own brains will provide the SusDrug. They'll feel the ecstasy because they'll be wired to, and they'll submit to, me. But I'm just not sure. And now with word that Dahl operatives are slinking around the planet . . ."

Smartun frowned. Dahl had a bad reputation on this planet. "By *operatives,* my General, you mean . . ."

"Might be a wet team here to assassinate me. Or just some armed scouts. Either way, they'll want their goods back, and they'll want me dead. That much is certain."

He shrugged, as if he wasn't worried. "There's no taking over a planet without making enemies. May as well deal with them now as later. They take enough casualties, they'll probably decide it's too expensive to pursue you any further."

She smiled. "I like that about you. You stay upbeat and loyal. That's good. I hate whiners."

He felt a lift in his heart at that. "I'll be loyal forever, my General."

She nodded, as if saying, *Of course, that's just how it should be*. She put her drink aside and stood up. She was so very tall . . .

"Come on, Smartun, let's talk to Vialle, see what he's got for us."

She led him out of the headquarters office, past her deformed bodyguard, who leaned against the wall outside her chambers muttering unintelligibly to himself.

They walked down the scuffed concrete hall to a door marked in big red stenciled letters:

VIALLE LAB 1
UNAUTHORIZED ENTRY IS DEATH

Smartun followed her in, closed the door behind them, and looked around curiously. He had taken the sign on the door seriously and had never seen the lab before.

It was a medium-large rectangular concrete room, chilly and only spottily lit. Two walls were bare, except for a few cluttered shelves. A third wall was a tangle of transparent tubes filled with yellow and red fluid, blipping with bubbles of green and blue gases. There were a couple of rusty, mucky sinks on opposite walls, and the far wall to his right was covered by a single big screen, a flat digital monitor, which glimmered and flashed with intricate biological readings Smartun couldn't decipher. He assumed the readings related to the semihuman figure floating in the transparent sarcophagus just in front of the screen.

He found he was a little afraid to approach that naked, distorted, armless figure twitching in green fluid.

There was someone else in the room: a Bruiser bandit lying in a kind of trance on a gurney. The Bruiser was an enormous man of exaggerated musculature, bald head, most of his nose missing—it looked as if it had been bitten off. He was naked and grubby, and Smartun could smell him from ten strides away.

Vialle looked up from studying the image his floating lozenge-shaped AI projected onto the translucent plastic table—it was an image of pulsating viscera. The AI module started to follow him as he came toward Gynella. The scientist waved the module back to the table and turned anxiously to the General Goddess. His long, cadaverous face was pensive, although ordinary emotion was hard to read on that skull-like visage: taut blue-tinged skin, sunken eyes, and mossy teeth. Vialle wore a bloodstained white jumpsuit, and he twined his fingers over his crotch as he spoke. "Is it true about Feldsrum, Gynella?"

Vialle was the only one of her followers allowed to call Gynella by her first name.

She nodded curtly. "It is, Vialle. I just got the

report in from our operative. I'm afraid our agent isn't likely to get much farther. They've identified him—he's on the run. I expect they'll kill him."

"They'll interrogate him first if they can."

"Yes. I paid him well, but money doesn't buy loyalty." She glanced at Smartun and smiled knowingly.

He looked at the floor and tried to seem humble.

"So," Vialle said, wringing his hands and staring into space. "Mince Feldsrum will be here, on this planet, looking for *us*."

"Yes," she said calmly. "Your old boss!" She chuckled.

Smartun cleared his throat. "May I ask who this Feldsrum is?"

She sighed. "He's underhead of Dahl security. It appears he took our . . . appropriation of Dahl goods a bit personally."

Vialle snorted. "Naturally! It made him look like a fool. Their most top-secret project, stolen from under his nose."

Gynella made a wry moue with her mouth. "I think what really infuriated them was when you destroyed the other prototypes." She clicked her nails thoughtfully on the ActiTone around her neck.

"Feldsrum!" Vialle shivered visible as he spoke the name. "I just never thought they'd come back to this hellhole. He always said they have as little to do with this planet as possible."

"That's right. Smartun made a good point in my office: too many Dahl operatives have ended up as skag snacks. It gets expensive. Leave it to me, Vialle. I just thought you should know." She waved a hand dismissively. "Now, you had a demonstration slated?"

"Hm? Oh, yes, yes." Vialle walked toward the hulking man on the gurney, rubbing his hands together as he went. The scientist had a curious way of walking when he was bent on a task, leaning forward so far it was odd that gravity didn't pull him flat on his face.

Vialle wheeled the gurney toward Gynella. The nude, noseless Bruiser on the wheeled table groaned, and his eyelids fluttered.

"You have a new formulation of the SusDrug?" Gynella asked, looking the Bruiser over with distaste.

"Yes indeed. Much more intense—to try to ensure that they don't fight the effects of the conditioning. After the ActiTone is used, the subject won't be in this sedated state any longer. You'd better bring your bodyguard in."

She nodded, went to the door, and summoned Runch. The ponderous, disfigured bodyguard lurched into the room and took up a post behind her, looming protectively, his bulging eyes looking this way and that, his pincer hand convulsively opening and closing. In his human hand he carried a spiked steel club; a sheath on his hip held a sawed-off shotgun. He had a strange, vinegary smell about him.

Vialle charged an air syringe with the new formulation of the drug and immediately injected it into the Bruiser's arm.

The Bruiser gurgled deep in his throat, and his eyes popped open. Runch took a good grip on his spiked club.

The General Goddess took a step back from Vialle's human guinea pig; she put a hand on her pendant and twisted the knob, with her other hand pointing at the Bruiser—though that was unnecessary. It was pure habitual stagecraft.

The ActiTone chimed and vibrated, and the Bruiser, primed with the new supercharged Sus-Drug, arched his back and let out a long, pealing shriek of mixed delight and terror. His arms flapped, his fists banged on the gurney, and his sexual organ pointed, very suddenly, with what Smartun could've sworn was a twanging sound effect, straight at the ceiling.

"Whoa," Gynella said, taking another step back.

The Bruiser began to claw at himself, giggling. Then he laughed madly, snapping his head back and forth, pummeling his feet on the gurney, until his long-nailed, probing fingers dug deeply into his own skin, and deeper yet, till they burst through, ripping a wound that spurted blood into the air. But he seemed to feel no pain; he kept tittering with mad laughter, every vein in his taut skin standing up, throbbing, his semen staining the ceiling even as his liquefying entrails burst like an oil-well geyser from the rent in his belly, his intestines and inner organs whipping up like eager creatures of the deep sea, eels snapping at their prey.

It didn't stop there. His outsides buckled and folded under; his insides expressed through the widening wound, muscle, bone, and organs bursting out to declare themselves to the world.

Viscera exploded; blood fountained; bones crackled and flew apart . . .

And the Bruiser turned completely inside out.

Smartun backed away, gagging, and rushed to the nearest sink and vomited so thoroughly and furiously he was afraid he was heaving his own guts out. Then he thought of his Goddess and turned to see that Gynella was all right. She was standing well out of the way of the expanding puddle of shattered entrail matter and blood, shaking her head sadly.

"Oh, that's not a good outcome at all, Vialle," she said, seeming only mildly annoyed. "I don't like to criticize, but I do think the dosage might've been too strong."

Vialle nodded mutely.

A minute passed as the thing on the gurney shuddered, occasionally spouting blood and fecal matter and bile, and at last settled down.

It quivered a few times more and subsided into mushy inertness.

There was silence then, except for the *drip-drip-drip* of blood from the gurney. They stared at the bloody wreckage of the Bruiser.

"Ah, well," Vialle said at last, handing Runch a mop. "I suppose I'd better tweak the new formula just a tad."

FIVE

"Now this," Mordecai said, as the dawn broke and the sun speared them with new light, "is a good, peaceful campsite. I had a decent rest. We should remember this one, Roland."

Mordecai was sitting on a rock by the smoking remains of their campfire, which was in the center of the stony, craterlike hilltop. They'd found the campsite a few klicks southwest of the hill where the varkids had tried to make dinner of them. The rocky rim of the hilltop gave them a little cover; there were a couple of outcroppings, too, and three big, stumpy, green growths, side by side, looking like something between trees and cacti and almost as hard as rock. The growths cast long shadows that striped across the camp in the morning sun.

"Where's Bloodwing?" Roland asked, as he packed his Scorpio turret into the back of the outrunner. They'd had the self-aiming machine gun set up, watching over them all night long.

"Feeding somewhere," Mordecai said, standing and stretching. "On something. Or somebody. Ah—here he comes. Uh-oh."

"Uh-oh what?" Roland asked, looking around for his shotgun.

"I don't like the way he's flapping his wings—and the way he's screeching."

"What's he trying to say?"

"Not sure yet."

Bloodwing screeched again.

Roland snorted. "Like you can tell anything from that."

"Actually—" He looked around. "That sound like an outrunner engine to you?"

Roland listened. "Some kind of engine. Where's it coming from?"

Mordecai pointed confidently to the south. "Way off that way. To the south. Can't be very close."

But it wasn't an outrunner, it was an *outrider*, a low-slung hot-rod-like vehicle with the skulls of beasts for its fenders, and it came from the *north*, so close it was already there, jumping the edge of the crater of the hilltop as if it was a ramp. It came down with a crash in between Mordecai and Roland. Broomy jumped off, a knife in one hand and a pistol in the other, as Cess spun the outrider in a tight circle, trying to run Mordecai down.

Mordecai had to leap headlong to the side to avoid being run over, sliding facedown close to his Cobra rifle. Bloodwing came screeching and diving at Cess, talons just missing her face.

Roland saw his shotgun, several paces away, leaning on a boulder.

Broomy rushed toward Roland, shouting, "Surrender, and you can live to serve me—or die right here!"

Roland snarled, "Broomy, blow it out your ass!" and half turned to lunge for his shotgun, but Broomy was on him then, firing wildly. The rounds ricocheted from the energy field of his shield. She slashed at his face, using a knife like a half-size machete.

Roland slipped past the blade, knocked the pistol from her left hand, grabbed the wrist of her right—and was surprised at how wirily powerful she was. She broke loose, punching him with her fisted left hand, and swung the big knife at his throat. He threw himself backward to avoid the slash, falling, but at the same time kicking out, catching Broomy solidly in the crotch. She bellowed with pain and staggered back, falling.

Roland landed heavily on his back, the wind momentarily knocked from him. He gasped, glancing at the outrider in time to see Cess hit Bloodwing with a fist as she braked the outrider. Mordecai's loyal flying predator was knocked away, cawing, wings beating at the ground as it tried to get back into the air. Cess moved to fire the outrider's machine gun, shouting curses as she strafed a burst up the ground to Mordecai. But she was too slow, and the strafe tore up the ground behind him as he ran, Cobra in hand now, ducking behind Roland's outrunner.

Roland was just getting to his feet and had to throw himself to the side to avoid the strafing machine gun. The bullets almost struck Broomy too, as she scrambled to get out of the way.

"Cess, you damn she-fool you almost shot me!" she shrieked.

Roland got his feet under him, saw Mordecai firing over the hood of the outrunner. Mordecai's aim was sharpened with adrenaline-honed precision, the bullets striking the magazine of the outrider's machine gun with two close, static-charged rounds. The magazine exploded, fragments of the wrecked gun shrapneling Cess's face and shoulders.

She grimaced in pain and climbed clear of the outrider, shaking her head to clear blood from her face, staying low, snatching a shotgun from a gun rack on the back of the outrider. Mordecai couldn't get a good shot at her. Bloodwing was in the air again and dived at her, slashing, snapping with its beak. She fired the shotgun, missing Bloodwing.

Roland turned to look for Broomy—didn't see her.

Then he felt the blast of his Vladof, heard the shotgun boom as it struck him, Broomy cackling with sick glee as he was knocked back, staggering against the back of his outrunner.

He looked down at his shield, crackling on his chest—it had barely stopped the shotgun, and now it was damaged, flickering out. He was unprotected, and Broomy was stalking toward him, weapon in hand. She'd gotten his shotgun before he had.

He cursed himself for an amateurish fool, not having his weapon within reach. One good night's sleep, and a man got sloppy. He was going to have to rush her and hope for the best—

Then Mordecai was firing past him, the rounds crackling on Broomy's shield, which flickered and went out. She stumbled back with the impacts, and that gave Roland time to turn, vault up on the back of his outrunner. He cocked the turret and then had to flatten himself as he caught Cess firing toward him from the outrider. The shotgun charge buzzed past his head like a swarm of angry bees.

"I had enough of you two ungrateful snobs!" Cess yelled—a clue to the source of her fury with Roland and Mordecai. A woman scorned.

Cess started the outrider, began driving it around the circle of the flat crater of the hilltop—as Mordecai tried to get a bead on her with his Cobra. Bloodwing was flapping after her, screaming warnings.

Roland was getting up, but Broomy was already standing, coming at him, shotgun in her hands—as something the size of a medicine ball, gray and massy, flashed past the outrunner and smashed into the shotgun, knocking it sideways against her chest. The small boulder shattered, and Broomy staggered but kept her feet. The gun wasn't so fortunate—it had taken most of the impact, and she dropped its broken halves to the ground and turned to run.

Roland smiled as he heard Brick's familiar rumbling shout, then: "Brick's here, bitch!"

He turned to see Brick with another boulder in his hand, a chunk of rock about three times as big as his head, which he threw with one hand straight at Cess's oncoming outrider. The boulder smashed into the engine, blasting it into smoking scraps of metal. The outrider kept coming from sheer momentum, and Brick stepped aside with surprising agility, sweeping an arm to swipe Cess from the driver's seat. She went tumbling across the ground, rolled, got up, pulling a pistol—but then a dark blur intercepted Cess from her left, a flying kick: Daphne Kuller, slamming Cess hard with both boots.

Cess went down. Daphne did too, but she did a tuck-and-roll and came up, immediately lunging at Cess with a drawn knife in each hand, teeth bared. Cess, still on her back, tried to bring her gun into play, but it was all over in less than two seconds. One knife slashed down to pin Cess's gun hand to the ground, blade slamming through the bandit woman's wrist; the other came down to slice down through Cess's throat, parting the trachea, then the spine, pinning her upper body to the ground.

Cess choked and died, eyes going glassy, blood brimming between her lips.

Daphne got up, breathing hard, eyes bright with excitement, but calm and contained, merely brushing her hands together.

Roland looked around. "Where's Broomy?"

"Gone!" Mordecai said. "That harridan dived over the rim rock there and . . . I guess we could still catch her in the outrunner. She's on foot." He didn't sound eager for the chase.

Roland shook his head. He had never killed a woman. He'd been ready to do it, but he'd rather not have to. "The hell with her."

"I wouldn't mind going after her," Daphne said, going to the edge of the hilltop. "She's going to think of me as an enemy now. I'd rather not have her running around loose, looking for a chance to shoot me in the back." She peered over the rock. "It's rugged out there. I don't see her . . ."

Brick pointed at the burning wreck. "See there? That's how you save rocket shells. Just throw a boulder."

"Don't think that'd work for me," Mordecai admitted, flexing a spindly arm. Bloodwing landed on his shoulder, and he scratched under the creature's beak. "You okay? She slammed you good once. Don't see anything broken . . ."

Bloodwing cawed and nestled its bony head against him.

Roland picked up the shattered pieces of his shotgun, shaking his head. "Man, did you have to wreck my only good shotgun?"

"You're lucky he did," Daphne said, walking over to pick up her knives. She wiped their blades on Cess's clothing.

Roland snorted. "I'd have taken her out, all right."

"Sure you would have."

Roland kept his temper. He really did not want this woman around on this mission. Just didn't trust her. Didn't like her attitude.

But Mordecai was gazing big-eyed at Daphne, licking his lips, as if trying to think of something to say to impress her.

Roland shook his head. *Smitten.* The way she'd dispatched Cess had won Mordecai's heart.

"Now," Daphne said, just a bit of swagger in her walk as she crossed to talk to Roland. "You ready to stop jacking us around about this mission of yours? We need a gig, me and Brick."

Roland wondered if Brick truly took to Daphne talking as if she and he were a team. He looked at

Brick, who was scratching his bristly head, seeming mildly confused. "You and Brick, huh?" Roland chuckled. "Well, I'll tell *you and Brick* about it later. Now you can tell me how you happened to turn up here just now."

"Me, I'm glad they did," Mordecai said. "Those bandit females caught us with our pants down." Daphne looked at him with raised eyebrows, and he added hastily, "It's just an expression!"

"We're here," Daphne said, with a note of defiance, "because we *felt* like being here. And we don't like it when people blow smoke up our asses."

"I knew a girl once liked smoke blown up her ass," Brick mused, with a look of nostalgia. "Not just any kinda smoke. But, uh . . . aw, never mind."

Once more, Roland wasn't sure if Brick was joking or not.

"This is a good camp," Daphne said. "Brick's outrunner's right over there."

She pointed the way they'd come, and Roland could see the top of Brick's outrunner and its turret sticking up; it was parked just on the other side of the rimrock, opposite the big plant growths. Which gave him an idea . . .

Daphne went on. "We oughta stay here. Me 'n' Brick have been tracking you lowlifes for half the night. We need some rest and some grub."

"Sure," Roland said. "But who gets the best spot? Most of it's solid rock. Tell you what, we'll have a little contest of strength to see who picks the best spot in the campsite. Brick here always wondered which of us was the stronger, him or me—"

"Ha!" Brick interrupted. "I never wondered that. I *know*."

"You sure?" Roland grinned at him. "Let's just test that assumption." He glanced at Daphne, saw she was tossing wood on the embers of the fire, not looking at him. "See those things growin' over there, Brick?" He waited till Brick turned to look, then made a sign to Mordecai, a hand gesture known across Pandora. And he nodded toward Brick's outrunner. Mordecai frowned, glanced at Daphne, but shrugged and muttered something about going to relieve himself. He walked toward Brick's outrunner, whistling softly.

"Those tree things over there, you mean?" Brick asked, squinting at the growths.

"Yeah, Brick. Now, those things are *hard*. Not exactly petrified but close to it. Whoever can knock all three of them down using nothing but his body—fists, whatever—why, we crown him the strongest, and he gets to choose the primo camp spot. Agreed?"

Brick rubbed his jaw. "What? Uhh, okay."

He balled his big, metal-sheathed hands into fists, the knuckles cricking loudly as he tightened them, and stalked over to the trees.

As Roland had hoped, Daphne went over to

watch. "What the hell are you two up to?" she asked, following Brick.

Roland picked up Mordecai's rifle and climbed up into his own outrunner as Brick squared off before the first big, stumpy growth, set his feet, and—*wham!*—smashed the growth to flinders with a single smash of his powerful, armored fist.

"Ha!" he crowed, stepping up to the next tree. "You wanna take me on, tree?" He laughed. "It's punch time!" And he smashed the second tree. "Now for you—this is easy!" *Crash,* the third growth was shattered.

Then he and Daphne turned, startled, at the sound of Roland gunning the outrunner. He drove it straight toward Brick's outrunner, jumped the ramplike rimrock, and came down on the other side, slamming on the brakes.

Mordecai came running up to the outrunner from behind, laughing nervously, Bloodwing cawing on his shoulder. "Oh man, Roland, I don't know about this!"

But he jumped into the outrunner, and they were off downhill.

"You fix his outrunner?" Roland asked.

"I unfixed it, if that's what you mean. I saw your signal and pulled out a few wires. They won't be driving that thing for an hour or so. But Roland—" He glanced over his shoulder. "I'm not sure it's so smart to piss those two off this way."

Roland looked back to see Daphne and Brick staring after them, two outraged silhouettes against the sky.

"You win, Brick!" Roland shouted back at them as he gunned the outrunner away. "You get the campsite! The whole damn thing! Enjoy it! See you later, big guy!"

He could see Daphne run to the outrunner. She'd soon find out that it was sabotaged.

"Look out!" Mordecai yelled.

Roland returned his attention to the terrain in front and veered hard to the right, just managing not to slam into a boulder twice the size of the outrunner.

"Whew!"

Then he heard a whistling sound, glanced over his shoulder in time to see a small but solid-looking boulder spinning through the air to make impact with the back of the outrunner in an explosion of rock chips. The vehicle took the impact, jerking forward, fishtailing, but continuing to drive.

"Shit!" Roland said. "That Brick's got an arm! You see if he did any damage?"

Mordecai looked and groaned. "Oh man. We're so underweaponed already. You really should've loaded up in Fyrestone. Looks like he bent the muzzle on your Scorpio, man."

Roland swore long and colorfully.

"See, Roland, if we'd just made nice with them—"

"You mean you wanna make nice with Daphne. 'Oh Daphne, my darling!'"

"Roland—come on, seriously—that woman is tough! She'd be a great partner!"

"She'd probably cut your throat first time you slept with her. She's Kuller the Killer, man. I'm sure of it. She's got enemies across half the galaxy. We don't need that. 'Cause her enemies would become our enemies. You can't see her straight because you're sweet on her!"

"Well, *so what* I'm sweet on her. She's a babe!" He glared at Roland, as they jounced down to the flatland at the edge of the Salt Flats, and then frowned as Bloodwing seemed to caw laughter at him.

A bullet from behind cracked by overhead, just missing Mordecai. Almost certainly fired by Daphne.

"That babe of yours almost blew your head off!"

"See?" Mordecai said admiringly. "So sweet! She coulda killed me, but she missed on purpose!"

On purpose? Roland wasn't so sure.

He floored the accelerator and quickly got the outrunner out of gunshot range. Daphne sent no more high-caliber love notes.

They continued on around the edge of the Salt

Flats, generally southwest, the light glaring off the white surface of the plain, making Roland reach for his shaded goggles.

"Where's that army Brick was talking about?" Roland wondered aloud, pulling the goggles on.

"I don't know, it's a big country. Maybe we'd better head down into that draw, keep out of sight." Mordecai pointed into a declivity to the left, a canyon off the badlands close by the edge of the Salt Flats. "Far as I remember, there's a way out on the other side."

"You better remember right," Roland said, turning the steering wheel. They veered down into the draw, into a shallow canyon rimmed with irregularly shaped blue and red boulders and the occasional spike of glittering crystal. The floor of the canyon was smooth blue dust, almost like a man-made dirt road. They passed through most of it without incident, drove up a rise on the other side—and then Roland hit the brakes.

Up ahead, against the sky, he could make out the movement of men, numerous men, and passing outriders.

"This canyon was your idea, Mordecai," he said. "Get out and scout it, and keep your head down."

Mordecai slipped soundlessly out of the idling vehicle and, Bloodwing on his shoulder, went quietly up the rise.

Five minutes passed. Roland waited impatiently.

Mordecai came running back down the slope, looking pale. "It's Gynella's army. Or part of it. Maybe two hundred heavily armed men up there. And they've surrounded the canyon. I saw a few at the place we came in, too. They've just set up at that end. I don't *think* they know we're here—but we're trapped. And they're bound to spot us."

SIX

She stood alone on the plain, dirty, bloody, and footsore.

There were bruises and welts across her. One of her teeth had been knocked loose. She was dizzy from dehydration, and her feet were bloody in the shreds of her boots. But she'd found the supply lines, just as she'd figured on, and she'd waited—and here they came.

She watched the dust rising in quivering lines, approaching across the plain. She knew just what it was. She waited some more.

The engines rumbled, and the rumbles became roars, as the vehicles approached closer and closer. She could make out the marching men, some distance behind them, a rough line, not genuinely orderly but with a unified purpose.

The dusty plumes arrived, their metal cores throwing off splinters of light. Then the engines slowed, the dust cleared, and the vehicles, approaching ahead of the supply column, ground their brakes. The outriders came to a halt near her, their drivers—and the soldiers hanging on, poised on the running boards—leering at her as they arrived: a panoply of deformed faces, masked faces, goggled faces. The skull-shaped *G* of Gynella blazed red on every outrider, every breastplate or tattooed bosom.

A chunky, short Psycho sergeant she knew to be called Skenk climbed out of an outrider and approached her, shotgun in hand. "You! You're AWOL, you are. Absent without leave and likely to be fed to the skags for it!"

"Kiss my fragrant ass," she said, spitting on the ground between them. "I have important information for General Goddess."

"They've been trying to find you, Broomy. And here you are, looking like a trash feeder tasted you and spat you out. Lost your ECHO, didya? Where's Cess?"

"Dead. So's Khunsuela. I've got information the General needs. And I need to see her in person."

He scratched his crotch thoughtfully, then shrugged. "All right. I'll give you an outrider. But you better have something she can use."

"You bunch are supplying what, Hatchet?"

"Yeah, Hatchet Legion."

"If they're where they should be, they need to be told about something. In fact, I'll show 'em myself before I head back to the Footstool."

"They're three klicks off, breaking camp. Watch out for that bunch. They like a kill before breakfast."

"They're the ones better watch out."

"I think maybe I can fix this," Brick said, looking at the engine. "Maybe he didn't know how to wreck it good. Or maybe he wasn't trying."

At Daphne's urging, Brick had pushed the outrunner into the center of the hilltop camp, near the dead campfire left by Roland and Mordecai. That way the outrunner was out of sight of potential enemies on the lowlands below. And this being Pandora, pretty much anyone down there was a potential enemy.

Daphne leaned on a bumper and looked at the engine. "Mordecai wasn't trying to cripple us for good. Just slow us down."

"How do you know?" Brick asked, removing his studded gauntlets so he could reach more deeply into the engine.

"Oh, Mordecai wouldn't do that to me." She looked out over the desert. She could just see the dust of Roland's outrunner in the distance. "Mordecai's kind of cute in a way. I wonder if I could get him to shave off that beard."

"Kind of *cute*? That one? Ha! I could crush him with one hand!"

"And that contradicts kind of cute, how?

Anyway, he's a damned good shot." She heard a rumble of engines from the north side of the hill. "What's that?"

Gruff voices followed the engine noise, accompanied by the sound of metal clanking.

"What's what?" Brick asked distractedly, re-attaching a wire.

"I just remembered something—" She picked up her rifle, an Atlas Pearl Havoc, and checked the load. "Cess was saying something about how the General Goddess's second division is divided into Knife Legion and Hatchet Legion. And Knife Legion was headed off to the southwest, to prep for some assault on a settlement. But Hatchet Legion . . ."

Brick looked up from the engine. "They're here? Time for me to bust heads!" He pulled his gauntlets back on. "I'm *ready* to bust heads. I'm hot to trot for punch time!"

"Maybe you'll get your chance, Brick," she said in a low voice. "But I'd rather give that fight a miss right now. Stay low, let me see if—"

But it was too late. She fell silent as Psycho soldiers bearing the skull-like *G* rose up over the rim of the hilltop—on all sides. They scrambled into view almost simultaneously, stepping onto the rim with a clop of many boots, as if choreographed. They grinned at her, and hooted, and pointed their rifles and shotguns . . . and seemed to wait for permission to start killing.

Daphne swallowed, looking around. So many of them, so well armed, and they were all around. There really was no way out.

She'd fought for her life a dozen times, across the galaxy. She'd killed numerous men, all of them scumbags . . . and then she'd gone to the scumbags who'd hired her, to get her pay. She'd survived the torpedoing of her spacecraft in orbit around Vargas Two, a bullet that'd just missed her heart on Grimm's World, a cloud of deadly toxins on the Choking Moons, and having to fight her way past two eight-legged, tusked guard mastiffs twice the size of a full-grown skag on Cerberus III. All that—only to die here, it seemed, on this hellhole of a planet.

Brick saw it differently. He was delighted with the arrival of an army of enemies. "Now *this* is odds I like!" He cracked his fists together, backing toward the rear of the outrunner, probably planning to get to the turret gun.

Then Daphne saw Broomy, climbing up to the hilltop and into view, her scarred face creased with a grin. "I found the Goddess's army!" Broomy crowed, with a sweep of her hand, "and I brung it back with me just fer you!"

"If you're looking for Roland, he's not here!" Daphne yelled. "Neither is Mordecai! You can find their outrunner tracks on the other side of the hill! Your fight is with them, Broomy, not with us! We got no grudge against the General!"

Broomy laughed, and the others laughed with her, a psychotic chorus. The smell of their mouths, rank and rotten, rolled over Daphne with their laughter.

Broomy pointed at her. "You know how many of our people that Brick there killed?"

Brick hooted at that. "*I* know! Ask me. Thirty-seven!"

"And you," Broomy went on, glowering at Daphne. "The General knew you was with him, but she wanted to recruit you anyhow. She gave you a chance! And what'd you do? You walked away! Well, you lost your chance!!"

Doesn't much matter if I die here, Daphne decided. *Everybody's got to die somewhere. It's probably never going to be where you want it to be.*

She raised her combat rifle, very slowly . . .

"Who gets to git some offa that little woman first there?" asked a bare-chested Psycho in a plastic industrial mask, tittering after he asked it. His chest showed Gynella's insignia—but in scars.

"Not *you!*" Daphne told him, and she shot him in the head—twice. He fell back stone dead, his shield flickering.

"Cheap shield," one of the Psychos observed, looking at the body.

"*Get her!*" Broomy howled.

Guns were trained on Daphne; the Psycho soldiers started toward her and Brick.

"Don't kill her yet!" a Psycho howled gleefully, stepping down from the rim onto the hilltop. "I likes the bodies warm!"

But before the others could fire at Daphne, Brick vaulted into the outrunner; he scooped up a rocket launcher and was working the outrunner's machine-gun turret with one hand while firing the rocket launcher—tucked against his side—with the other.

"Yeah, bringing the pain!" Brick shouted as he fired.

Broomy dived out of the way just as a rocket shell blasted a chunk of rock near her, the blast flinging three Psychos into the air.

"Show me some blood!" Brick cackled.

Four more Psycho soldiers were shot off the hilltop, ripped in a strafe of his concentrated machine-gun fire. "Damn, I'm good!" he yelled.

Daphne had turned, was firing methodically at the Psycho soldiers ranged behind Brick, to protect his back, blowing away the top of one Psycho's skull, knocking another backward off his perch on a boulder—but the soldiers were firing too, and she was hit. She staggered and danced with the impacts of their bullets on her energy shield.

Another burst of gunfire knocked the rifle from her hand, and Daphne spun with the force of the burst and went down. Her shield was struck again and again. It weakened until a bullet penetrated the energy shield and hit her grazingly in the shoulder, and then she was hit by three electrically charged shots fired by a Bruiser. The rounds caused her to arch her back and convulse with shock—

And she lost consciousness.

Brick blasted half a dozen more Psycho soldiers off the hill with his rocket launcher, till he ran out of shells and tossed it aside, emptying the machine gun with his other hand.

Then the Psychos rushed him, firing, bullets rebounding from his shield. But the shield wouldn't last long with this barrage, he knew.

Brick let the *feeling* rise up in him.

Normally, he tried to keep that feeling down— it was dangerous. Sometimes he killed the wrong people when it took him over.

But today—right now—it was time to go . . . *berserk*.

That special something he called the *berserk feeling* took him over the top at times like this.

He passed into that state, and he began to kill. A crimson light suffused his senses, and he roared wordlessly—*"Yarrrrrrghhhh!"*—and leapt off the outrunner into a throng of his enemies, scattering them like a runaway train hitting a herd of animals.

The Psycho soldiers were flung backward from

him, their blood splashing, bones flying, teeth spinning away, as he jackhammered into them with his fists, faster and faster, right left, right left, right left, faster than the eye could follow.

A Bruiser rushed at him, and Brick smashed his fist right through the man's breastbone, yanked out the still-beating heart, and stuffed it down the dying man's throat, all in less than a second. Fist still bloody, he turned to strike another Psycho before the ripped-open Bruiser had quite fallen dead. Brick smashed every bone in his next target's head: jaw, cheekbones, cranium flew to flinders all in one blow.

Bullets cracked into his shield, and it began to give out. He felt the protection slipping away from him, but he didn't care; he was mad with bloodlust as he gripped a Psycho by the neck with his right hand, another by the face with his left. With his right hand he squeezed hard, crazy hard, and caused the man's blood to explode out of his eye sockets, making his eyeballs fly out with it; with his left, Brick dug his middle and index fingers squishily deep into the other Psycho's eye sockets, got a grip, and ripped the front of the man's skull off.

Those two Psycho soldiers fell, and he smashed two more with fists slammed left-right to their sternums, then turned to another—

Who was pointing a very large-caliber weapon at his head? It was a Tediore Avenger, aimed at him from about a meter away.

Brick roared defiance, his bellowing kill rage echoing across the Borderlands as he prepared to rush the Tediore—and then his enemy fired.

The bullet struck Brick glancingly in the side of his head, gouging but not penetrating—still he kept moving, grabbing the Tediore's barrel. And he used the weapon as a club to brain the gunman, and then the bloodied rifle slipped from his fingers.

Brick swayed . . .

And stared wildly around him . . .

And fell onto his back, toppling down like an ancient tree chainsawed at the base and crashing to the ground. The impact of the bullet had finally penetrated his thick skull enough to knock him cold—and now darkness closed over him.

It was a hot, dusty day on the parade ground, and Smartun was tired of supervising the marching drill. The soldiers, so called, were barely capable of keeping order, as they tramped in ragged lines back and forth, and he had to break up fights every ten minutes. The army typically lost a man every couple of days to a casual murder in the barracks. Smartun tried to avoid deaths on the parade ground when he could. But these knuckleheads seemed untrainable sometimes.

It didn't matter. Gynella wanted them trained anyway. And Smartun wanted whatever Gynella wanted.

Still, he was relieved when she sauntered up to him and made a peremptory wave of her hand that allowed him to dismiss the soldiers.

"Take it easy in the barracks!" he called after them. "And don't kill each other! It's against the rules!"

Grumbling, and with many hungry, backward looks at Gynella, they filed off to the barracks.

"My General?" he asked, turning to her, inclining his head respectfully. "Something's up, no?"

"Something's up, yes. I have the Second Division down on the southwestern frontier of the Salt Flats. There's a ripe settlement down there we want to overrun; we want to loot it and enslave it. Place called Bloodrust Corners." Almost as a vagrant afterthought, she added, "And of course, be sure to kill anyone who resists."

He nodded. *Of course.*

"But," she went on, "someone there has had the clever idea of setting up a big, high metal wall, guard towers, and other barriers around the settlement. They knew we were coming, and . . . well, there are moats of fire, there are kill-mechs, a lot of nasty things."

"Kill-mechs at a settlement? Where'd they get those?"

"It appears that they were a mining settlement. The kill-mechs double as mining robots, with drills and the like. They may have been retrofitted for the extra duty . . . there's someone clever there. But I won't be stopped, Smartun. I need that territory—it's all part of the plan!"

He nodded. He'd seen her charts, knew she had a strategy for taking over the planet by taking over key territories, especially those heavy with resources that could be embargoed till she was accepted as ruler of the planet.

She shaded her eyes and looked out across the Salt Flats, below the Devil's Footstool. "I want you to go there, Smartun, take half the First Division, reinforce the Second, and deal with these problems. I need someone cleverer than they've got with the Knife Legion, and I'm hoping you're the man. I've got to stay here for now and make sure we're ready for the Dahl operatives. But I will come out and inspect the battlefield, and soon. I'll be looking to see what progress you've made."

He bowed deeply this time. "I will not disappoint you. I would rather die, my General."

She smiled thinly. "That's the spirit."

He watched her, lovingly and achingly, as she walked back to her headquarters.

SEVEN

Roland was thirstier than a miner on payday.
They were trying to keep from drinking
too much of their water. But it was hard to
conserve in this baking heat.

"Suppose we break out of here before they find
us," Mordecai mused, as he trimmed his beard.
"Where do we go? They'll pursue, and they've got
long-range weapons . . ."

Bloodwing, sitting on its perch in the outrunner,
squawked as if concurring with its master's view of
the situation.

They were parked in the shade of the western
canyon wall, as far as possible from Gynella's army.
Roland was sitting on the ground, his back to the
outrunner's warm metal. Mordecai was sitting on a
rock nearby, looking in a little hand mirror as they
talked and trimming his beard with the tiniest pair
of scissors Roland had ever seen.

"I don't see how they haven't found us yet," Roland said.

"They're kind of oriented to the southwest—they're looking mostly out that way, focusing on that settlement over there. Pretty well-reinforced place called Bloodrust Corners. I was there overnight once."

"Must be pretty damned well defended if Gynella's bunch is waiting this long."

"Yeah. They got some kill-mechs, a wall shield, some other stuff. They thought it through. See, it's a co-op mine, run by the settlers, not a corporation effort. The miners do the work, share the profits. Kind of a new deal on this planet. There's a guy there named Dakes, same color as you are. He's got the place organized for good defense."

"Huh. They got a ECHO antenna there?"

"Yeah. Kind of short-range, I'd guess."

"We won't need much range," Roland said, standing and dusting himself off. "I'm gonna get close, and you're gonna talk to them on the ECHO."

"Get *close*? How? There's an army between us and them!"

"So? You wanna die here of thirst? Or wait till they notice us and start firing shells in here?"

Mordecai sighed. "What the hell. Let's do this. I didn't figure to live forever, anyway."

"Okay. You're driving, I'm on the turret."

"Nah, man," Mordecai said. "You're a better target standing up there than me. Turn me sideways, I almost disappear. And I'm a better shot than you, Roland, face it."

"So you say, Mordecai. Now's your chance to prove it. There are only twelve explosive shells left in that thing. Put that beauty on single shot, and fire it carefully. Now, let's take us a real long drink of water. We're gonna need it."

Two minutes later, they were tooling up the slope, headed right for the rear lines of Gynella's Knife Legion, Second Division.

When they got to the top of the slope, Roland slammed the accelerator and yelled, "Fire at will, man! But pick those targets!"

The army had pitched camp about a quarter-klick from the outer front gates of Bloodrust Corners, and they were lolling about, drinking, floundering in wrestling bouts, when the yawning sentries noticed the outrunner roaring up on them from the badlands. Roland was driving, Mordecai standing behind him at the big gun turret. Bloodwing was clinging to Mordecai's shoulder, its head ducked, its red eyes glaring a challenge at the enemy.

They got closer, closer yet, and now the sentries were taking aim at them, and Roland wondered when Mordecai was going to get around to firing the turret gun.

Bullets cracked overhead and zinged off the armored front of the outrunner. Roland hunched down far as he could and still drive.

"Mordecai? You still back there?"

"You said to pick my targets. Let me concentrate!"

The enemy lines were forming up now, about fifty meters off. Forty. Thirty . . .

"Mordecai?"

A bullet cracked into the outrunner's roll bar.

A Psycho was stepping out with a big rocket launcher on his shoulder and a grin on his face.

"Oh, *Mordecai*?"

Mordecai fired a shell—*whoomf!*—and it went directly into the rocket launcher's muzzle, down the tube, and struck the rocket inside, which was just then coming up the barrel.

The rocket launcher exploded in a ball of fire, taking the weapon, the Psycho, and four other soldiers standing on either side of him with it.

"Good shot!" Roland admitted.

Especially good, he thought, since the outrunner was bumping along on the uneven ground, bouncing on its shocks, and sometimes jumping hummocks.

Roland steered for the gap in the lines that Mordecai had made with that shot.

Mordecai fired again, three times more in quick succession, taking out a sniper, a Psycho with a submachine gun in each hand, and four men reaching into a box of grenades. He hit the box, and they all blew up with it.

Then the outrunner was careening right through the enemy lines, men running to get out of their way, some of them firing after them. Roland drove right over one of General Goddess's standards, her sign on a dyed cloth hoisted on a wooden pole, the pole snapping and flipping past him.

Mordecai shouted an order at Bloodwing, something Roland couldn't clearly hear, and the creature was suddenly flapping and soaring, then diving at the face of a man swinging a tripod machine gun toward the outrunner. The man screamed as Bloodwing, hovering in front of his face, scratched both his eyes out with a practiced double motion, one eye with each set of talons.

Roland dodged the vehicle past a rocket launcher, so that the rocket missed and killed two Psychos; Mordecai blew up that launcher too as they were passing it.

Up ahead he saw a cluster of three Psychos with combat rifles trying to get a bead on him. Roland's only weapon at the moment was the outrunner itself, and he knew better than to slam it into those beefcakes head on. That'd probably wreck him. Instead he acted as if he was veering completely around them, ducked under a spray of bullets, and then cut sharply back toward them, hitting the group glancingly. *Bing bang boom,* he hit the three in sequence, and he could hear bones popping with each impact.

They plowed through tents, Roland feeling the outrunner roll over a Psycho bandit lying in a tent, the guy's bones audibly crunching, the man's scream even more audible.

"Sorry, buddy," Roland said.

He drove on, and startled faces turned toward him as Psychos leapt out of the way. Three bandits in a row peeing in a trench jumped into the sewage to get out of Roland's way as he drove past the urinal ditch.

He drove on, bullets smacking against the outrunner, even as an energy bolt from an Eridian rifle struck the seat beside him, burning a hole through it, and another bolt caused a charge explosion to detonate just in front of the outrunner.

"Dammit!" Mordecai said, as the vehicle jumped at the near impact.

Roland glanced over his shoulder in time to see Mordecai with his feet bounced into the air, his hands desperately holding on to the turret grips, till the smaller man fell back down on his feet again.

Roland chuckled, returning his attention to crossing the enemy camp, and saw a big man—a damned *big* Psycho—looming up: a Badass Bruiser, just a stump for a left arm but an overgrown right arm; in his right hand he carried a mace-like weapon crackling with electricity. His eyes were hidden in goggles, his head in a striped helmet, his chest decked out in a *G* breastplate.

They were hard to bring down, this variety of Bruiser—the radiation had mutated them into gigantic killing machines. And one sweep from that weapon might well smash into his outrunner engine, with the next swipe aimed at his head.

Bloodwing was suddenly there, raking at the Badass Bruiser's exposed arms, then deftly avoiding the swish of his electrified mace.

Just before Roland came into the Bruiser's reach, five shots from the turret cannon on the outrunner *whoomed* in quick succession, and the Badass Bruiser staggered back, his energy shield taking the impacts but not all of the force.

The fourth and fifth shells penetrated the shield, and the Bruiser's head parted company with his neck. Roland tried to avoid the heaving fall of the enormous headless cadaver, but it fell half across the outrunner, gushing blood from a neck stump into his vehicle.

"Crap," Roland muttered.

Then the last few sentries dived to avoid being run down, and he was through the enemy lines, with bullets whining past him from behind. Bloodwing was flying ahead of them, and Mordecai was shouting into his wrist communicator, trying to raise Bloodrust Corners.

Roland drove in an irregular pattern to throw off the enemy's aim but working his way toward his goal, that rusty metal gate up ahead.

They were getting damned close. He wondered if he could smash through it with the outrunner.

More likely he'd smash *on* it.

A rocket shell exploded just to the right of the outrunner, raining dirt and rocks on Roland and Mordecai.

The gate was only another ten meters ahead . . .

And then the big rusty barrier grated open, and Roland drove through, into the settlement of Bloodrust Corners.

They stood in the open steel chamber, Dakes and Mordecai and Roland, at the top of a lookout tower. The tower jutted up at the corner of the western wall of the settlement. Reticulating energy fields protected the lookout from snipers. Below them, outside the wall, were the Salt Flats and a lot of level open ground, here and there pocked by shell craters. Past the open ground, smoke rose from fires, unruly lines of men marched, sentries leaned on rifles, Gynella's symbol flapped on standards, pitched tents of cheap yellow plastic looked like disease blisters . . . and the desert was choked with milling Psycho soldiers.

Turning around, Roland looked over the fifteen-acre spread of Bloodrust Corners. The small settlement was enclosed by a rusty metal wall three times higher than a tall man. Within the boxy confines of the walls were humplike houses of concrete and wattle, roofed by curved slats of tin, and boxy outbuildings for pumps and storage. Smoke rose here and there, and a few children played in a central commons. People chatted in groups or pushed carts; the occasional mining tractor putted along slowly through the narrow lanes. Against the farther wall were the low entrances to the three mines, where elevators carried miners down to the digs—low, roughly pyramidal shapes against the rusty metal backdrop. The scene looked quiet enough, but at each corner of the walls was a watchtower, with two armed men. Gun slots opened in the walls at regular intervals, and three mortars stood ready to lob shells at the enemy should they get close. Kill-mechs waited just inside the gate; a strip of ground around the settlement was treated with an incendiary fluid.

Dakes was a large black man with salt-and-pepper hair matching his salt-and-pepper beard. He wore green coveralls and a bulletproof vest. When Roland shook his hand, it was like grasping sandpaper. The man had calluses. This was a working man.

Dakes stared at Mordecai. "Say, weren't you here before? A few months ago?"

Mordecai nodded, tugging his beard. Blood-wing shifted uneasily on his shoulder. "Yeah. I stayed maybe twenty-four hours. A while back."

Dakes kept looking him up and down. "You didn't happen to get one of our girls pregnant while you were here, did you?"

"What? Me?"

Roland managed not to laugh. *What? Me?*

"I mean, why would you say *that*?" Mordecai asked. "Someone accusing me?"

"No. I don't know who did it. We do get a lot of damn vagabonds through here."

"Vagabonds!" Offended, Mordecai sniffed. "So I'm a *vagabond*?"

Dakes looked evenly at him. "If you're not, what are you?"

"Me? Well, I . . . uh . . . I sort of . . . um . . ." Blood-wing cawed a laugh. "Shut your beak, Bloodwing."

"Mr. Dakes—" Roland began.

"You can call me Cronley, boy. Cronley Dakes."

"Cronley, you know what you're in for, with that horde of Psychos and bandits out there?"

Dakes nodded. "I just wonder why they're waiting."

"Waiting for orders, maybe. Or thinking to starve you out because they know you're pretty well defended. How are you set up for supplies?"

Dakes frowned at him. "Who wants to know?"

"You really think I'm a spy? You see how many of those so-called soldiers we killed, coming in here?"

Dakes nodded grudgingly. "You've got a point—you made quite a mess out there. We're pretty well supplied for a while. A week or two."

"Water supply?" Mordecai asked.

"That's the good news. We have an excellent well." Dakes scowled out at the horizon. "What a place. This planet—just try getting the settlements to help one another. Not much of that. Help under siege? Sorry, we're busy scratching our asses. We got a little help from New Haven but not much. No one does anything for anybody else on this rolling rock. Not outside these walls."

Mordecai blinked. "But inside these walls you're trying to build some kind of community? On Pandora?" He seemed mildly amazed by the concept.

Dakes smiled ruefully. "We're trying. We're going to build a schoolhouse. We have a clinic. We're trying to teach the kids it matters what you do for other folks—and what they do for you. Community matters. But that's a strange idea on this planet."

Roland remembered Cal, a boy he'd befriended, not so long ago, on Pandora. He'd been relieved when Cal and his mother had left the planet— relieved because this was no place to raise a kid. These people were either crazy or visionaries to try it.

"What do you mine here?" Roland asked. "Iridium?"

"No, that stuff's dangerous to be around much." He pointed at Gynella's army. "Look at them! That's iridium damage, from the radiation."

Roland nodded. He planned on limiting his exposure when he went after the crystalisks.

"No," Dakes went on, "we mine glam gems. They're a fairly new find on the planet—just last year big deposits of glam gems were located here."

"I don't think I know what a glam gem is."

Dakes drew two polished gems from his pockets. One pebble-sized gem was prevailingly green, the other red. "You never saw these?" He brought the two gems, one in each hand, into contact with each other. The red one took on some of the green one's color; the green one took on a strong tinge of red. "They're beautiful, and they're sensitive to one another—"

"Huh," Roland said, puzzled. "And people *buy* stuff like that?"

"People put them in marriage rings."

"Hey, I'd buy a couple of those," Mordecai said. "The ladies would totally—" He cleared his throat. "Well, anyway, you guys are making good money from this, I guess—and General Goddess Gynella wants to take it from you?"

"That's what our prisoner said. She wants the gems."

"You've got a prisoner, one of the soldiers?" Roland asked. He needed information. An imprisoned Gynellan could provide it.

He was trying to figure out how to get Gynella to give up on this settlement so her army would withdraw and he could go on his way . . . or figure a way out of there, just him and Mordecai. It kind of bothered him to leave these people on their own, with Gynella's Psycho soldiers waiting out there. The residents of Bloodrust Corners seemed capable but maybe a bit naïve. Earlier Dakes had said he'd only been on the planet a couple of years.

Dakes shook his head. "We're trying to treat the prisoner with decency, but it's hard. He bit off somebody's finger when they were trying to give him a sandwich. He tried to bite a Claptrap, too."

"Must've been hard on his teeth," Roland said. "Any chance we could talk to him? We need to get out southwest, need to know what he knows."

"You ask him, he'll spit blood in your eye."

Mordecai chuckled grimly. "Bloodwing'll get him to talk."

She woke to a banging sound, like someone hitting a big hammer on a slab of steel.

After a moment, Daphne realized the sound was coming from within—it was her head throbbing.

She forced her eyes open—it felt as if the eyelids might tear at the effort, as if they were glued shut.

But at last she was able to prise them open and blink blearily around her.

She was lying on her left side, on the ground, just far enough from a campfire to get no real warmth from it. She could see that the sky was dark beyond it, and little more. It was night, then. Psycho bandits, wearing the livery of Gynella, shuffled about, carrying weapons, cursing when they got in one another's way. Scuffles broke out; a ways off, a gunshot sounded, someone yelped, and a gruff authoritarian voice bellowed, "You damn fool, now he's wounded, and I'll have to shoot him! We got a shortage of Dr. Zed, we got no way to carry no damn invalids, and you've wasted a good soldier. He dug a latrine like no other man!"

Someone called feebly, "Don't shoot me, Sarge, I'm fine! Hardly hurts at all. You don't have to—"

There was a gunshot, followed by the echo of the shot—and silence.

Daphne groaned. She was alive, but she was prisoner of the Psycho bandits.

She tried to wriggle about, push herself up from the ground, but her hands were bound behind her, tied by a long cord to her ankles. Not a good situation.

She wondered if anyone had their way with her when she was out cold. And if they had, how many of them?

But she didn't feel as if she'd been violated.

Maybe they were saving her for something special. She turned her head to look right, as much as she could, and to her surprise saw a heavily chained, bound figure lying on his back, his head the only part of him unbound. It was Brick! She could see his eyes slightly open, the eyelids fluttering slightly.

So Brick was alive. There was a nasty splotch of dried blood on the side of his head. He'd been hit hard enough to put him down, maybe render him comatose. But he was alive.

That was something to hold on to. Despite the growing agony in her wrists and ankles, the strain on her shoulders from the awkward binding, she felt a glimmer of hope. She wasn't quite alone in this.

Only—if she was to get any help from Brick, he had to live. He had to wake up. And somehow he had to get free.

"Well, now, opened her itty-bitty eyes, has she, the little thing?" said a harsh voice from behind her. She couldn't see the woman speaking, but she knew from the sound and the smell just who it was.

"Hello, Broomy," Daphne said raspily. "How are you?"

"Me? Pretty good! Had some food, some medicine, took a nap on a nice bedroll. Had a good crap. Plenty of water to drink, too. And of course I don't have my little wrists tied to my ankles like some people do. How's your circulation? Hurt, does it?" Broomy creaked with laughter.

Daphne forced an insouciant smile. "Could be worse. I could be an ugly mama-skag like you."

Shouldn't have said it. She knew that. Knew it even more sharply when Broomy kicked her, hard, in the middle of the back.

"You enjoy that? It's only gonna get worse. They've got something planned for you. They're gonna let a Goliath kill Brick in the coliseum. And for his reward, the Goliath gets to play with you! You know what a Goliath'll do to a little girl like you? He'll pull your legs apart, keep pullin' an' pullin' till you rip in half, right down the middle, and he'll dance in the mess, n' laugh as he does it!"

EIGHT

There wasn't much room in the stone storage shack Bloodrust Corners was using for a jail cell. Roland was crowded in with Mordecai and Dakes, with the prisoner lying on the dirt floor at their feet.

"I want to know what Gynella's little army out there is waiting for," Dakes said. "I want to know what she plans for us. You tell us that, you'll get better treatment."

"Okay, here's my conditions for telling you all about Gynella's army," said the Psycho prisoner, his grin displaying a mouth in which the few teeth were snaggled and red with blood. His bare, bloodied ankles were chained to the wall; his fox-narrow face was tattooed with a pattern like a web of broken glass, centered on his nose. His scalp was scabby and hairless. "First, you bring me a bee-yew-tiful girl, make that two girls, and leave me alone with them and a bottle of fine narcojuice. Then you take their bodies out, and you bring me in a feast, maybe a big juicy steak of a—"

"I've got another idea," Mordecai interrupted. "How about if I stop my friend Bloodwing here from taking *both* your eyes? One might be enough. He does like to eat both, though. He's partial to a man's eyes."

The prisoner stared. "Your friend who?"

Mordecai smiled thinly and opened the door of the jail cell. He whistled, and Bloodwing flapped into the cell and landed on his outstretched hand. It cocked its head to eye the prisoner hungrily.

The prisoner recoiled into a corner. "What *is* that thing?"

"It eats carrion, and it doesn't care," Mordecai said, "if the carrion is alive or dead."

"Can there be living carrion?" Dakes asked, as if academically curious.

"There can be, in this case. So—" Mordecai smiled coldly at the prisoner. "Which eye do you want to lose first? Left or right? Your choice."

Roland winced at this. Torture was not his style. But he knew that Mordecai was largely bluffing. He'd maim anyone who was trying to kill him, but an unarmed man in a cell? No, he wouldn't really order Bloodwing to rip a man's eyes out under those conditions.

Or would he?

The prisoner swallowed hard, and Roland could see him working up his courage. He spat at Bloodwing, which squawked and snapped its beak with a clack.

The prisoner snarled, "Go to the pit of darkness and rot there! I'll twist that thing's neck if it gets anywhere near me!"

Mordecai sighed and murmured something to Bloodwing, something inaudible to Roland. Bloodwing sprang into the air and immediately dove at the prisoner, who flailed his arms to keep Bloodwing back. Bloodwing hovered, flapping its wings rapidly, deftly avoiding the man's hands, then pointed its wings at the ceiling so that it dropped at the prisoner's face and dug its talons deeply into the skin just over the Psycho's right eye. The prisoner grabbed at Bloodwing, but it performed a remarkably adroit twist with its entire body, pushing off the bloodied face to leap into the air, out of reach. It screeched mockingly, flying over to light on Mordecai's shoulder.

"You *missed* his eye, Bloodwing, you only got close to it," Mordecai said chidingly.

Bloodwing ducked its head as if in sorrow and shrugged.

The prisoner was furiously wiping blood from his eyes. Mordecai grunted and said, "Well, one more time, then. This time, see if you can get both eyes, really rip them up good—I know you can do it! This is a great training opportunity, Bloodwing!"

"No no no!" the prisoner screamed. "I'll tell you! It doesn't matter, because you can't stop her! Gynella's just waiting for her new commander. She's waitin' for Smartun, and when he gets here he's gonna take the whole place down. And Gynella's gonna waltz in here, and she's gonna take her pick of the prisoners, and Dr. Vialle's gonna use some for experiments, and she'll use some for slaves to help build stuff, and they'll kill anybody that resists, and if there's women or girls, they'll be given as prizes to the soldiers for good behavior—"

"Good *behavior*!" Dakes burst out, laughing and shaking his head. "Oh, for the Angel's sake."

"Obedience to her is good behavior!" the Psycho prisoner insisted, pointing a filthy, bloody finger at them. "And you'd better obey the General Goddess! Because she's going to come here, and she'll tear you right in half! I *promise* you she will! Why, she could kill any one of you *personally*! There's a reason we call her Goddess! She has the power in her hands to take a man to heaven! And she has the power to take his life—" He snapped his fingers. "Like that! And she's coming to you, to destroy you or enslave you. And you can't stop her. Because she is the vengeful soul of this world!" He tittered madly and howled, "She is the vengeful soul of Pandora!"

They were standing in front of the mine entrances in Bloodrust Corners—Roland, Mordecai, and Dakes—as the dusk gathered and the sky got slowly more gloomy. "That's one of our kill-mechs," Dakes said, pointing at a big tri-wheel robot trundling by, the mech shaped like a cylinder with arms. It was a little taller than Roland, and it had a ring of sensors all the way around its cylinder, near the top; from its upper sides extended long mechanical arms, one ending in a rifle that had been built seamlessly into its metal forearm, the other ending in a jackhammer. Behind it came a much smaller robot, a Claptrap, jigging as if dancing as it came, singing to itself in an artificial tenor,

> *"I gotta program that lets me sing*
> *Everybody oughta try this thing*
> *I gotta chip that lets me dance*
> *Come on baby take a chance."*

Despite amusing itself with song and dance, the Claptrap seemed to be directing the mech in some way.

"Unit seven," Dakes told the Claptrap. "See that mech gets charged and serviced quick as possible. We don't know when the attack might come!"

"Gotcha, boss! Gotcha, I'm on it! I gotta program that lets me sing . . ." The robots trundled past.

"Glad that big mech's on our side," Mordecai said. "How many do you have?"

"Only three mechs programmed for fighting," said a woman's voice. Roland turned to see a young black woman striding confidently up to them, a look of amused curiosity on her face.

Dakes smiled, seeing her. "Ah, here's my daughter. Roland, Mordecai, this is Glory."

"Sure is," Mordecai muttered. He winced when Roland gave him a shot in the ribs with his elbow.

But both he and Roland were staring at Glory, Dakes's beautiful daughter, a shapely, poised, young woman, wavy dark hair tied back, eyes set off by white eyeliner. She wore shorts on her taut, muscular legs; a desert camouflage top tied off over her belly; on her hip was an Atlas pistol, and she wore large miner's boots, but they somehow didn't spoil the effect.

Glory was staring at Roland. "Hi," she said. "You're Roland, yeah?"

Roland was surprised. "Yeah. Your dad tell you?"

"Naw, it's a . . . well, people talk about you." She seemed a little embarrassed and turned to flash a smile at Mordecai. "You'd be Mordecai, I bet. I've heard about you too. Maybe you could teach some of us how to shoot better."

"I'd give you lessons anytime," Mordecai said. Then he quickly added, "In shooting."

"You going to join our little town here?" she asked, looking back and forth between them—but her eyes lingered on Roland.

"I, uh . . ." Mordecai began. "Well, I *could* consider it, actually . . ." He tore his gaze from Glory and pointed at the mines. "So, these mine shafts all finish in dead ends? I mean, suppose you got to give up this outpost for a while? How do you retreat? That prisoner made it clear Gynella's not letting anyone go. It's either die or surrender to slavery. So if we can't beat 'em, how do we get away from 'em?"

Roland looked at him, not sure what he meant. "What's that got to do with the mine?"

But Dakes was nodding. He spoke in a low voice. "Yes. That center mine, there, connects with a cavern. And there is a way out to a canyon, a little farther south, through that cavern. But it's a narrow way—and anyhow we don't want to just give up what we've worked for here."

Roland shrugged. "If it comes to that, this place could be retaken later, like Mordecai says. You've got money from all this. You could hire mercenaries."

"Mercenaries," said Glory, her face clouding, "are scum."

Dakes put a protective arm around his daughter. "She had a bad encounter with a merc. But she waited her chance—he's buried outside the walls."

"Not all mercenaries are quite the same," Roland said softly. "Anyhow, I think you ought to have a plan B, if this thing goes sour here."

"*You're* here now," Glory said, looking at Roland. "Now I've got more hope."

Mordecai rolled his eyes, and Bloodwing rolled its.

Voices drew their attention to the nearest mine entrance. Four tired-looking men shuffled out, talking wearily, all wearing miner's coveralls, energy-charged mining jackhammers in their hands. They were followed by a cylindrical mech lacking the rifle arm, pushing a cart of gem-bearing ore.

One of the men, the youngest, a pale, dirt-smudged man with a thatch of brown hair, paused, seeing Glory, then hurried over to her, wiping dirt off his face with his free hand.

"Hi," he said. "What's going on?" He frowned, looking Roland and Mordecai over, taking in their weapons and their innate spring-coiled wariness.

"This is one of our engineers—we call him Lucky," Dakes said, nodding at the young man. Roland could see by the warmth in Dakes's eyes that Glory's father liked Lucky. "He's foreman of mine number one, there. Lucky, this is Roland and Mordecai. They broke through Gynella's lines out there while you were down below. Did some real damage. Mordecai got something out of that prisoner." Dakes looked at Roland. "Lucky here's the one who caught the prisoner. He snuck out at night, and dragged him back. Almost got shot doing it."

Lucky turned to Glory. "You guys sure these mercenary types are . . . trustworthy?"

He shot Roland and Mordecai a hard glance, as if daring them to take offense.

"Dad's a good judge of character," Glory said. Her eyes softened when she looked at Lucky. "You oughta go clean up, get something to eat."

"Come over to our place," Dakes said. "We'll give you dinner, Lucky. We all need to eat. I've gotta feeling we're going to need our strength." He turned to Roland. "You both are invited too."

Roland nodded. "Thanks."

Dakes pointed at a hut. "That little place is empty. You can bunk there for now. We'll talk at dinner. About . . . what Mordecai suggested. I don't incline that way, but no reason to not have options."

He nodded at them and walked off with Glory, his arm around her, the two of them talking in low tones. Roland could see how strong their relationship was in their relaxed body language.

Something in him ached. What would it be like to have children? To have a daughter like that?

He shook his head. *Ridiculous.*

"So, you two," Lucky said, hefting his jackhammer. "Where'd you come from before here?"

Mordecai pointed. "That way." He seemed annoyed by Lucky's obvious mistrust.

But Roland didn't blame the young miner. "We're not sure we're staying," Roland said. "But we're not going to do you any harm. We already cut down the odds against you people out there. We'll do what we can—if we decide to stay here."

"Don't do us any favors," Lucky said. "We'll do all right without your type." And he walked away.

Mordecai looked after him and snorted. "He doesn't trust us. It's jealousy, is what it is," he whispered to Roland. "He's into that girl, Glory. Big-time."

"Is he? Real perceptive of you, Mordecai," Roland said dryly. "Almost as hard to see as that goddamn beard on your chin that nearly puts people's eyes out."

"Very funny. Well, anyhow, it's obvious what we have to do. Get out through that center mine, there. We'll go out through the cavern, and we'll have to steal an outrunner somewhere, or hire one, and then . . . what?" He lifted his goggles from his eyes and squinted at Roland. "No! You're not really thinking of . . ."

"I don't know. But it's a little hard for me to leave these people without any backup at all. They've got kids running around in here. Actual—" He stared as a little boy and girl ran by, chasing a Claptrap. "Children."

"Sure, well, that was their dumb mistake, bringing kids here. I mean, who does that? Kids on this planet?" He shook his head.

"It's not unheard of. But I agree, it was foolish." Roland sighed. "I just don't see how we can just walk off."

"You don't? You just watch me. I'm gonna eat, I'm gonna rest, then I'm getting out of here. With or without you."

"Okay. But suppose General Gynella finds out about that cavern? Suppose while you're using it to get out, she uses it to get in?"

NINE

Smartun was tired, aching from the long drive in the outrider. But in another way he felt good, driving along with the wind in his face, the engine growling defiance to the world, crossing the Salt Flats in the moonlight, two protective outriders flanking him. It felt good to be away from the Devil's Footstool, roaming a world once more, on a mission for his mistress, his Goddess...

The feeling of renewed freedom whispered to him, suggesting that he could get away from those idiots Gynella had sent as his bodyguards. He could kill them when they weren't expecting it, or give them the slip, and he could heave off in another direction entirely—maybe just head full blast to Fyrestone, and then the shabby little spaceport, and just get himself free of this planet entirely. He was sick of the sight and smell of the

Psycho soldiers. He had some money tucked away in his coat for emergencies.

Pleasant to dream about. But he knew he could never do it.

He could never abandon Gynella. If he tried, he'd only come back on his knees, begging her to forgive him. She'd probably kill him for desertion, then and there, and he wouldn't blame her at all.

He'd never desert her. Not really.

Smartun drove on and on, and soon he saw the campfires of the Knife Legion, burning against the horizon like the multiple red eyes of some nightmare predator.

The mine was well shored up; nothing was likely to fall down on him, but Mordecai felt anyway as if it was about to. The helmet light he'd cadged from the supply shed illuminated the down-slanting interior of the mine with a glaucous glow, the carven stone walls looking slick in the light, descending into shadow like the gullet of some giant saurian.

"I'm being swallowed here," he muttered, making his way down.

Maybe the feeling of being trapped wasn't from the outside. Maybe it was from the inside. Maybe he was bothered by something.

It did bother him that he'd left Roland back there. They were almost friends, sort of, kind of, in a way . . . and he was leaving him to fight the Knife Legion with a few confused miners. Sure, Roland and Mordecai had spent the afternoon giving shooting lessons to the settlement's men and offering advice on how to deal with the Psycho soldiers.

"If you haven't got a good kill shot, try to shoot out their knees before they get too close. Once they get close they're deadly . . ."

But that wasn't what the settlement needed. It needed backup. It needed as much firepower as it could get. More important, to Mordecai, *Roland* needed backup—from his sort of, kind of, friend. Closest thing he had to a friend lately. Roland . . .

Stop being a sap, he told himself, as he stepped over a hummock of loose rock and worked his way deeper into the mine.

Stupid, feeling sorry for the settlement. That kind of thinking would get you killed on this planet. Dakes's settlers, especially, coming here to start a legit co-op business, bringing children.

Someone like him or Roland, why, they didn't fit in anywhere but on a world where killing was the norm, where life balanced on a razor's edge, where adrenaline and a good weapon were a man's only salvation. But to bring your *family*? To bring children here? Why, it was practically suicide. Who was he to stand in the way of suicide? Mass suicide at that.

The hell with them. All of them. Even those damn

kids, running and playing in the street, counting on the adults to keep them safe . . .

Damn kids.

His grim rumination was interrupted by a blast of chill air. He'd come to the end of the mine shaft. It widened there, and to one side were carts on rails. Up ahead, the way was blocked by a barrier made out of thin sheets of metal. The cold air came from a thin gap in the metal barricade.

"Crap," Mordecai muttered. That must be the way to the cavern—blocked off.

Looking around, he found a pair of heavy gloves lying beside a cart and put them on, then began to pry at the metal sheets, slowly peeling them back.

Smartun was glad to see that the equipment he'd ordered had gotten there ahead of him. The two new catapults reared in dark skeletal shapes against the sky. It'd been relatively easy to have them built from scrap materials at the last settlement the army had razed.

Stretching his legs with a walk around the encampment, Smartun strode ahead of Skenk and Bulge. They followed loosely, still acting as bodyguards—and possibly as Gynella's spies, to make sure he was doing what he was supposed to. He walked past tents and campfires, where men gambled and grumbled. A rank smell swept over him as he came upon a sewage ditch, a mix of running water and waste, in which one Psycho was, it seemed, drowning a smaller one; the big Psycho was holding the Midget's head under sewage.

"Yes, you choke in that!" the big Psycho bandit snarled, as he held the thrashing Midget down. "You choke good!"

"Skenk, stop that waste of resources!" Smartun ordered.

Skenk went to the edge of the ditch, raised his auto shotgun, took careful aim to blow the bigger Psycho's head off, so he could save the little guy from being drowned.

"No, dammit, Skenk, don't kill that one either! They're both resources. We need them both."

Skenk turned him a puzzled look. It was hard for the Psycho soldiers to understand the "don't kill him" order.

Then Skenk shrugged and fired the gun over the man's head. Someone, somewhere in the background, yelled in pain.

Smartun sighed.

The gunshot got the attention of the bigger man in the ditch. He let go of the choking Psycho Midget and turned to gape at them. "What?"

"What you killing that one for?" Skenk asked, as the Midget sat up, sputtering.

"He tried ta steal something from me!" the bigger Psycho said. "I think. Maybe."

"I did not!" the little guy said, and sank his teeth deeply into the calf of the big one's leg.

The bigger Psycho howled and kicked the Psycho Midget loose.

It took another several minutes to get them separated and pacified.

Smartun had been joined by the subcommander of the Knife Legion, Bolkus, a difficult-to-control Badass Psycho. Now he pointed at the Midget Psycho. "Bolkus, take this one to the special munitions enclosure."

"What's that?"

"I sent instructions. Don't you have the Midgets we captured in a corral? The special munitions enclosure?"

"Oh, that's what you call the corral? But this one isn't captured. He's one of us."

"Now he goes in the corral with the bunch you captured. See that they're watched. I don't want any of them getting away. We'll need them." Smartun looked toward the settlement of Bloodrust Corners. "We'll need them fairly soon. Just before dawn."

About a half hour before dawn Roland gave up trying to sleep. Some instinct seemed to insist he get up and look around the settlement.

Carrying a Tediore Genocide Stomper in one hand, his other hand on the pistol in his holster,

Roland left the hut and stretched, then went to the watch fires glowing in pitted metal barrels. Several men stood in the circle of firelight. Dakes was up too, staring pensively into the flames; beside him were Lucky and a muscular, shirtless miner, Gong, a scarred man with filed teeth. A former nomad who'd changed his ways to marry a settlement girl, Gong rarely spoke, but he was the only one in the camp besides Dakes who hadn't needed extra instruction with a weapon. Roland intended to keep Gong close to him when the fight came.

Dakes glanced up at him. "You're up early. Where's that little partner of yours?"

Roland suspected that Mordecai had slipped out the back way, as he'd said he would, but he didn't know for sure, so he only shrugged. "Any movement from out there?"

"Some. They've been moving catapults into place—I think that's what they are. They arrived a few hours ago."

"No kidding? I've never seen a catapult on this planet. But it figures. Gynella's always got to scrounge for ammo. Smart to use catapults. Stick a boulder in one of those, there's your free ammo, lying right on the ground."

Roland remembered how Brick had used a boulder as "ammo" and damaged the Scorpio turret. He wondered how Brick was doing—had he run into Gynella's people? At some point, Brick would have to confront the Psycho soldiers again. The thought almost made him feel sorry for the Psychos. Almost.

Maybe he should've stuck with Brick, even if it meant keeping that dark little female killer with them. Brick sure would've been a help here . . .

"There's extra ammo for that combat rifle," Dakes said. "It's in that stack just inside the gate."

"Good, thanks. Right now I'm thinking about the possibility of a sortie. I might be able to—"

"You might be able to slip away and desert us?" Lucky interrupted, looking at him.

Dakes shot a glare at Lucky. "Dammit, shut up!"

Roland chuckled. "Kid—" He grinned at Lucky. "You really that worried I'm going to take your girl?"

Lucky ground his teeth together. "You saying she'd go anywhere near you, you Arid Lands bum?"

"Lucky," Dakes hissed, "the man's only got so much patience. You're gonna get yourself killed!"

Roland shook his head. "Kid, the girl is too young for me. Not my style. Even if she throws herself at me, I'd have to disappoint her. So you can stop with the adolescent hostility—"

"Throws herself at you!" Lucky sputtered in disbelief. He balled his fists and rushed at Roland.

Roland simply stepped aside, extending his leg

a little, so that Lucky tripped over it and fell face-down.

The other men laughed. Roland reached down and hauled Lucky to his feet by the collar. "Take it easy, kid. I was just ribbing you. I'm not going after your girl. We need to work together, all of us, if we're going to stay alive. If you and that girl are gonna live to have your kids someday."

Lucky glared at him, twisting from his grasp, then glanced at Dakes, who nodded, smiling. Finally, Lucky said grudgingly, "Yeah. Okay. But you got lucky just now."

"Heh heh—he sure did 'get Lucky.'" Dakes chuckled as Lucky stalked off toward a watchtower. "He got him facedown in the dirt."

Mordecai was sick of tramping through this cavern. He was cold and tired, and he wanted to sleep, but it wasn't safe to close his eyes for long—he was too vulnerable there, with only minor weaponry on him. He had only four grenades, and the Cobra combat rifle. He hadn't wanted to take gear that Roland might need.

The cavern smelled heavily of dissolved minerals, and underneath that was a gamy animal smell. What *was* that? Seemed like he'd smelled that once before . . . nasty sort of smell.

He continued on, noticing that the slope angled upward. He was constantly watching for sudden crevices, trying not to trip over stalagmites, wary for subterranean predators.

And then he heard someone singing, up ahead in the cavern.

> "... I gotta chip that lets me dance
> Come on baby take a chance."

It was that annoying little Claptrap robot with the pointless song-and-dance chip. Mordecai could hear the robot's piping voice echoing thinly off the stalagmites and the natural stone dome of the ceiling.

He passed into another, wider chamber of the cavern, and there was the Claptrap, dancing and singing in the middle of the dirt floor. About fifty long paces ahead, light was coming in from the outside—thin, pale, silver light, probably moonlight. That must be the way out of the cavern.

The curved walls and floor there seemed more like packed dirt than stone. That smell was stronger there too, that odd animal smell.

And the robot was there, jigging and singing. "I gotta program that—"

"Hey, robot!" Mordecai barked.

The Claptrap spun around—literally spun around, more than once, till finally it was facing him. "Wha-a-at? Oh! Oh, you gave me a fright! You almost made me pee lubricant!"

"What the hell are you doing down here?"

"Why, don't you know, Mr. Dakes set me to watching the back entrance! Of course the guardian is here, but I'm here too 'cause Dakes wants me to come and report to him if the bad lady finds the back way in and— Wait, what's the password? You gotta say the password!"

"Never mind that. What guardian are you talking about?"

"Just the Thresher, that's all. There was two of them, but one of them ate the other one—"

"Wait, did you say a *Thresher*?"

"Oh, yes. He tried to eat me and spat me out, halfway down his gullet. He learned I'm not digestible 'cause I'm metal. But most of *you'd* be digestible. Like what's not left of that guy—" The robot pointed a mechanical hand at a skull, a few bones, a rusted gun, and some bits of armor left piled in a shaft of moonlight across the chamber.

"Where is this Thresher now?"

"Oh, I don't know, it could be outside the cavern—it goes down into the dirt and comes up outside and eats people and things out there. It eats dirt too if it has something tasty and disgusting in it. If you want to see the Thresher, we could sing and dance while we wait for it, if you want. Everyone sing: I gotta program that—"

"Cut that shit out. You think it's not here now, right? Okay, I'm leaving, before it comes back."

Mordecai started across the dirt ground of the cavern chamber.

The robot chirped up. "I didn't say the Thresher wasn't here! I said it might be outside. But come to think of it, I do think I feel its vibration in the floor, and is that a tentacle over there near your foot? Oh, dear."

Mordecai turned in time to see a tentacle whip up from the dirt, and the tentacle stared at him: the gray and yellow tentacle had an *eye* on it partway down its sinuous, barbed length. It was a black, shining eye but clearly an eye. Then the tentacle slapped toward his leg. He leapt back, just out of reach, hopping awkwardly, remembering being dragged underground by the varkid. And Roland wasn't there to pull his ass out of the fire this time.

Mordecai tracked the tentacle with his gunsight as it came toward him, the Thresher's rubbery limb cutting the dirt like a periscope from a sub-aquatic craft; it was a big, hefty, barbed tentacle, with a sharp black hook on the end, a hook that now slashed up at him.

Mordecai fired the Cobra and hit the tentacle in its eye, cutting the whipping pseudopod right through, as the gun's boom echoed in the cavern.

"Ooooh, nice shot!" the Claptrap shrilled.

Mordecai thought about turning back to the stone-floored part of the cavern, but he'd come a long way, and this creature was between him and the way out.

The remains of the tentacle darted below, but Mordecai had seen these strange, enigmatic creatures once before and knew there were many tentacles and a voracious body down below. There was only one way to kill it—he had to get that hidden, burrowing head and body to show itself. And the only way to do that was to shoot the—

Tentacles whipped upward suddenly, two of them coming from right and left, as if they were trying to trap him between clapping hands. He saw more eyes glittering on the tentacles, hooks flashing, and he lurched and fell on his back, cursing himself for his clumsiness.

A tentacle twined around his ankle; another poised over him, about to strike. Mordecai fired instinctively, his hands finding a target, and the burst cut the poising tentacle in half. Ichor flew from its severed ends. The other tentacle began to drag him across the dirt . . . and down.

"Hey! Claptrap! Come on over here, grab my arm!"

"Not me, can't do it. Dakes wants me to stay here and watch for bad lady people, not get pulled under the dirt where my parts can get grit in 'em! That would be contraindicated!"

"I'll disassemble you with a rusty wrench, you little—" He didn't get any more out; he had to use every ounce of energy to resist the inexorable pull of that tentacle. He aimed with the gun, balancing it on his knee, his hands shaking, thinking there was a very good chance he was about to blow his own foot off. He had to be precise. The Thresher was pulling harder, and in a moment—

He fired, just one round exactly aimed, barely missing his own ankle, cutting through the tentacle. It spurted fluid, and he was able to pull his leg back and had just managed to scramble to his feet, when the thing's head burst up from its burrow, dirt spilling off its sides. The Thresher was big, big enough to swallow him whole. It reared over him, and he knew that swallowing him whole was exactly what it had in mind. Its big head, shaped like some sleek aerodynamic vehicle, was silvery-gray trimmed in yellow, with a row of ventlike gill structures, behind which were two large green-black eyes on each side, with a third behind and above them. Its head tapered into a serpentine body, knobbed with yellow spikes; rubbery, finned underparts whipped about as it prepared to lunge for him. Its rubbery mouth gaped . . .

There was a message in the green-black glitter of its eyes: *I hunger . . . I hunger for you!*

Mordecai's mouth was dry, but years on Pandora had formed his reflexes. Another man would have been paralyzed with horror, but Mordecai was already firing. He directed three bursts of the Cobra combat rifle into those big vulnerable eyes.

The Thresher squealed in agony, thrashed,

spurting red and green fluid. Mordecai backpedaled, just out of the reach of its death throes.

Then it sank, revolving slowly, into the dirt . . .
and in a few moments was gone from sight.

"I wonder if you killed it," the Claptrap chattered.
"I wonder, I wonder if you killed, killed, killed it, that
could make a good song. I wonder wonder if you—"

Mordecai turned furiously to the Claptrap. "You!
You'd better do your job for those people. Because
you're useless to me. You don't do your job, and I'll
spend a long, leisurely night taking you apart!"

The Claptrap spun about and jigged away, muttering bitterly to itself.

Mordecai stepped gingerly out onto the dirt, waited,
then rushed across it, to the stone on the other side. A
few moments more, and he'd reached the egress, the
mouth of the cave that led out to the canyon.

He made his way to the opening, stood there
smelling the night air outside—and turned to see
two Psychos standing beside a red outrider, guns
in hand, talking, about ten paces to his right. They
wore Gynella's livery. There could be a lot more of
them around. If he killed these two, he could at-
tract half of Gynella's army there . . .

They hadn't seen him yet. But they would. Unless he went back through the cave, and the mine,
to the settlement.

No. Roland would laugh at him if he went back.

Mordecai waited in the shadows, listening.

TEN

It was the edge of dawn, and Roland had just finished eating a meager breakfast, when the first
assault came.

The moon had slipped quietly away, and the
sky was going from black silk to gun metal as day
stalked them like a creeping skag.

There were fifty miners in the camp, most of
them men; there were twelve women and five
children. That was the whole settlement. And all
the men but the guards on the watchtowers were
gathered around the dying fire in the barrel, eating hot gruel, drinking stimutea, or cleaning their
weapons.

Roland was just picking up his combat rifle
when he heard a shout from a watchtower: "Some
of them are coming closer!"

Dakes shouted orders, and three miners rushed
to man the mortars. Quick instructions came on

range and angle, and the middle mortar, set up directly behind the gate, fired with a throaty cough. The shell rose at a steep angle, reaching its apex and visibly tipping, falling on the other side of the gate. Roland heard a triumphant shout as he headed toward the nearest tower.

"Got two of 'em! But there's more, some kinda weapon set up!"

Then came an odd sound—a *twang*, a whistling. He figured that was the catapult, heaving boulders. He hoped they would waste the boulders on the wall. Besides being steel, it was protected by an energy shield—a series of them, really. Not very strong shields—they wouldn't stand up to a pounding for too long.

Dakes and other miners, including Glory, fired out through the horizontal rifle slits in the walls. The metal barricade clanged and racketed with bullet impacts from the army outside.

Then Roland heard a cackling shriek from above. He looked up to see a Psycho Midget hurtling through the sky, flying like a creature of mythology, without aircraft, without wings; it had been simply hurled over the wall by a catapult and the little loon was arcing down, now—right at Roland.

The Psycho Midget had lost his "vault mask" in the air, and his deformed face was grinning, all clownlike, protruding tongue fibrillating with the rush of air as the mad bandit got closer and closer, yodeling as it came, angling head downward to crash into—

—into the ground just behind Roland as he simply stepped nimbly out of the way.

Roland expected to hear a horrible *splat*, but the Psycho Midget had an energy shield, strong enough to withstand the impact, and the malformed bandit bounced in a flash of sparkling energy and hit the ground at an angle like a skipping rock, skidding on the glowing purple resistance of the shield, which fluttered out just as the Midget crashed headfirst into the rusty old metal barrel used for a central campfire.

The Psycho Midget's momentum punched his head and shoulders through the thin corroded metal, and he screamed as his head was thrust into burning coals.

Dakes took pity on the Psycho and shot him— just as another *twang* and whistle announced another one catapulting into the camp.

Gynella's men had rethought their catapulting. This time the Psycho Midget came over the wall feetfirst, hurtling down to Roland's left, the Midget's field crackling as the little lunatic hit. The shirtless bandit bounced a little, fell flat on his back, spun like an overturned turtle on its shell, then scrambled to his feet and rushed toward the nearest miner, brandishing a hatchet and shouting,

"It's time to paint this body with blood!" The stunted Psycho was still wearing its full white and black vault mask, complete with Mohawk-style fin across the cranium and luminous blue eyepieces.

The miner was Glory's friend, Lucky. He seemed stunned by the shrieking, glowing-eyed, masked apparition charging him.

Lucky fumbled at his gun and backed away, but the Psycho Midget was closing fast, the blade of the hatchet gleaming.

Roland was already tracking the Psycho Midget with his sights, and he could see the bandit's shield was weak, flickering out near his head. He fired and sent a burst right through the side of the stunted madman's skull. The Midget fell dead at Lucky's feet.

Lucky stared at the corpse, then gaped up at Roland. He closed his mouth and nodded his thanks, then ran to reinforce the guards at the front wall.

He's a good kid at heart, Roland thought.

Another *twang*, another whistle, a burbling shriek as a third Psycho Midget came down, and this time a fourth was flung over the wall, from the back of the settlement—they were coming from two directions, babbling miniature madmen with axes, hurtling through the air, arms and legs waving, screaming for blood.

A group of miners were arguing about a possible sortie to destroy the catapults, and the fourth

Psycho Midget dropped into their midst, hacking wildly with his hatchet as he came down.

Blood splashed with his arrival; men screamed; bits of skull flew.

Then the survivors, most of the men in that group, closed around the Psycho Midget and began using their jackhammers on him.

The Midget's shield didn't last long. Neither did his mask, his face, or his spine.

Roland saw all this as he ran up the stairs to a watchtower on the northwestern corner of the settlement's walls. The stairs quaked under him as a round from a rocket launcher struck the front gate. The gate held, the shield shimmering, sparking, but not giving in entirely. It was a heavy steel gate, and it'd take quite a few rounds to blast it down even without the shield. He got to the watchtower, where he found two bodies. Their heads were shot neatly through.

Recognizing the work of snipers, he ducked quickly down—and not a moment too soon. A bullet meant for his head smacked off the ceiling of the watchtower. That meant that at least one of the settlement's external shields had failed.

There was no point in exposing himself with a sniper targeting the watchtower. But how was he going to hit Gynella's Knife Legion where it most hurt?

Another *twang*, another whistle, another gibbering shriek, and another Psycho Midget came flying over the wall into the defenders. A man yelped as a well-placed hatchet clove his head. Guns boomed. The Midget giggled and shouted imprecations. Another man screamed.

Keeping low, Roland looked down the stairway in time to see a mob of miners tear the Psycho Midget to pieces.

He looked away. It'd been a long time—a time in the distant past for him, on another planet—since he'd been in a fight this big, in war-scale combat. Fighting skags and bandits on Pandora was one thing—getting caught up in the ugliness of war, that was another. Still, Roland was committed—for the moment.

Another *twang*, a whistle, and a defiant screech from a descending Midget.

How many damn Midgets, Roland wondered, did they have for ammunition out there?

It was pretty obvious what he had to do.

He descended the stairs and shouted to Gong when he got to the bottom. "Hey, pal, can you drive an outrunner?"

Gong looked up from the rifle slit in the wall; his grin revealed his sharpened, fanglike teeth. "Better than you ever did!"

"Okay, you up for a sortie? We'll make it quick and get back in. Set some guys on the door to let us in and out. I'll be on the outrunner turret. What do you say?"

"Let's go!"

Just then, another Psycho Midget came flying over the wall at the back of the settlement, at a fairly low, oblique angle that took him over most of the settlement, coming down close to the front gate.

"Crap, look at that!" Roland said, as the Midget bounced in his energy field, rolled, then came up on his feet and scurried between the miners who tried to take him down, dodging left and right, heading for the gate. "I was afraid they'd try that. He's trying to get to the control box. He's gonna open the gate!"

Gong ran after the Psycho Midget, Roland at his heels. The Midget was well ahead of them, using a small electronic device in his hand to send activation sparks into the control box for the gate. The gate shuddered and began to move slowly open.

Beyond it came an answering roar of murderous glee from Gynella's horde.

The riflemen at the slits fired furiously. But the Psycho soldiers came, a wave of them rolling toward the opening gate.

"The fire!" Dakes shouted.

A miner fired an Eridian rifle through a slit, hitting the swath of ground impregnated with incendiary fluid, igniting it. A wall of blue and yellow fire roared up around the settlement, and the first phalanx of Psychos was caught in its licking flames. Psycho soldiers screamed and writhed, running in random directions. But the flames quickly fluttered down, turning to smoke, and more Psycho soldiers came, leaping through.

Then Gong reached the Psycho Midget, grabbed him by the ankles, jerked the little lunatic off his feet, and, the muscles in Gong's broad shoulders standing out, swung him in a rapid arc, smashing the stunted Psycho's head open on the metal wall.

Roland was trying to figure out how to operate the box; then he spotted the instrument the Psycho Midget had dropped. He picked it up, activated it, and the box responded—the gate began to close.

It shivered shut . . .

But not before six Psychos, all in vault masks, including a Badass who was on fire from the defensive wall of flame, came roaring in, firing their weapons, swinging glowing axes. The one-armed Badass swung an enormous energy-charged battle axe with his single, oversized arm——he didn't seem to notice or care that he was on fire, that his skin was bubbling and charring even as he knocked the brains from an onrushing miner.

Three more defenders went down, spinning into death. Lucky was rushing toward the invaders, shouting defiance.

The Psycho soldiers shouted maniacally, "Time

to play, time to play! I'm gonna eat you when I'm done!"

And then Roland and Gong were among them, Gong picking up a fallen jackhammer as he came. Firing his Cobra—aiming carefully so as not to hit a settler—Roland knocked down two of the Psychos.

The Badass cut his weapon at Lucky, screeching, "I'll take pleasure in gutting you, boy!" Lucky ducked under the sweep of the Badass's axe, shoved a shotgun up into the huge Psycho's mouth, and pulled the trigger, blowing his head off from within.

"Good work, kid!" Roland shouted, as he swung to blast a hulking, goggle-eyed Bruiser Psycho, this one firing at Gong.

The big miner took a round in his arm, didn't even twitch in response to it—as he and Roland fired at once, cutting the Bruiser down.

Roland looked around. All the Psychos who'd slipped through the gate were cut to pieces by the miners—and the gate was closed. The first penetration of Psychos had been repelled, but misery stayed behind. Men lay dying, or wishing they were dead, on the blood-soaked ground. Glory was kneeling by an elderly miner, trying to stanch his gouting neck wounds. She burst into tears as blood gurgled from his mouth and nose and, convulsing, he died.

Lucky went to her and helped her stand. He tried to comfort her, but she shook her head, smiled weakly at him, and went to find another fallen defender she might try to help. The bandages in her hands already dripped with blood.

Dakes was there, surveying the scene. "Lucky, Muddflap, Gannon! You three stay close to that gate! They'll try it again for sure!"

Roland strode up to the gate. "I'm gonna make a request you're not going to like, Dakes. Open that gate for me."

"What?"

"I'm going out with Gong in an outrunner . . . if Gong's still up for it." He glanced at Gong, who was using Dr. Zed and spraying his wound with closer. Gong gave him a thumbs-up. "We're going to see what we can get done on a quick sortie—we'll circle the settlement, then come back in. While we're out, you'll keep the gate closed. Open it just enough when we come back—if it looks safe."

"And suppose it doesn't?"

"Then we'll take our chances out there."

Dakes shook his head. But then another Psycho Midget came shrieking over the wall, laughing as he fell among the miners, spraying with a submachine gun. He didn't last long, but he took two miners down.

"We're going to run out of defenders pretty soon," Dakes muttered. "All right. When?"

"Right now!" Roland declared. "Time is bullets!"

Five minutes later, Gong driving and Roland at the turret gun, the outrunner rolled up to the gate, which creaked open, under Dakes's control, just enough to let the outrunner get out.

Roland got a good grip on the turret as Gong accelerated through the gap and roared toward the enemy.

Both men—and the outrunner—were defended by shields, but there was so much firepower out there Roland wasn't confident the shields would last long.

The outrunner gunned through the wall of smoke where the "moat of flame" had been, and then they were on the open plains, looking at a line of Psycho soldiers just thirty meters away.

"Cut hard left for that catapult!" Roland yelled, pointing.

Gong twisted the wheel, and the outrunner cut left so hard it almost turned over, going up for a moment on two tires. Gunfire roared, bullets cracked, and energy blasts flashed by. Roland felt a powerful jolt to his shield, on his right shoulder, and had to hold hard to the turret to keep from falling over.

Then the vehicle banged down onto all its wheels, Gong flooring the accelerator to slam through a line of four Psychos trying to keep them away from the catapult. The Psychos screamed as the vehicle plowed through, blood spraying like a wake around a speedboat's prow, and then they were clear and within ten meters of the giant mechanical slingshot. Two guards close to the catapult fired submachine guns at him and Gong. His shield held—for now.

Roland aimed carefully—the catapult was primed with a Psycho Midget sitting in the cup, waiting to be flung into the air, cackling to himself. Roland fired at the crude metal cup holding the Psycho Midget first and blasted the Midget with the shell from his turret cannon. His next shot was at the wires holding the catapult's arm down, knocking them away so it flung its load of Midget remains into the air. It flew sloppily to splatter against the settlement's outer walls.

Then Roland blasted the support beams of the catapult, and it collapsed onto the two guards firing at him from its base.

"They won't have that workin' anytime soon!" Gong crowed, as he swung past the wreckage toward the settlement. A burly Psycho soldier loomed up, tried to jump onto the outrunner. Gong jerked the wheel so the man fell clear; then he bumped the vehicle over another Gynellan soldier, the smaller man howling with pain as the outrunner crunched his rib cage.

Eridian rifle pulses zinged past, making the air smell as if it had been cooked in chemicals, and then they had reached the nearest corner of the settlement's boxlike wall. They gunned past it, for the moment no longer a clean target for the Psychos behind them—but in seconds they'd passed the back corner and were facing another phalanx of Gynella's soldiers, arrayed around the other catapult at the back of the settlement.

A Psycho Midget was loaded up in this catapult too. Roland aimed carefully and shot out one of the stretch wires under the catapult's arm, so that when it released a moment later, its living missile went crookedly and fell short, smashing on the very top of the metal wall, then dripping down both sides in a wet mass of bones and entrails.

Bullets cracked into the outrunner, Roland's shield flickered, and then he saw that the machine-gun turret firing at him was right under the catapult, and its gunner had a big box of ammo handy. He grinned and shouted, "Mess with the bull and you get the horns!" as he fired at the box of ammo. It exploded, blowing up the machine-gunner and the catapult team, pieces of them trailing blood into the morning light.

"Mowin' 'em down!" Roland yelled.

"What now?" Gong shouted.

"That's it! Back to the front gate, Gong. We'll take out what we can on the way."

Gong drove past a clutch of Psycho soldiers, and Roland fired a cannon round at their feet, knocking several of them down, killing one. Then the outrunner veered around the corner, roared up past the wall toward the front of the settlement; it whipped, skidding, around another corner, then headed for the opening gate, its shield fading as bullets cracked into it—until . . .

A rocket launcher round hit the outrunner squarely on the front end—there was a gush of fire and flying dirt, and the outrunner flipped up and back. Roland let go of the turret and jumped free, rolling himself into a tight ball before he hit the ground, grunting with the impact on his right shoulder, rolling, then coming down flat on his belly, skinned up but not badly hurt.

This was as dangerous a spot as he'd ever been in—especially now that his shield had gone dead.

He jumped up, ears ringing from the blast, and saw his Cobra lying nearby. Bullets kicked up dirt at his feet as he ran for the weapon. He scooped up the Cobra, kept running, looking for Gong. Then he saw him crawling out from under the overturned outrunner. Gong's face was masked in blood, but he didn't seem too badly hurt.

Roland reached the outrunner and threw himself down behind it, as bullets slashed through the place he'd been a split second earlier, just missing him. He growled with pain as he skidded on his belly, already raw, then got to his knees, looked over the smoking wreck. He saw about thirty Psycho soldiers running toward him from their lines, weapons in hand, howling for his blood, shrieking about how they were going to kill him and eat his flesh raw.

"Well, ain't that just dandy," he murmured, glancing at the gate.

It was at least forty meters away.

The miners on the tower fired furiously, trying to give him and Gong cover. Gong got up behind the outrunner, firing at the oncoming Psychos with a pistol. Roland fired several rounds, but he was running short on ammo.

There was nothing for it but to run for the gate. It seemed suicidal, as metal rounds cracked on the outrunner and *spanged* into the air, and Eridian blasts seared past. Another rocket sped toward the outrunner, but it flew too high and exploded on the metal wall behind him. Shrapnel screamed by from the explosion.

This wasn't looking good. He and Gong had to cross a lot of open ground to get to that gate. How were they going to do it before that wave of Psycho soldiers mowed them down with gunfire or just overran them and cut them to pieces, up close and personal?

"We'd better give it a shot, Gong! You ready to run for it?"

Gong gave him one bobbing nod and then seemed to freeze in place, staring. He pointed, and Roland saw a red outrider come roaring across the open ground, from the west, as if bent on colliding with the wreckage of Roland's outrunner.

There was only one occupant of the outrider. Roland couldn't make him out clearly yet, but he saw that he was driving with one hand and firing explosive shells from his turret gun with the other.

And the outrider was firing at the Psycho soldiers. Flame blossomed, smoke plumed, Psychos were flung left and right.

Confused by gunfire from one of their own vehicles, the charging Psycho soldiers slowed down, tumbling into one another, gawking at this new adversary.

The outrider gunned up to the outrunner, and Gong jumped up to take a shot at it.

"Hold your fire, Gong!" Roland shouted. Because now he could clearly see Bloodwing clinging to the seatback of the outrider's driver.

Mordecai spun the wheel and hit the brake, skidding, so the outrider did a donut and screeched to a stop within a meter of the wreckage, turned sideways to it.

"Jump on fast, dammit, right *now*!" Mordecai yelled, as bullets started to hum past from the Psycho soldiers.

Roland and Gong ran to the outrider, jumped

onto the running boards, and held on tight. Mordecai spun it about and, fishtailing, almost losing control, managed to turn it toward the gate. The gate was only one-third open—Dakes had stopped it there, to discourage the Psycho soldiers from rushing it en masse.

Roland was distantly aware that someone—a Gynellan officer of some kind—was shouting from the top of the catapult's ruins, urging his men to storm the open gate. The Psychos started toward it, close to a hundred of them surging that way, but then the kill-mechs rumbled out of the gate, one following another, and rolled full speed at the front lines of Gynella's legion.

Mordecai drove past the kill-mechs and through the gate, into the settlement. The gate closed behind them.

And three minutes later, all hell broke out.

More precisely, hell broke *in*.

ELEVEN

"So, what were you doing out there in one of their bony-ass hot rods, Mordecai?" Roland demanded, as they stepped from the outrider. Roland was feeling bruised, contused, and shaken by the narrow escape, and he kicked at the skag skull on the front of the outrider, knocking it loose. "Where'd you get this thing?"

"Where do you think?" Mordecai said, stretching. He accepted a cup of water from Glory. "Thanks. Need this." He drank the water and went on. "I came out of the cavern, after I went through the mine, and there were some of Gynella's bunch, scouts maybe, looking for a back way into the settlement. Arguing over whether the cave could be it. So I picked them off—only one of them even had his shield charged—and I took the outrider. I came to warn you guys that they're snooping around back there. And, you know, see how you were . . . if anybody . . . well, I was just passing by."

"Bullcrap!" Roland snorted, rubbing Dr. Zed's salve on some pretty extensive scrapes. "You were *worried* about us! You were coming back to help, you damn fraud! You're as softhearted as any—"

"Softhearted!" Mordecai interrupted, glaring at him. "*Me?* I tell you I was just passing, and I thought I'd let you know that, uh . . ."

Dakes had been listening to all this as he walked up. "You think they're coming in the back way?"

"Not from what I can figure," Mordecai said. "I got rid of those scouts. Still, that robot you've posted down there isn't much use. And, uh, I had to kill that Thresher watchdog of yours. Way things look now, you ought to get your injured, your kids, anybody that's not in the fight, and get 'em into that mine."

Dakes shook his head. "I don't know. I thought maybe the kill-mechs would drive 'em off, but two of them are down already—rocket launchers. We took out maybe a dozen of the bastards first, but . . ." He wiped blood and soot from his eyes. "I just don't know."

Roland said, "Mordecai's right. Be ready to head out through the mine if it's—"

A painfully clangorous triple explosion, *clang-boom, clang-boom, clang-BOOM*, made the ground shake, and they all looked toward the front gate.

It was buckling inward, and badly cracked.

"I was afraid of that," Mordecai said, as Bloodwing landed on his shoulder. "When I drove up, I saw 'em moving in some more rocket launchers. They're concentrating fire on that front gate! You'd better get your people under cover!"

Dakes was already turning, shouting to Glory to get children and any women not prepared to fight into the center mine. He tossed Roland a shotgun. "You'll need this for close fightin'!"

Roland nodded and turned to Mordecai, as another clanging boom announced the demolition of the front gate. Now it was breached, bent inward like the lid of a roughly opened tin can. Miners rushed to the gate, firing at the oncoming Psycho soldiers. Guns roared, the marauders shouted their obscene challenges, and men screamed in pain.

"So are you staying here or what, Mordecai?" Roland asked, having to shout over the racket.

Another ear-shattering *clang-boom*, and the gate shattered completely, in an explosion of spinning, fragmenting metal and a gush of smoke.

"Looks like I'm not going out *that* way," Mordecai said, staring at the smoking breach, where Psycho soldiers were already rushing in. "Guess I better stay. I sure as hell hope you gotta plan!"

"Get in the driver's seat of the outrider. I'll get on the side; we can nail some of these bastards up close and still be hard to hit!"

"Okay, but the outrider's shield is almost dead, man!"

"It is what it is!" Roland yelled, jumping onto a running board. "Let's do it!"

Bullets were whining overhead as Mordecai jumped in, Bloodwing still on his shoulder, and Roland grabbed a hand-hold bar with his left hand, his right propping his new weapon on his hip, an Atlas Hunter's Hydra, one of the most effective combat shotguns around.

Gong jumped onto the other running board with a Torgue Boomstick in his left hand, and they were off, Mordecai gunning the outrider straight at the twisted wreckage around the gate. Bloodwing took to the air, flapping furiously overhead, working hard to keep up. They passed between two buildings, then crossed an open area, driving full-bore at the gate. Mordecai reached up with his right hand and tilted the turret gun on the red outrider's hood, the small rocket launcher aimed toward three Psycho soldiers clustered to the right of the gate. Mordecai fired, and two well-placed shells knocked them up into blood-splashing backflips. Bloodwing darted down and slashed at two other Psychos, keeping them distracted, ruining their aim, so that Mordecai was able to drive past them without taking fire.

Mordecai spun the wheel, and the outrider whipped about, Roland and Gong white-knuckling on the grips to hold on. A big Bruiser—with a black mask, red goggles, a Mohawk, and Gynella's face tattooed right on his chest—came rushing toward Roland, leveling a combat rifle. Roland fired the shotgun propped on his hip, three rounds in less than a second, two of the powerful shotgun's big loads slamming through Gynella's tattooed-on face, the third shot blasting the goggles off the Bruiser's eyes, blinding him.

Roland lost sight of the Bruiser as the outrider continued its turn, making a complete circle, Gong firing at another Psycho, Mordecai shooting at a blue outrider coming through the gate, blowing the driver's head off. Two Psychos clinging to the outrider lost their grip as the vehicle spun out of control. It rolled, crushing them, as Bloodwing circled overhead, cawing.

Roland was only peripherally aware of this carnage. He was gritting his teeth as he tried to hold on to the red outrider against the tug of inertia, firing the shotgun again and again at vault-masked Psycho faces flashing by. Mordecai brought the outrider around again, and Roland sent his last few rounds through the still-smoking gap in the gate. He caught a glimpse, as they sped past, of the last kill-mech, on the plains outside, using its jackhammer to slam a Bruiser to pieces, shooting another with its rifle arm—before exploding as three grenades hit it at once.

"I'm outta ammo!" Mordecai shouted, firing a last round. He angled the outrider toward the back of the settlement, and bullets cut the ground just to Roland's left. Then they drove behind the cover of several low rusty-metal outbuildings near the mines. Mordecai pulled up, and Roland jumped off, having to skid to stop his momentum. Mordecai whistled, and Bloodwing flapped up, landing on his shoulder. Gong was no longer on the outrider.

"Whew!" Roland said, breathing hard. "Some ride. You should sell tickets."

Roland looked for Gong—and saw him lying facedown about ten paces back. He jogged back, alert for Psychos as he went, and was relieved to see that Gong was alive, getting dazedly to his knees, but shot through the back of the left shoulder.

"I couldn't hold on, with that bullet in me," Gong said, shaking his head in self-disgust.

Roland helped him to his feet. "Come on, get into the mine. You've gotta keep an eye on the families, help Dakes get them through."

Gong nodded and plodded grimly toward the mine. Roland turned at a tittering sound and saw a strange sight: three Psycho soldiers charging at him, all wearing Gynella's livery. But they represented three types of Psycho, and they were coming in a row, one behind the next; first came the smaller one, a Midget Psycho; then directly behind him came a standard Psycho, midsize but fully insane; then a Badass Psycho. Far taller than the standard Psycho, the Badass had a disproportionately long and powerful right arm but a shriveled and stunted left one—the left arm was useless, but the hugely muscular right arm and the big glowing axe in the big Psycho's right hand almost made up for it.

All three attackers wore full-face vault masks with glowing eyes. All three were coming in single file but fast, the first one tittering, the second one gibbering, the third one howling for blood.

Roland was a little amused by the graduated display of Psychos but also a little intimidated.

Still, Roland was a pro. He aimed the Atlas Hydra carefully, fired it when the Midget Psycho was just three paces away, and blew its right kneecap in half. He did it that way so it'd fall right in front of the medium-size Psycho and so it'd still be lively enough to thrash about and entangle the second Psycho's legs—and that's how it worked out, the second Psycho falling on the Midget underfoot.

Roland was going to dispatch the second one when the third, the huge Badass Psycho, gave a short leap and jumped on the back of the second Psycho, crushing the Psycho's spine. Roland had the shotgun ready, and he fired as the Badass came at him like a truck bearing down. But the blast from the Hydra didn't stop the Badass Psycho. The lunatic bandit's shield was a tough one, a powerful Pearlescent, and the Psycho stumbled but didn't take any real damage.

"Come here, meat puppet!" the Psycho shouted.

Roland stepped back, but the enormous, energy-charged axe was swinging at him and struck the barrel of his weapon just as he fired again. He got off a shot, the powerful shotgun weakening his enemy's shield, but a moment later the gun was knocked from his hands with such force his fingers felt numb, and he stumbled back, almost falling.

"I'm gonna skin ya, put on your face, and say hi to your mama!" the Psycho shrieked, raising the axe.

Roland got his feet under him, decided to rush the Psycho, but then two rattling bursts from a combat rifle sounded close to his right, and the Badass staggered, the side of its head half shattered, helmet cracked.

Roland drew his big knife and rushed in, using all his strength to penetrate the Psycho's failing shield. He forced the blade through the energy field and up, through Gynella's *G*, and into the huge Psycho's heart.

The malformed soldier shuddered and fell on top of Roland, stone dead. A true deadweight, the corpse slammed Roland onto his back, crushed the breath from him as he struck the ground.

Mordecai strode up, grinning. Bloodwing rode on his right shoulder. "Good thing for you I can hit a moving target! Tough shield! You hadn't have weakened it, I couldn't have gotten those rounds through."

"Will you . . ." Roland wheezed. "Get this . . ." He took a hoarse breath. "Stinking carrion off me . . ."

Mordecai laughed and set to work. It took both of them, straining hard, to roll the Badass Psycho off Roland.

"Well, stop loafing around, Roland," Mordecai said, as Roland got gasping to his feet. "Let's move—there's another wave of them coming."

Roland picked up his shotgun, but the barrel was bent. The weapon was useless.

He tossed it aside, then noticed another dead Psycho lying facedown on a Vladof Glorious Havoc, a formidable machine gun. He strode to the body and pulled the weapons and extra magazines of ammo free, just as a red outrider came careening down an alley between two low metal buildings, with a group of Psychos running behind it. The outrider fired a small cannon shell that burst just behind Roland, making him stagger. The outrider flashed past him, screeching into a turn.

"Come on, Roland!" Mordecai shouted.

They ran full tilt toward the mine entrance, Mordecai just ahead.

"Where are Dakes and the others?" Roland called, between puffing breaths.

"They're all inside!" Mordecai shouted, as Bloodwing flew above him, screeching.

They got into the opening of the center mine just as the outrider came up behind them, almost running Roland over. He had to dive headfirst into the mine to keep from getting clipped by a bone-studded fender. He shoulder-rolled, careful of his new weapon, got up, and saw that Mordecai was already stationing himself at the door, firing out at the Psychos.

Moving stiffly, muscles aching from the falls he'd taken, Roland ran to hunker behind the partial shelter of the metal girders framing the entrances, across from Mordecai.

"Concentrate fire on that damn outrider!" Roland suggested. "Hit the driver!"

They had to take him down fast. One good shell from that outrider's mounted turret cannon would kill them both in this enclosed space.

Mordecai nodded, and they both aimed at the driver as the outrider spun around, came back for another pass. It fired its turret cannon at the entrance to the mine. The other Psychos, an increasing throng of them, were taking up firing positions to either side of the buildings across from the mine entrance. Roland aimed the combat machine gun and squeezed off a long burst, the powerful weapon bucking in his grasp.

The red outrider's turret missed the entrance, raising two fireballs just outside the mine—and then their concentrated fire penetrated the outrider's shield, and the driver's head vaporized in a red mist. The outrider spun wildly, completely out of control. It rolled over and exploded against a side wall of the settlement.

Lucky suddenly appeared, coming from behind, crouching down between Mordecai and Roland. He fired an Atlas combat rifle at the Psychos in quick bursts. He wore a mining helmet with a light on it, and there was blood dripping from under the helmet, but he didn't seem badly hurt—Lucky's eyes burned with hatred for the invaders.

Roland glared at him. "Lucky, get back in there, dammit, you're too exposed!"

"Kiss my ass!" Lucky shouted back, grinning, firing till his clip was empty. Two of the enemy had gone down to his fire, but more were rushing to fill the gap, as increasing numbers of the Knife Legion penetrated the wrecked front gate of the settlement.

Bullets sang past and struck sparks from the frame of the mine entrance. Roland emptied another magazine, mowing down half a dozen small Psychos and two or three bandits.

But the press from behind forced the front line of the legion into action. Two big Bruisers roared in fury and rushed at the mine entrance, firing submachine guns and leading a general charge.

"Come on!" Lucky shouted at Roland. "The mine's entrance is wired! Back inside! Get to the cavern!"

"Go, you two!" Mordecai yelled, knocking one of the Bruisers off his feet with a burst from his Cobra. "I'm gonna be right behind you!" He set the Cobra aside, took four grenades from his belt, gave two of them to Bloodwing. And he threw the others, in one handful, at the charging Psychos. Bloodwing was already flapping toward the Psychos, and Roland was afraid Mordecai's winged partner would get caught in the grenade blasts, but it dropped its grenades like a bomber in the thick of the Psychos and then swooped back, just ahead of the blast cloud.

The four grenades blew up almost simultaneously, about fifteen meters out, momentarily obscuring the onrushing enemy in a cloud of dust and spraying blood.

"Come on, Mordecai!" Roland shouted. "While they're eating dust!" And they followed Lucky back into the mine, Bloodwing swooping in after them.

Back and down they went, slipping at times on the slick, gradually descending ramp of stone, hurrying but not able to run full tilt for fear of slamming headlong into girders or the occasional cart. Most of the time they were in darkness, following the bobbing glow of the light fixed to Lucky's helmet.

"The whole settlement make it in here?" Roland asked, as they reached the bottom level of the mine. "I don't see anyone."

Lucky came to a stop, looking back the way they'd come. They could hear the guttural shouts of the oncoming Psychos, working their way down the mine shaft. Another minute, and the Knife Legion would catch up with them. "The others are in the cavern—the ones that survived. About half the men are dead."

"Come on, Roland!" Mordecai said, climbing through the opening at the back of the mine. "This way!"

"Lucky!" Roland shouted. "Come on!"

"I'm coming," Lucky said, opening a metal box fixed to the wall. "I've gotta prepare a welcome for those plug-ugly bastards."

Inside the metal box was a switch.

TWELVE

Smartun climbed the metal steps to a corner watchtower overlooking the plains outside Bloodrust Corners. He felt a mixture of elation and disquiet. Would she be happy? Casualties had been surprisingly high. And there was that little debacle at the end. But still . . .

He reached the watchtower proper and looked out at the legion's encampment. Bandits and Psychos, Gynella's men, were milling about the camp, some of them fighting, some drinking liquor cadged from the settlement. A great many others were looting the settlement, arguing over newly discovered caches of money and weapons and food. Skenk was having difficulty keeping more soldiers from rushing into the settlement. But there was no room for them—and there could be more traps . . .

It was time to make a report.

Smartun tapped his ECHO comm, activating

its link to the device he had plugged into his ear, and heard the clicking of its decrypter. After a moment Gynella herself answered.

"Is that you, Smartun?"

He shivered with pleasure as her voice, the blessed voice of his living Goddess, reverberated within his ear, a kind of sonic intimacy . . .

"It is, my General Goddess. We have possession of Bloodrust Corners—we took considerable casualties."

"How many casualties?"

He told her. He thought she'd be angry, but she only chuckled. "We have reports that the mercenaries Roland and Mordecai entered Bloodrust Corners right before your attack. Does *that* account for the high casualties?"

"In part. The settlement had good defenses. Their kill-mechs took out quite a few of our best fighters. We used up a lot of rocket-launcher ammo on the mechs and the front gate—we'll need more, as soon as it can be supplied, as much as you can spare."

"All in good time. Meanwhile you will scavenge weaponry as you find it. We'll have to start expanding our range, and if you go to . . ." A crackle interrupted the transmission, and then her voice came back in. "Fyrestone, probably, soon. There are a lot of weapons in and around Fyrestone we can use. The weapons dealer Marcus has a good many tucked away around the settlement, I'm told."

"As you wish, General Goddess."

"But first, secure the area. How many prisoners did you take? We have need of work slaves. I have to shore up the new ramp off the Footstool. I'll need a good many workmen . . ."

When they'd first come to the Devil's Footstool, the only access to the top had been to crane men and supplies up in the cumbersome shell of an old bus lifted creakingly up and lowered creakingly down. Gynella had ordered a ramp cut in a zigzag pattern down one face of the giant stone column, so her fighting forces could be moved out to a battlefield with less delay—and less vulnerability. A single good cannon shell could blow that old bus up en route, and all the men inside.

"Ah, unfortunately there are no prisoners, my General. The few wounded who were left behind were killed by our front lines. You know how . . . impetuous they can be."

"What? The settlers escaped?"

He winced. "The surviving settlers . . . essentially, yes, ma'am, they've escaped—so far. We hope to locate them."

"But you were to have the place surrounded!"

"We did surround it, my General, but there seems to be a hidden exit through one of the mines.

The mine appears to lead to a cavern, which could be traversed, we believe, to a hilly area in the—"

"And you didn't *pursue* into the mine?" she interrupted, her voice harsh with impatience.

"A large contingent of our men rushed into the mine, to pursue—before I could stop them."

"Why would you stop . . . oh. It was a trap?"

"Yes, ma'am. The mine was wired with explosives. We lost about sixty men. Killed or buried alive when the mine collapsed."

"Really! Then the settlers committed suicide in the mine, with explosives?"

"I don't think so. While the other mines appear to be dead ends, ending in solid rock, this one seems to have had a back way out. We found a prisoner in one of their storerooms—one of our people—he says that he heard a miner talking about a cavern, a back way out of a mine. I had heard other rumors of it when I first arrived, from a captured miner before he died under interrogation. I sent scouts to find this back entrance. But they never returned." On Pandora, if someone went on a mission and didn't return, they were invariably assumed to have been killed. "I will find the cave entrance, I promise you!"

"The settlers will be well away from there by the time you find their little escape hatch!"

"Perhaps so, my General, but they will have left tracks. We'll locate them!"

"Do it only if you can do it expediently, but don't expend too much energy or manpower on it. We have to stay on schedule! Best to search for them with drones."

"I do have two new drones, just in. I'll set them to it, my General Goddess."

She said nothing for a moment. He imagined her clicking her nails as she took the news in. "So . . . we have the mines, anyway, and the glam gems?"

"Two of the mines are intact, and we found a large storeroom packed with gem ore."

"Good! When I turn the gems into cash, I can hire a force of mercenaries from off-planet. They'll be more trainable than these lunatics we have now."

He looked out onto the squalling, contentious, psychotic soldiers of the encampment. "Yes, that'll be preferable to what we have to work with now. They're getting more quarrelsome. Difficult to control."

"They're growing restless. Vialle warned me that they would need their conditioning reinforced. I'll come out, fairly soon, and give them one of my special blessings. How did your catapults work?"

"Ah—very well! We successfully propelled the Psycho Midgets inside. They created considerable havoc in the ranks of the defenders."

"A very creative idea, on your part, using those little wretches as missiles."

He glowed inside at the compliment. Then felt

an inner plunge, realizing that he must again miti-
gate his triumph with a failure. "Thank you, my
Goddess—but . . ."

"Well? What now?"

"This man Roland did a sortie in an outrunner—he destroyed the catapults. We rocketed
his outrunner, nearly nailed him. But Mordecai
showed up, and then, ah . . ."

"And then they escaped into the settlement?"
She made a *tsk* of disgust. "Let me guess. After
that, he and Roland spearheaded the resistance
against our forces?"

"Yes, that is essentially what, ah . . . yes, ma'am."

There was a crackling silence. Then Gynella
said, in a cold voice, "Your successes are badly
blemished, Smartun. Still, you're new on the job.
But I expect to see improvement. I demand it!"

"Yes, ma'am."

"If you find Roland, if you get a chance to com-
municate with him, take it. Try to recruit him. If
you can't get the offer across to him, if he won't talk
to you, simply kill him any way you can. Don't take
any chances with him—clearly, he's a great danger
to our plans." She sighed. "It'll probably come to
that, and it does seem like a waste. There are so few
men of his kind on this planet. Very few indeed . . ."

Roland and Mordecai stood in the cool of dawn,
gazing out from the top edge of the small plateau

that overlooked the badlands south of the settlement. They were silent, standing with weapons in hand, keeping watch on the stony road up to the top of the plateau and the badlands. Bloodwing was perched on the rough point of a nearby boulder, dozing with its beak tucked under a wing. Beyond the rugged, still-dark maze of hills was the white blaze of the Salt Flats. Roland could just make out the distant smoke of what he supposed might be the encampment fires of Gynella's Knife Legion.

"So, do we move on soon, Roland?" Mordecai asked, at last. "I'm ready to harvest some Eridium. A lot of money and a little luxury sounds good to me right now. Between you and me, I don't think I'm developing a taste for fighting entire armies."

"I'm not a fan of it either," Roland said. "Brick probably loves it, though. If he's still alive."

"I wouldn't count that big chunk of muscle out," Mordecai said. He yawned. "I don't much care for early-morning watches."

"Yeah. Old Dakes just took it for granted we'd take a watch. Gave us our orders and went to bed."

"But here we are."

"We went to a lot of trouble, trying to keep some of these people alive. Wouldn't like it to be for nothing."

"If they're going to expect something of us, they should pay us. We're pros, Roland."

Roland shrugged. "Seems like most of their gems and money were left behind in Bloodrust Corners."

"Great. So we're . . . volunteers?" Mordecai made a face. "Hey, I risk my ass all the time. I don't mind doing it. But not for free."

"I figure we'll get them settled in, make sure they're pretty secure, and move on. Head for those crystalisk dens."

"Sounds good." Mordecai paused, squinting at the sky. "Are those rakks?" he asked, pointing. "Wouldn't be good if they decided to go for a settler's kid."

Roland looked up, shading his eyes, and saw two birdlike shapes, hard to see against the dim gray of first light, flying about a third of a kilometer away, not far above the altitude of the plateau top. They flew in a surprisingly neat circle, around and around. He could make out their wings, their lean bodies. "Looks more like trash feeders."

Mordecai went to the boulder and poked a finger at Bloodwing's breast, waking the creature up. It made grouchy squawking sounds and then listened with its head cocked as he whispered to it. Bloodwing cawed in response, hopped a couple of times on the boulder, then sprang into the air. It flapped up and up, spiraling higher and higher, then broke off to soar toward the trash feeders—if that was what they were.

Bloodwing seemed to approach the flyers as if it planned to pass above them, on its way somewhere else—then it suddenly dived. There was a flutter of close engagement, as the two figures became one, Bloodwing and the trash feeder thrashing in the air. Then one of them fell away, turning end over end as it dropped. The other one flew swiftly back to Mordecai—Bloodwing, carrying something in its claws.

Bloodwing circled just overhead and dropped its burden at Mordecai's feet.

He bent down and picked it up. "I thought there was something odd about the way those things were flying around and around in the same spot. Not a rakk or trash feeder motion, really." He showed Roland the piece of the flyer that Bloodwing had brought back. It was mechanical, a thing of metal and glass and synthetic skin designed to look like animal hide.

Roland stared. "A lens? A surveillance drone! Camouflaged as a trash feeder."

Mordecai nodded. "And by now it's transmitted back to whoever sent it here. They know just where we are."

INTERLUDE

Marcus Tells a Tale, Part Two

"... So Roland and Mordecai had a big decision to make," Marcus said. He cleared his throat. His voice was giving out. He'd been talking for hours.

Marcus, the woman, and the Claptrap were in the back of his broken-down bus. They had a little light from a lantern sitting on the floor of the aisle. It was too dark to see the woman's face. Darkness, broken only by a few patches of moonlight, engulfed the world outside. "I need a drink before I can go on with the story. Getting hoarse."

"Oh, *do* finish the story!" piped the Claptrap, suddenly sitting bolt upright up on the seat behind him. "Tell some more about that brave dancing Claptrap!"

"Shut up, or I'll pry out your voice circuits," Marcus growled.

The robot sagged back down on the seat.

"Near as I can tell," the woman said, "there are only two of those bastards out there. We're not as weaponed up as we ought to be. But . . . maybe if we take the fight to them now, we can catch them at their camp. I don't like sitting here waiting for them to decide they're going to use that rocket launcher on this heap of slag you drive."

"This bus is no heap of slag. This is a finely tuned mechanism! They shot the damn engine, remember? You want to go after them, I'm game. But then what? We'd still have to wait for Scooter. Too far to walk to Fyrestone in the dark. This is Pandora. It's dangerous out there. Only place you're anything like safe on this planet is in a locked room in a well-defended settlement. And maybe not even then."

The woman shrugged—he still didn't know her name, although he'd been talking to her all night.

"You sure your buddy Scooter can be relied on?" she asked, peering out the window.

Marcus snorted. "He's not my buddy. I don't think he's anyone's buddy. But he'll show up eventually. And he'll bring some firepower with him."

She looked at a chronometer in her thumbnail. "Just a couple of hours to go before the sun comes up. You could finish your story."

"I'll need a drink, a good long one," Marcus said, looking toward the front of the bus. He got up and, crouched over, back aching from the odd position, moved toward the front of the bus. He tried to scan the dark wasteland outside the windows, but he couldn't see much, just the outlines of a few stark growths throwing shadows in the attenuated moonlight. He reached the front, his boots crunching on broken glass, and squatted down to reach under the driver's seat. His fingers groped and found the bottle. He tugged it out—and a muzzle flash flicked beyond the front window, just past the boulder. A rifle burst sizzled past his head, smashing through the back window.

He threw himself flat, cutting his hands on the broken glass. "Lady, you hit back there?"

"I'm fine!" the Claptrap robot called. "Thanks for asking!"

Marcus gritted his teeth. "I said—"

"I'm not hit!" the woman called. "You'd better get back here. It's better cover!"

He got up to a crouch and, carefully sheltering the bottle in his hands with his body, hurried back down the aisle, expecting to be shot in the back at any minute. But no shot came. Instead, a grizzled voice called to them from somewhere in front of the bus.

"Why dontcha come back over here? I got a little present for you!"

"Ooh, a present!" the Claptrap said happily.

Marcus reached their little camping spot in the back of the bus. He sat cross-legged on the aisle floor, grunting, his back cricking. "Whew!"

"I'm gonna rip off your arm and beat your baby with it!" yelled the Psycho in the darkness.

"We haven't *got* a baby!" Marcus yelled back, opening the bottle. "Think of a different one!"

There was a puzzled silence. Then the voice shouted, "I'm gonna cook you over a slow fire, meat puppet!"

"That one makes more sense," Marcus said, raising his bottle in salute. He took a long drink of the liquor and offered it to the woman.

She shook her head. "One of us has to stay sober."

"Don't you worry," Marcus said. "I put this stuff on my breakfast cereal. Ah! That's better. Now, where was I?"

"You were telling us all about the brave little Claptrap!" the robot chirruped.

"No, I wasn't. I was talking about how Mordecai and Roland figured out they were gonna have to move the settlers to a new hiding place, because the camouflaged drones had found them, and Mordecai was getting pretty frustrated about not being able to stay on mission. He hadn't signed up to wet-nurse a bunch of foolish miners. But see, Roland never did have an operation to have his conscience removed, like a lotta people do. Neat little bit of brain surgery . . ."

"Why didn't he just have the chip taken out?" the robot asked. "I had a conscience chip once. It totally confused me. I mean, what's in it for me? So I had it taken out. I feel much better now. By the way, based on your current stress patterns, I calculate an eighty-nine-point-four-percent chance that you will encounter an unfortunate death experience very soon. You'd better be careful, or that unpleasant person out there will suck your brains out like crappucino!"

They ignored the Claptrap.

"What about the assassin, Daphne?" the woman asked. "And Brick? What happened to them?"

"Oh yeah, well, I'll tell you, it wasn't real pretty, what they'd fallen into, not pretty at all . . ."

THIRTEEN

Sitting on the grit in the corner of the reeking, metal-link holding pen—a cage, really, with a ceiling of links over it—Daphne was feeling almost luxurious. They'd taken the chains off her wrists, and she had a little food, her first in twenty-four hours. The soup stank, and she was definitely not going to ask what the chunks floating in it actually were, but as she drank it down from the dented metal bowl, it seemed to give her strength, and that's exactly what she needed. So she choked it down.

Survival started with strength, and as the food strengthened her, she found her mind clearing, too. She'd been dazed while being hauled there in a cart pulled behind an outrider. An old self-driving truck, cadged from a Dahl construction site, had toted Brick there, and he was now chained up—triply chained—in the center of the coliseum's dirt floor across from her.

They would set Brick up to fight, to be their entertainment, in this rinky-dink, shabby, patched-together little coliseum Gynella had had built on the edge of the Salt Flats. They would have him fight a Goliath. An almost unbeatable adversary was a Goliath, hand to hand. And already, before his gladiator duty had begun, Brick was injured—more than that, he was concussed, wounded, half starved, and dehydrated. When it came time for the Goliath, could even Brick survive? It seemed unlikely.

Daphne sighed, thinking about it. It wasn't as if she was close to Brick. She couldn't quite imagine being in any kind of physical intimacy with him. If he lost control, for one thing, he might break her in half. Besides that, he wasn't her type. Mordecai was more her style. But still, she felt a fondness for Brick, that great brute. Perhaps it was the mummified paw of his lost doggy, worn around his neck, that touched her. Perhaps it was a kind of crude gallantry he'd shown her from time to time. But she'd come to think of him as a slightly mentally handicapped big brother. And it was hard to see him brought this low.

She forced herself to drink the dregs of her execrable soup; she wiped her lips and tossed the bowl aside.

You're going to survive, Daphne told herself. *No giving up. There's always a chance.*

After all, she'd never thought she'd survive that tight spot on top of the hill, with Gynella's army wherever she looked, bullets flying from every direction, and Broomy squalling for her blood.

But she had. She was still alive.

They thought they'd use her for a little toy, once Brick died. But she was going to surprise them. She was going to—

"Well, you squirming little slag," came a voice like a rusty saw working its way through hardwood. "Still alive, I see."

It was Broomy, looking at her through the wire of the containment pen, a submachine gun in her hands.

"Yes, Broomy. I'm still breathing. I'll be breathing, walking around, and laughing when you're long dead."

Broomy showed the snags of her teeth in a gruesome leer. "Will you? After Brick's dead and the Psychos use you for their little hump toy, I'll come to find what's left of your body—and I'll wipe my shoes on it. Then I'll squat over it. And you know what'll happen then."

"Keep dreaming, Broomy. Just keep lying to yourself. I'm making you a promise. I'll kill you before I'm done."

Broomy tittered. "Says the girlie with chains on her ankles. Very convincing!"

And Broomy walked away, laughing.

• • •

"You really think they're gonna be safe here, Roland?" Mordecai asked, looking at his newly trimmed beard in the little hand mirror.

Bloodwing, on his shoulder, looked into the mirror too, turning its head this way and that, seeming to admire its own reflection. Mordecai glared at the creature. "Stop that, you leather-winged scrap-eater!"

Bloodwing cawed as if laughing, and Mordecai put the mirror away.

They were standing across from the Steel Incisor, keeping an eye on the street. The town had a good many unoccupied huts and shacks—unoccupied because the occupants had died or mysteriously disappeared. Those rude domiciles had been easy for Dakes to rent for his people.

"No way I can be sure the settlers are safe here," Roland said in a low voice. "But—" He paused to watch two children from Bloodrust Corners walk by, looking around them at their new settlement with large, uncertain eyes. "I feel like this place makes good cover. See, nobody takes this town seriously. Jawbone's like a . . . a blot on the map. I just don't think she'll look for 'em here. And there aren't any of Gynella's people here now. The settlers can regroup here, keep their heads down, make a plan to retake their settlement. If they stick to the cover story—that they're new settlers, looking for a place to settle on the planet—they'll probably be overlooked. Long enough, anyway."

Mordecai chuckled dryly. "You sound like you're trying to convince yourself, Roland."

Roland shrugged. He smiled, very slightly, seeing Glory and Lucky walking across the street together. Glory was still pretending that she wasn't quite sure about Lucky, but she was allowing him to hold her hand—tentatively. She'd set her cap for him, Roland had no doubt about that.

"You don't think they saw us caravaning here?" Mordecai asked. Adding bitterly to himself, "Giving the last of our money to Scooter to do it."

"Your pal Bloodwing got the other drone before we left. We covered up our tracks pretty well. With luck, the settlers are safe for a while. Meanwhile, you and I head out, scout the territory, find the safest way to that crystalisk den . . ."

Dakes emerged from the Steel Incisor and, hands in his pockets, crossed the street to Roland and Mordecai. He seemed a little drunk. His expression was hangdog, his shoulders slumped. He had a rifle on a strap over his shoulder and Roland hoped Dakes wouldn't have to use it while he was drunk.

"Roland," Dakes said. "Mordecai." He rubbed his forehead. "The stuff they sell in that bar! Ugh."

"Wouldn't drink that stuff, if I was you," Mordecai said.

"Trying to relax," Dakes muttered. "Couldn't rest all night. Every time I try to stretch out to sleep, I start seeing all those bodies back at the settlement. Half of us stone-cold dead. Seven more men maimed. We used up every bit of Dr. Zed we could get our hands on." He sighed. "We got two orphans to take care of now. Just little kids—they don't understand. My fault, getting their folks to come out here."

Roland shrugged. "I don't know. This world needs more settlements like yours. New Haven, a few other places—other than that, there's not much real civilization on Pandora." But privately Roland thought it was a mistake bringing children there, until the planet was tamed.

As if reading Roland's mind, Mordecai remarked, "Not sure this planet could ever be tamed. It's psychopathic, this world. Far as I know, pretty much any animal here is predatory. Everything's trying to kill and eat everything else."

"But you stay here," Dakes pointed out.

Mordecai tugged at his beard thoughtfully. "Guy like me, I need the action. That's the one thing on this planet you can count on."

Dakes glanced at Glory and Lucky, strolling down the street. "Shouldn't have brought my daughter to this world. She's gone half savage here. I just . . ." He shook his head. "Shouldn't have brought anyone."

"You're here now," Mordecai said. "I don't like seeing that lunatic Gynella win this one. Especially using those lunatics. How she ever got 'em to follow orders, I don't know. But once they start in on a settlement, it's slaughter. Torture. Cannibalism sometimes. She's not going to be able to control 'em forever. And you've got a right to take that place back."

Dakes looked at him. "That mean you're going to help us do it?"

Mordecai blinked. "Me? I didn't sign on for that. We've already gone way off mission. That's not professional, Mr. Dakes. And me, I stay pro. Me and Roland are going to head out. But if we get another chance to help . . ." He glanced inquiringly at Roland. And Roland nodded. Mordecai went on. "I mean, while we're on our mission, you know, just along the way, well then . . ." He sniffed. "If there's something we can do to reduce the odds against you folks, why, I wouldn't mind."

Bloodwing cawed and nuzzled Mordecai's ear.

It was only a couple of hours after dawn, but it was already warm out—it was going to be a hot day.

Daphne watched from her cage as scores of sullen Psychos were roughly lined up in the middle of the coliseum's gladiatorial ground. All of them were unarmed except their drill sergeant and Skenk, who stood at the back with a shotgun.

Listening to her captors, Daphne had learned the names of some of the principals of Gynella's army: the scar-faced sergeant was Flugg; the semihuman with eyes on the sides of his head was Runch. The enormous bodyguard was standing near a small pavilion, a large colorful tent with the stylized *G* on the side. Runch held a rocket launcher in his hands, as easily as an ordinary man would have carried a small rifle.

And then an extraordinary woman stepped out of the pavilion and surveyed the troops. Runch stepped up close to her, just a little behind, watching the troops with his own kind of surveillance.

The Psycho soldiers gaped at her, many of them trembling, moaning at the sight.

Daphne had never seen Gynella, but this had to be her. She was tall, powerful-looking, carrying herself with a feminine grace somehow perfectly combined with megalomaniacal confidence. Someone else might've looked absurd in the sexy armor, the high ornate boots, the cape, the long glittering nails, that long flowing white-blond hair, but Gynella, the General Goddess, carried it off easily. Daphne was quite impressed.

"My warriors!" Gynella called out, her voice carrying powerfully throughout the coliseum. "We have succeeded in capturing Bloodrust Corners!"

There was a ragged cheer of approbation from the Psychos.

"That will mean riches for all—once our mission is done!" She raised both fists in the air and shook them at the sky as she declared, "We will conquer this world and divide it up! We will feast on it!"

A real roar erupted at that one.

"And now, you are among those who've gone too long without your reward. The time for my blessing is here!"

The men murmured in anticipation. Several of the soldiers stepped forward, gasping in desire, hands outstretched. Runch snarled and pointed the rocket launcher at them. Flugg cursed at them to keep their places and pointed an assault rifle.

Gynella stood there calmly, waiting.

The soldiers looked at the weapons—and stepped back in line.

Gynella nodded. "And now—" Her voice reverberated loudly throughout the small stadium. "Will you follow me into battle?"

The men responded in litany, "We will!"

"And will you fight to the death for the banner of a new world?"

"We will!"

"Then . . ." She smiled seductively, and her fingers twisted the circle of metal on her ActiTone medallion. The men moaned in unison as she pointed her finger at them. "Then feel my love!"

Even from there, Daphne could see the medallion vibrating, could hear the weird chime emanated from it. The men fell to their knees, writhing, foaming at the mouth, clawing at their crotches in sensual rapture, many of them reaching orgasm—judging by the bucking of their hips— and all of them ecstatic. She noticed that Flugg and Skenk seemed unaffected; they stood and watched the others impassively. Doubtless the "goddess" needed them to keep their wits—probably she gave them their "blessings" in private. Could be they had to be specially treated first.

Watching the writhing Psychos, Daphne shook her head. "Wow," she muttered to herself. "Where do I get one of those medallions?"

Panting, the men gradually settled down, and Flugg walked around them, growling commands, occasionally smacking someone with a gun butt, bullying them back into some semblance of order. At last he gestured to Skenk, who pushed a prisoner out ahead of him, a medium-sized Psycho walking clumsily in his ankle shackles. The prisoner, looking blearily around, was without his mask or helmet; there was a bloody crater where his right eye had been.

The prisoner was brought to within ten paces of Gynella, and then he was halted by Skenk. The bald, one-eyed prisoner cocked his head to focus his single remaining eye on her, and he swallowed, over and over, licking his lips between swallows.

"Goddess," he whined. "Goddess!" He began to shuffle toward her, stretching out shaking hands.

"Stop!" Gynella ordered, giving him a wilting look.

He stopped, blinking his single eye in confusion.

"This one!" She pointed at the prisoner, shouting to her men. "This one tried to touch me at the last blessing. Normally I would simply have killed him, but this time I've saved him . . . to show you something special! A quick death is too good for a man who breaks my rules! Watch and learn what happens to those who do not keep a proper distance from their General. See what becomes of a soldier who does not respect what is sacred!"

She turned to the prisoner. "So—you want a blessing from me, do you?" she asked him.

He gaped and then nodded slowly. "Goddess . . . Goddess . . . touch you . . . *touch*!"

Gynella's eyes gleamed; her teeth flashed in a cold smile. She pointed a finger at him, her other hand twisting the medallion. "You wish to feel me? Then feel this!"

His back arched. She kept pointing, kept turning the ring on the medallion, staring at him. He bucked in ecstasy—and then a look of sickened horror came over his face. His entire body quivered like a plucked wire. He screamed, "No, Goddess . . . no!"

His hands ripped at his belly; blood spurted from a gash just above his navel, and then it erupted. His innards exploded from the gash, and he fell onto his back; his body contorted, and his skin seemed to have a will of its own, wriggling away from him, as if he were a hideous gift unwrapping itself. His mottled intestines whipped up and flailed in the air; his bones jolted from the widening wound and snapped upward.

As Daphne watched, the man turned inside out. And still he lived. He was beyond screaming, and yet his agony could be felt vibrating in the air, at some pitch higher than men could hear.

The Psychos watched in a kind of sick fascination, almost seeming to enjoy this nightmarish death. Gynella turned to them. "So, you *like* that, do you? Would you like it to happen to *you*? Is *that* what you want?"

The men began to fall to their knees, some of them kowtowing, slamming their heads to the dirt in obeisance. "No, Goddess, no! Please . . . We will respect . . ."

The smell of the man who'd turned inside out rolled across the open ground to Daphne . . . the smell of feces and blood and ruptured tissues.

She turned away and retched.

A few moments later, when she had herself under control again, Daphne heard the sound of footsteps. She turned to see Gynella strolling up to her cage, hands on hips; Runch followed close behind her.

Gynella stopped a step beyond the steel-link fence and looked imperiously down at Daphne.

"Do you know why you are still alive?" Gynella asked, her voice pitched low.

Daphne shrugged. "The way I heard it, I'm part of a show."

"Oh yes, there's that, but I wanted to make sure you lived till I could watch you die in person. You see, I know who you are. And I know what you did."

Daphne's heart sank. "You . . . are from the guild of assassins?"

"No. I have my own reasons for wanting you here. For wanting to see you debased. To see you slowly—very slowly—put to death."

Daphne's heart thudded, but she set her expression of cool defiance in stone. "Yeah? Going to share your reasons for wanting that?"

Gynella licked her lips, just once. "You are Daphne Kuller. And you assassinated Merritt Granick."

Daphne considered denying she'd done the hit. But this woman seemed so convinced she'd probably found proof.

Daphne waved airily. "Granick was a mass murderer. A crime lord. I killed him because his rivals wanted to take over his territory. It was just another job. What of it?"

"Oh, nothing. Except that Merritt Granick was my husband. The only man in the galaxy who could possibly be worthy of me. And you killed him. *You* are the creepy-crawly little assassin who snuck past his defense system. You shot him from hiding, with a poison dart, like the sneaking little coward you are."

"He died quick and clean." Daphne nodded toward the mess that used to be a human being out in the center of the coliseum field. "Not like that. I would never kill like that. I take pride in doing a good, clean job. But that—what *you* did, lady—is sick."

"Is it?" Gynella favored her with a twisted smile. "That's nothing compared to what's going to happen to you. And it's going to happen this very day, Daphne. Enjoy the show . . ."

FOURTEEN

"We're gonna need transportation, now that you got yours blown up, like the genius you are," Mordecai pointed out. "There's no Catch-a-Ride station around here."

Bloodwing squawked in agreement.

Roland nodded. "That's why we're in the cemetery."

"Somebody buried an outrunner?"

"Funny. You're gonna *win* us an outrunner." It was almost high noon in the Jawbone Ridge cemetery. A thin breeze blew scraps of paper through the grave markers.

"Cemeteries," Mordecai remarked, looking around. "There are so many on this planet. More graves on this planet than living people."

Roland heard engine noise, spotted the outrunner he was waiting for, showing up right on time. "Here he comes!"

The outrunner came rumbling down the dirt access road and pulled up. A big man jumped out of the driver's seat. He wore a red leather helmet, red goggles, a scarred black sleeveless leather vest that showed off his muscular arms. The man reached into the back of the outrunner, drew out an Atlas combat rifle, then strutted confidently toward Roland and Mordecai. As he came he bared his teeth—more of a feral challenge than a smile, his teeth coated in metal. That was a fashion around Jawbone Ridge, getting your teeth coated with steel. Roland didn't get the appeal, although it probably helped if you had to bite somebody's ear off.

"Mordecai, this is Gumble," Roland said. "I know him from New Haven. Ran into him today while you were buying ammo."

"Ammo for *that*?" asked Gumble, scowling at Mordecai's Cobra combat rifle. "Kind of a worn-out-looking piece of junk you got there."

"Once I get to know a gun, it works for me," Mordecai said, sounding bored. "And I know this one. You got some kind of competition in mind, Roland?"

"If you're game for it, Mordecai. Target shooting! You win, we get the outrunner. He wins, we pay him ten grand."

Mordecai's eyes widened. They didn't *have* ten grand, as Roland well knew.

"You are out of your mind, Roland," Mordecai said, in a low voice behind his hand.

"I've got faith in you, is all."

Gumble looked Mordecai up and down. He snorted. "This guy is a better shot than me? He looks like the recoil of a decent gun'd knock him flat on his ass."

Mordecai pushed his goggles back and stared at Gumble. Then his eyes narrowed and his nostrils flared.

Bloodwing made a gravelly *heh heh heh* sound deep in its throat.

Roland chuckled. He knew he had Mordecai hooked now.

"Let's do this," Mordecai said, between clenched teeth.

There was an open grave someone had started and not quite finished; above it was a grave marker made from planks that had no name on it yet.

Roland reached into his open jacket, pulled out a poster he'd torn from a fence in town. The poster had a large picture of Gynella looking like an empress, smiling regally, a rifle in one hand like a scepter. Above the picture were the words:

THE GENERAL GODDESS
WILL BRING PEACE
TO ALL THE WORLD
JOIN HER
AND MARCH TO GLORY!

"Ha, look at that!" Mordecai said. "Pretty pro-paganda!"

Roland hung the poster on the grave marker, using a couple of nails sticking out from it.

He stepped back and nodded. "You'll shoot for targets on the poster. Shoot out the O's in 'God-dess' and 'Glory.' And, say, her eyes." He turned and pointed. "Take your shots from way back there. Far as you can go and still see the targets. No sniper rifles, of course—just standard combat rifles. Single-shot setting."

Gumble snorted. "Is that all? Hell, I could shorten her eyelashes for her. Let's do this. And start counting that money out!"

Mordecai turned and stalked back, back, back, away from the open grave and the target, Gumble following. Roland moved to one side of the grave, well out of the line of fire.

"Hold it, hold it," Gumble said, when he'd gone so far Mordecai couldn't make out the words on the poster at all anymore. "We gotta get close enough to shoot at those O's and all that."

"This is close enough," Mordecai said calmly. "How about another twenty paces farther?"

He kept going, and Gumble reluctantly came along. At last Mordecai turned and looked at the target. "You want to shoot first, Gumble?"

Gumble muttered something inaudible, shook his head, but set his Atlas combat rifle to single shot, adjusted the sights, raised it, tucked it into his shoulder, and squinted. "I'll go for the top *O* and two of her eyes."

He took a long breath. He licked his lips.

He fired. Once. Twice. Three times. The cemetery echoed with the gunshots.

Mordecai shouted to Roland. "Well?"

"He hit her around the navel once!" Roland shouted. "The other two missed the poster, just chipped the marker!"

"Bullshit!" Gumble snapped. He strode quickly back to the grave marker. Mordecai waited behind.

Gumble stared. Roland was right. "Bah!" Gumble grumbled. "No one could do any better from that range."

Roland shrugged. "I guess we'll find out. Let Mordecai have his shot."

Gumble drew back, with Roland, out of the line of fire. Roland waved.

Mordecai pushed back his goggles, aimed his Cobra, and fired. Once. Twice. Three times. The gunshots echoed.

Roland looked at the poster. Mordecai had punched out Gynella's eyes and the first *O* in the text.

"What the—!" Gumble yelled. "Fakery! He's using some kinda secret sniper scope, maybe had his eyes altered! Cheat! It's a cheat!"

Mordecai walked slowly toward Gumble.

Gumble shook his fist at Mordecai. "I'm telling you, I know when I've been cheated! You used some kind of electronic cheat! I don't know how you did it, but you did it!"

Mordecai kept coming.

"You're not getting away with this!" Gumble bellowed.

Mordecai walked up to Gumble and Roland. He calmly handed Roland his rifle. Then he took four steps back from Gumble. "You have a pistol on your hip there, Gumble. Drop the rifle. Then take your time. And go for that pistol. I don't take accusations of cheating lightly. You can examine my rifle, and you can examine me. I didn't cheat." He looked Gumble in the eye and said, carefully, "I'm just . . . plain . . . better . . . than you are."

Gumble glared. "What? You're challenging me to a gunfight?"

Mordecai shrugged. "You could always hand Roland the key to your outrunner and . . . walk away."

Gumble shook with barely suppressed rage. "So you cheat me, and now you think you're gonna kill me when my back's turned! Well, you've got a little surprise coming. And I'm gonna send that surprise right through your heart, you little prick!"

"Talk is cheap," Mordecai said calmly.

Gumble took two slow steps to his right, sidling so he and Mordecai were face-to-face.

"Wait a minute," Roland said. "Let's make this clean and fast. No shields."

Gumble frowned. "He turns his off first."

Mordecai switched off his shield. Gumble licked his lips, glanced at Roland, who hefted the Cobra combat rifle meaningfully. Gumble swallowed and switched off his shield. Then he looked at Mordecai. And prepared himself for a kill.

Mordecai's hand hovered near the pistol on his hip. He had equipped himself with a Dahl Anaconda revolver early that morning, bought from a Jawbone Ridge weapons dealer. But he didn't touch the gun yet. He simply kept his hand near the butt of the pistol, watched Gumble, and waited.

The big man in the red helmet let his fingers slide over the butt of his Hyperion Lightning Nemesis . . .

And then Gumble snatched it up—

Mordecai was already leveling his revolver. He fired two neat shots, so fast they almost blended together.

Gumble's eyes vanished, replaced with bloody pits. The bullets went right through his eyes and into his brain. He swayed. And fell backward . . .

. . . into the open grave.

Roland nodded. He'd never doubted the outcome. He knelt by the grave, reached down, fished in Gumble's pockets, found the key to the outrunner. Then he stood up and kicked a little dirt over Gumble. "Well, that's buried enough. What the hell, the trash feeders have to eat too."

He looked at Mordecai, who was replacing his gun in its holster and walking toward the outrunner. "Nice shooting, Mordecai. I didn't know you could fast-draw."

"Neither did I."

The day was wearing away, Daphne saw. Soon the moon would rise. The lights would flare up around the coliseum. The show would begin.

Brick was awake and alert. They'd given him some Dr. Zed, and some food. Not enough to get him back to full strength but enough to make for a good show.

She waved to Brick, who was standing in another cage, about ten meters to the right of hers. He glanced at her and winked. "Wait'll I get my hands on 'em!" he called. His fingers were clutching at the metal link, and he fell to examining it. She supposed he was thinking about tearing through that fence. But she knew what it was—molecularly reinforced steel. You couldn't break through it without a nuclear flamecutter.

Brick tried anyway, squeezing the metal links with his powerful fingers. To her surprise she saw it bend—but it held, and when he released it, it snapped into place, just as it had been before.

Brick shook his head. He wasn't going to have the initiative.

"Another couple hours," came the rawboned voice to Daphne's left.

She looked, knowing who she'd see: Broomy, leering at her with yellow, snagged teeth.

"What do you want, you pathetic old cow?" Daphne asked mildly.

Broomy laughed. "Keep it up, girlie! We'll see how brave you talk when they start in on you. Do you know what they're going to do? After Brick is killed by the Goliath, why, they're gonna chain you down on that Brick's dead body! And they're gonna let the Goliath rip into you and pull you apart and—"

"I've already had the preview on that, thanks. Charming stuff."

"Soon, girlie! *Soon!* When the moon rises, the fight commences!"

"Suppose Brick wins?"

"Against a Goliath? It'll never happen! But if it did, why—" She laughed. "They'll kill him with four or five rocket launchers! And they'll chain you down on what's left of him and then—"

"Right. You already mentioned that. Have *I* mentioned, by the way, that I'll kill you . . . before the moon sets?"

"Ho ho ho! Keep telling yourself that, little girlie!"

And Broomy walked away, laughing.

• • •

The outrunner was bumping and grinding through the raw countryside in the dusk. There was a thin trail, winding along between outcroppings. They were following the southern edge of the Salt Flats, heading west.

Roland came upon a sudden small gulley where they glimpsed a big, armored badmutha skag they wanted no part of. He accelerated around the gulley away from the skag and its whelps as fast as Gumble's beat-up old outrunner would go.

He looked over his shoulder at Mordecai, who was standing at the machine-gun turret. Mordecai swung the turret around to watch their backs and sent a judicious burst of machine-gun rounds into the badmutha skag just then leaping up to pursue them. It was a big, bristly creature, like an oversized armored wolf with trisected jaws. The burst didn't take the badmutha out but discouraged it, along with their outdistancing it with the outrunner, and the skag turned away.

Roland looked back at the faint trail up ahead just in time to avoid smashing headlong into an outcropping of stone.

"Hey, Roland!" Mordecai shouted, over the engine noise. "We on track to get to the Eridian Promontory?"

"Yeah, if we don't have to detour too far around that bunch of Psychos playing soldier!"

"We need to get there, harvest some crystalisks, load up on Eridium, and get the hell to Fyrestone!"

Roland chuckled. He knew it wouldn't be that easy. And suppose they found a lot of Eridium? How would they move it? Not in this outrunner. They'd need to hijack a truck somewhere.

"Roland?"

"What?"

"You notice anything tracking us, in the sky?"

"More of those fake trash feeders?"

"Naw—looked like some kind of flying craft, maybe an orbiter!"

Roland hit the brakes, and they squealed to a stop. Dust swirled around them. Mordecai coughed.

Roland turned to him. "When were you gonna tell me this?"

"I wasn't exactly sure of what I saw," Mordecai said, shrugging, glancing at the sky. "There was some cloud cover, and it just dipped down and seemed like it was pacing us, and then it was gone. But we were hitting a lotta bumps, and I was trying to hold on, and . . . I couldn't be sure."

"When was this?"

"It was—" Mordecai stared and pointed at the sky up ahead. "Right now."

Roland looked the way Mordecai was pointing and saw a three-strutted orbiter, like a salt shaker on a tripod, burning its way down, down, retros slowing the vessel as it approached the desert sands about fifty paces ahead.

"Roland, could it be Gynella? She's from off-planet—maybe she brought that with her."

"I don't think so. Markings on it . . . Dahl Corporation!"

They could see the Dahl insignia clearly now, as the vapor cleared away around the orbiter. And they saw a hatch open, in the side of the gray metal cylindrical vessel, and a ramp lowering from the open hatch . . .

They didn't have to wait long. Three men came out. Two of them were heavily armed, probably protecting the smaller one in the spray-on suit. An exec type. He waved at them, real friendly.

"We oughta either kill 'em or steer clear of them," Mordecai said.

Roland nodded. "Yeah, we should just back off and go around." But instinct changed his mind for him. "No. We need information. We'll get it from this slick son of a skag—a guy like that likes to talk. They're here for a reason . . . Just keep steady on that machine gun, Mordecai. But don't get jumpy."

He accelerated the outrunner slowly, eased it toward the orbiter, and stopped a few steps from the ramp. He left the outrunner in idle, grabbed his new Hyperion assault rifle as he climbed out. Roland was careful not to seem as if he was going to shoot at anyone right away, holding the gun casually—but also in plain sight to let them know he was not going to go down easily.

He walked toward the man in the suit, a black-haired man with a sculpted beard, piercing dark eyes, flashing white teeth when he smiled. Behind him were two red-armored Dahl specialists, highly trained killers who'd almost forgotten they'd once been human. Both men were cyborgian, their eyes replaced by whirring scopes that focused on Roland, with precise digital irising.

Each specialist carried a big, smoothly contoured weapon Roland didn't recognize—some new Dahl armament, maybe a form of Eridian rifle.

Roland didn't want to find out what those rifles could do unless he had to.

"I believe you'd be the one they call Roland," said the dark-eyed man unctuously.

"You *believe* that's who I am?" Roland asked. "Or you know?"

The man chuckled. "Very astute. Yes, I know who you both are. We've been observing Gynella's army, from suborbit. And you. We did a facial-recognition scan, ran it through our files. We noticed your work at that settlement. You were effective, you and your friend. Gynella's quite surprisingly elusive. I'm interested in people who cause her difficulty. That would be you."

"And you are?"

"My name's Mince Feldsrum. Dahl security specialist, assigned to Homeworld Security."

Roland shrugged. "What do you want with us?"

"May I ask what, ah, goal you have set for yourself, at the moment? Are you planning to join Gynella? Maybe kill her?"

"Neither one. First one, I can't imagine it. Second one, too much trouble. Way off mission."

"Ah-ha! And what is your mission?"

"That's our business. We're . . . prospecting. A long ways . . ." Roland pointed past them. "In that direction."

"Suppose I offered you more money than you'd make on your mission. I'll double it. Good cash to kill Gynella for me. To take her on directly—with our help."

"Why? What do you care what she does here?"

"She's stolen something from us. Haven't you wondered how she controls her men? Considering that they're all Psychos."

"I've wondered."

"She took a mind-control drug from us. And my company is not yet aware I let it get it taken. I can't summon our full firepower without letting them know what it's for. It's all rather embarrassing. But you seem capable of doing the job. I could help you, provide you with a fast flyer; you could take them from the air. Kill her, and Dr. Vialle. Kill as many of her followers as you can—destroying her supply of the drug in the process."

"Why don't you do it, with your two boyfriends there?" Mordecai asked, from the outrunner, pointing at the specialists.

Something dangerous flickered in Feldsrum's eyes. But he made a careless, dismissive gesture and said, "Gynella is well defended. And it would take too much explaining, in all the wrong places, if I had to go after her directly. Let's leave it at that. Do you want the job or not?"

Roland turned to look at Mordecai, who shook his head, once. Roland turned back to Feldsrum. "Nope. You're hiding things from Dahl—so I figure you'd kill us after we got the job done, to make sure we don't talk about it. And anyhow, I don't like to go off mission."

Feldsrum sighed. Then he unclipped a small silvery metal box from his belt and tossed it to Roland, who caught it neatly in his left hand. "If you change your mind, call me on that."

He turned and walked between his guardians and up the ramp. The specialists backed up, keeping their electronically enhanced eyes on Roland—then they turned and followed Feldsrum into the spacecraft. The ramp withdrew into the vessel, and its hatch clanked shut.

Roland climbed back into the outrunner and

backed it up, just in time to avoid the burning backwash of the orbiter's energy pulsers.

He and Mordecai watched the vessel lift into the sky.

Mordecai sighed. "You get any of that useful information you were hoping for?"

"Maybe. I got a line on how Gynella controls her men. Could be useful, down the line."

"I got mixed feelings about the offer. Might've been faster to take the job, collect the paycheck, than to do what we were going to. But on the other hand . . ."

Roland nodded. "On the other hand they'd probably have killed us to keep us quiet, later on, first time we turned our backs."

"I was thinking that too. Well, let's hit the road."

They resumed their journey. The evening crept toward them across the plains. The sky shifted from dark blue to the color of lead.

After another half-hour they drove up onto a bluff and saw lights up ahead, shining from below—the ground rose to a cliff edge overlooking a valley. Roland pulled up, and they stared at the lights, coming on, in the coliseum down below.

"Looks like somebody's got a show planned," Roland said softly.

FIFTEEN

Brick was standing up now but chained to a block of stone flush with the ground, in the center of the coliseum's field. Unbreakable shackles were locked around his neck, wrists, and ankles. He glared at gathering Psychos, in the seats overlooking the gladiatorial arena, and every so often he shook his chains and bellowed at them in defiance. "You wanna take me on? Come on, let's dance!"

The crowd of Psychos responded with jeers and catcalls.

Brick pulled at the chains, trying to rip them from the stone they were pinned to, all the time howling at the audience: "Come on down here, chickenshits! You're looking at my fists? Then take off the chains and get a better look! Whatcha waitin' for!"

Gazing at Brick, Daphne was feeling increasingly

desperate, like an animal trapped in a cage—and maybe that's what she was. She turned away from the darkening field, the glare of the lights, the roar of the crowd—a crowd of Psychos, bandits, thugs lining up on the risers to watch the coming fight between Brick and the Goliath.

Each step clanking with her shackles, she walked over to the locked gate at the rear of the cage. That was the only weak point of this little prison. That gate. There was a lock on it—but locks could be broken.

Only she couldn't reach the gate. Her hands were free, but her ankles were locked into a long chain attached to an iron pole in the middle of her cage. She'd tried the chains over and over, never got any give in them.

Cursing in frustration, she turned away from the gate, walked back to the fence. There was no way under the fence—the links extended under her too, beneath a covering of dirt. And there was no way over it.

She had one hope, which was chained up on that slab of stone out there.

Roland had moved the outrunner back from the edge of the bluff, and now he and Mordecai lay flat on the verge, peering out over the shallow valley and the small, open-air, oblong coliseum almost directly below. The ramshackle arena was so close that if Roland were to back up, take a run and a long jump, he might be able to jump onto the top of its curved outer wall.

Mordecai stared at the arena, roughly built of random slabs of thin metal, with wooden posts at intervals, wooden bleachers. "Looks like they went to the Rust Commons, scavenged some junk, and built that piece-of-crap coliseum in no time."

"Using mostly slave labor—yeah. You think that's Brick down there?" Roland asked. There was a good deal of dust blowing by, and he wasn't quite sure. But it looked like his old "friend" Brick, chained up in the middle of the killing ground.

"Looks like him," Mordecai said. "And that's gotta be Gynella's little pets yelling at him from the cheap seats. I can smell 'em from here. And there's her banner. And—hey! Is that *Daphne*?"

There was a small dark woman in a sort of cage, half hidden by the nearer wall of the coliseum—shadow draped her, making it hard to be certain. "Might be her. I'm not sure. Wait—Gumble had a sniper rifle in the outrunner. It's got a scope on it."

He got up, trotted to the outrunner, got the sniper rifle, a loaded Atlas GGN350 Long Cyclops, and brought it back to the cliff. He lay down, got the rifle in position, and looked through the scope.

At just that moment, the shackles around Brick's neck, unlocked by a remote-control device controlled by Runch, fell away, clanking to the ground. And Brick was free . . . free to die.

But to die fighting—that was a beautiful thing.

Gynella's pavilion had been removed from the coliseum's killing field, and a wooden post stood in its place. Daphne didn't like the look of that post.

She turned at a clattering sound and saw a bald, hunchbacked woman in dirty gray armor and bullet-scarred leggings unlocking the back gate of the cage. The hunchback's name was Pestra, Daphne knew—part of Gynella's women's retinue. Instead of hair and eyebrows, Pestra had tattoos representing permed hair and arching eyebrows, the *appearance* of hair tattooed on her head.

She walked slowly toward Daphne, her steel boots thumping the ground.

Maybe this was the moment. Pestra would have to unlock her shackles—she had that pistol in her hand, but it wasn't pointed at Daphne . . .

"I can see it in your eyes, what you're thinking," Pestra said, in a low, dull voice. She made a low sound, *hur, hur, hur*, and after a moment Daphne decided it was this woman's version of laughter. "I see you're gonna try'n jump me. But see . . ." She stopped just out of reach and aimed the pistol. "Not going to happen."

She fired, and the pistol hissed. Daphne felt a small, fierce, stinging pain just over her sternum, and she looked down to see a dart sticking there. She plucked it out, but the drug was already in her.

Was it the drug that Gynella used on her men? Would it work on her? Would Gynella turn her inside out?

A tide of sickly greenness washed over Daphne, thick and cold, and she fell to her knees. She could see her own hands spasmodically clutching the air in front of her—they looked green. Everything looked green.

She tried to lift her arms—they were too heavy to lift.

The hunchbacked woman unlocked the shackles at Daphne's ankles, but Daphne couldn't make a move against her. She could barely keep on breathing.

Pestra took Daphne by the neck and dragged her to the door of the cage. Daphne was distantly aware of the Psychos in the audience clapping, hooting, demanding they be given their chance at her.

A green blur, a change of position, then Daphne saw the darkening sky, starting to show a few stars overhead, as she was dragged by the neck across the ground. She had difficulty breathing, but it didn't seem to matter.

Harder to breathe; harder yet. Time slipped into green ooze, and she must've lost consciousness for a few minutes. She wallowed in a toxic green sea . . . until suddenly light stabbed through. Her eyes popped open, and she gasped, sucking in air. She was awake and found she was lying on her back in the middle of the coliseum. She struggled to move and managed to sit up. The paralysis drug was wearing off; the greenness was draining away, and true colors were slowly returning. She looked behind her—the motion hurt a little, because of a tight metal shackle around her neck. It was attached to a chain that reached two meters before connecting with a steel pin in a wooden post.

Head throbbing, Daphne turned to look at Brick and was surprised to see he didn't have his shackles on anymore. He was standing on that flat stone, staring past her, at something beyond.

The crowd roared—and Daphne *knew.*

She looked anyway and saw the Goliath come through a wide rusty metal gate opening at the other end of the arena.

The Goliath was big, towering over any ordinary man, and must have outweighed Brick, she guessed, by about double. The Goliath had once been an ex-con, brought to this planet like so many others to work in penal servitude, then abandoned by the Dahl Corporation. Now he'd mutated, twisted by Eridium radiation and experimental steroids, into this obscenely muscular, oversized hulk with a swag belly and arms like tree trunks and a strangely small head. The Goliath's head was quite disproportionately small compared with his body, the entire skull encased in a crude gray metal, flat-topped helmet completely concealing his face. He wore a vest that was too small for the enormous barrel of his torso, brown leather trousers on rather squat legs, big rubbery boots. He didn't seem to be wearing a shield—probably usually didn't need one. Most bullets would be like mosquito bites to a Goliath, so long as that head was armored.

She could feel the ground shaking with each of the Goliath's thumping steps as it stumped toward Brick.

The Goliath shook his massive fists at Brick, rumbly voice coming muffled but audible through the helmet: "Get ready for . . . HURT!"—and the crowd went wild with sadistic delight.

"Brick!" Daphne hissed, as Brick stalked toward the Goliath. "Brick—how about if you just smash down that wooden post, set me free, carry me out of here! You can dodge past the Goliath! Bash the gate down! Let's just get outta here!"

Brick looked at her, eyebrows bobbing in surprise at her suggestion. "Run? *Me?*"

"Brick—you've been injured, weakened, and he's . . . big. Very, very big. And I've heard those things can change and get *bigger*."

"I will set you free," Brick said, nodding. "As soon as I kill this big slob over here."

Daphne groaned. Brick marched past her, toward the Goliath.

The Goliath threw his head back, pounded his fists on his chest, and roared, "ALWAYS KILL! GET READY FOR HURT!"

Not particularly articulate, is he? thought Daphne torpidly.

Brick responded with his own bellowed declaration of destruction as he leaned forward and rushed toward the Goliath. "You . . . better . . . RUN!"

Then Brick was upon the Goliath, ducking under the swing of the mutant's enormous right fist, slamming his own gloved, studded fists hard into the Goliath's belly, a left and a right blur-fast, deep into that swag belly.

The Goliath roared and took one staggering step back. "Ouch!" he yelled. "A little hurt!"

A wave of laughter swept over the crowd.

Brick kept coming with freight-train force, hitting the Goliath with a tackle around the knees, and the huge mutant fell over, facedown, his helmet ringing on the ground like a badly made bell.

The Psychos came to their feet in the bleachers, jumping up and down in outraged excitement.

Brick squirmed free of the Goliath's legs, was up, turning and jumping, body-slamming on the Goliath just as the mutant got to his hands and knees.

The Goliath grunted as Brick knocked him flat again.

Daphne grinned, thinking maybe Brick was going to win after all. Feeling the paralysis dissipate a little more with each passing second, she looked around for Gynella and spotted the General Goddess in a special, decorated viewing box, with her banner hanging in front of it, in the lowest row of the coliseum. She saw Presta standing protectively behind Gynella on one side, Broomy on another. Runch was standing on the field, just beside his Goddess's coliseum box, in case anyone should rush her. He had the rocket launcher in his hand and seemed impatient to use it.

Daphne heard an *oof* and a grunt of pain from Brick, turned to see the Goliath had turned the tables on Brick, slammed him to the ground, was now getting up and looming over him. Brick looked as if he was wheezing, breath knocked out of him.

Oh shit, Daphne thought.

She stood up, took a deep breath, and yelled, at the top of her lungs, "Hey, Goliath! Hey, dumbass! *Hey, bucket head!* Over here!"

The Goliath lifted his head and turned to see who was shouting at him.

He stared at Daphne. She blew him a kiss.

The crowd roared at that.

But in distracting the mutant she'd given Brick

a chance to get to his feet, and when the Goliath turned back around, he was met by Brick jumping up and smashing his mailed fist hard into the giant's crotch.

The Goliath howled in pain and bent double—and Brick cracked him with an uppercut to the chin.

The Goliath staggered back, three steps. Then got his feet under him and rushed at Brick, shouting, "Deathtastic! And DIE!"

And he clapped his fists together—with Brick's head in between. The double impact was an ugly sound to hear.

Brick yelled in pain and fury and quivered.

Daphne knew what was coming. Brick was going into his *berserk* state. She'd seen it when they were defending the mine by Jawbone Ridge.

Brick's muscles seemed to flex to twice their previous size, the veins standing out, his face going mottled, his teeth clenching, his eyes crazy wild.

"Rauugh!" Brick thundered. "BLOOD!"

And he hit the Goliath with a rushing shoulder slam, powering into the big mutant's belly with such force the Goliath backpedaled five times and went over backward.

"BLOOOOOD!" Brick howled, and rushed toward the fallen Goliath, who proved surprisingly agile. The Goliath rolled, got to his feet, turned—

And was met by the still-berserker Brick

leaping up to smash a fist into that helmet, just under the chin.

The helmet cracked down the middle and flew off the Goliath's head, spinning away in two halves.

The giant's exposed face was blanched, emaciated, flattened by the helmet—and as Daphne watched, aghast, the Goliath's head began to quiver within itself, like an egg with an infant reptile breaking out of it. Brick was hauling back for another powerful punch, but the Goliath planted those big hands on Brick's shoulders, held him at arm's length, as the mutant transformation was completed.

Daphne had heard of the phenomenon—the most perverse aspect of the Goliath's mutation. The Goliath's entire body swelled up; it grew—as if the giant were trying to show that its "berserk" was more berserk than Brick's—increasing in size, more than doubling its heft, somehow expanding its physical mass, and rapidly changing color, turning bright glossy red, head to toe, the veins standing out on its scarlet body.

Brick took an unsteady step back, unsure of what was happening. He watched in puzzled fascination.

But the head changed even more drastically.

Its mouth opened wide, wider, wider . . . *impossibly* wide. And something wriggled within it, the skull itself trying to break free from the sheath of skin and tissue. Some of the crowd gasped, some cheered, others fell gapingly silent, as the impossible elasticity of the Goliath's mouth allowed it to vomit forth the Goliath's skull.

That's how it looked to Daphne, as if the Goliath was vomiting out its own skull.

The skull, complete with eyes and tongue, came squirming out of the mouth like a profane birth, blood dripping from it, blood spurting from the nose—and the nose was now on the back of the head, as if the skin of the face and scalp and neck was part of a hoodie that had been pushed back.

The skull popped completely free and swayed like a cobra on the spine, which seemed to have a life of its own.

All the time the bright red body was still swelling, veins distending till they seemed about to explode from interior pressure, most of its clothing ripped away from it, torn apart from within.

The skull waved this way and that on the flexible, bloody spine, and it looked at Brick with its lidless eyes. The mouth opened, and the bloody skull tried to speak. But all that emerged from its clacking jaws was a burbling sound.

Then this doubled and doubly hideous Goliath charged Brick, swinging massive bright red arms—they were even more massive now, after this metamorphosis—and although Brick made a powerful defensive move with his forearms to block, the Goliath's blows smashed him off his feet, flipped him to the side. Brick rolled over onto his back, stunned, blood bubbling from his mouth.

Daphne groaned.

The Goliath's skull, like a sick joke on a jack-in-the-box children's toy, bobbled on its neck as it tried to speak. "Gubble . . . blooble . . ."

The enormous red mutant turned and stalked toward Daphne, and she thought, *This is it, it's going to rip my legs off and dance in what's left of me.*

She set herself to make a move, thinking she'd try to reach through a rent in the Goliath's torn pants, tear one of the monster's testicles off. Something, anything, to go down fighting.

But the Goliath stopped before reaching her. It was after something else. The giant red hands clamped on the wooden post and pushed at it, pulled at it, finally cracking the wood, tearing the pole loose. It left a short snag sticking out of the ground, and the post, in the Goliath's hands, was now a crude spear, its lower end splintered to a rough point.

The Goliath started back toward the still-supine Brick, who was just then trying to get up. And Daphne was dragged along by the chain, which was still fixed in the post. She yelled and dragged her feet, trying to hold it back, although she knew the metal collar on her neck might pop her head right off her shoulders.

The Goliath made a burbling grunt of irritation and turned, seeing that the woman was still snagged to its chain.

The crowd was howling, cheering, laughing— Gynella was shouting something at the Goliath, but she couldn't be heard over the tumultuous crowd hubbub.

The Goliath set the post on the ground, yanked at the chain attaching Daphne to it, pulling the connecting pin out of the wood. The mutant dropped the chain and pointed at her, the skull's exposed jaws moved, and it managed to say something like "You die next!" Only, the words came out more like "Yoofdy nescht."

Then the red behemoth, carrying the post, stalked to Brick, who was just then sitting up, shaking his head to clear it—but still on the ground. The Goliath lifted the post over its head, prepared to slam its rough point down like a giant spear, aiming it to stab through Brick's belly.

Daphne was gathering up the chain in her hands, hoping to use it to trip up the Goliath—

Then there was a *zing* sound. Twice. High enough to penetrate the crowd noise.

And the Goliath's cranium exploded, shot through with two rounds right through the brain. It swayed.

Daphne turned toward the source of the sound, a clifftop overlooking the coliseum, saw a glint along what might be the barrel of a sniper rifle. And was that a sniper lying on the edge of the bluff? Hard to tell—it was just a silhouette against the darkening sky.

She turned toward the Goliath; the mutant still hadn't fallen. The Goliath seemed to wobble, and still it just stood there, not quite completely dead, holding that post tremblingly over Brick.

Brick stood up, stared a moment, then walked around behind the Goliath. "Who did this?" Brick demanded, scowling. "Someone shot him! Dammit! I was going to kill him myself with nobody's help!"

He grabbed the post, jerked it from the Goliath's grip. The Goliath dropped his big red arms down to his sides, twitching. Brick shifted the broken-off post in his hands and swung it like a bat, cracking into what was left of the Goliath's head. The mutant's skull snapped off the waving spine and went spinning like a home run into the bleachers.

The Psychos in the bleachers yelled in mad glee and began to bounce the skull back and forth among them, as if it were a balloon at a concert.

And the Goliath's dying body fell forward, crashing to the ground in a gush of spurting blood.

Daphne heard Gynella shouting orders and turned to see Runch firing the rocket launcher.

Brick ran to Daphne and threw her onto the

ground, shielded her with his body, as the rocket shell exploded just a half-dozen paces away. Shrapnel screamed over them, and dirt pattered down.

And Daphne thought, *Now we die. She'll send her whole army down onto the field to tear us apart. At least we'll die fast.*

SIXTEEN

"You sure you know what you're doing, Roland?" Mordecai shouted over the noise of the outrunner's engine, as Roland drove them down the bluff. They were headed south, toward the only place that looked like a close entry to the unnamed valley where Gynella's coliseum had been built.

Roland turned his head partway to shout over his shoulder at Mordecai, who stood at the machine-gun turret with Bloodwing clinging to his shoulder. "No, of course I'm not sure! If I was sure, it'd be boring, and if I was into stuff like being sure, what would I be doing on Pandora anyway?"

Mordecai started to reply but cut it short as he grabbed for a better hold on the turret as Roland jerked the outrunner into a hard right, down an old erosion cut into the shallow valley. They bumped jarringly down, Roland risking the axles, and both of them felt their teeth clack as the outrunner hit the valley floor.

Then Roland jerked the wheel again, bringing the outrunner around to the north, heading for the coliseum.

"Yeah, Roland, I like action, you know I do, but there must be *two hundred* of those fuckers in that coliseum!"

"You like action, and I like to give you what you want, Mordecai! Now hammer that gate up there with the machine gun!" He slowed the outrunner so he could pull a couple of grenades from an ordnance box and have time to chuck them ahead of the outrunner.

"Brick!" Daphne yelled as bullets cut the air nearby. "Gynella wants to kill me more than she wants to kill you! Maybe you could join her and live, or maybe—"

"Woman, shut up and prepare to kill the enemy or be killed!" Brick growled. "We're going to take the fight to them, and we're gonna kick some Psycho ass!"

She was running along beside Brick as machine-gun bullets slashed the air and thunked into the ground near them. Broomy and Presta were toying with her, laughing as they fired the submachine guns. But Brick was running at the enemy—right at Runch.

A rocket shell whooshed past, missing Brick's left shoulder by a whisker, and then he was upon Runch. He slammed him hard in the chest, straight-arming him, and Runch crashed backward into the thin metal wall. He gasped for breath and went to his knees, looking more like a fish than ever, with his mouth open, sucking for air.

Daphne ran up to Runch—she'd seen the remote control for the shackles on his belt. She snatched it off, held it to her neck, pressed the button, and her steel collar fell off. For a moment she and Brick were beneath the shooting angle of Gynella and Presta, and no one dared shoot at them from behind—they were too close to Gynella.

Daphne tossed the remote aside as Gynella screamed furious orders. Brick was about to finish Runch off, but Daphne said, "Brick—pick me up, throw me at 'em! That'll distract 'em, and you can—"

Brick scratched his head. "Throw you?"

She didn't get the rest of it out, because several things happened just then. First there were two quick explosions behind them, from the gate. Gynella and her retinue were distracted by the blasts, looking toward the gate. Runch was getting up, and, responding to a shout from Gynella, he aimed the launcher at the gate. He fired, as Brick grabbed Daphne, in a way she thought was a bit indelicate—crotch and chest—and threw her underhand, up toward Gynella's coliseum box.

Daphne felt herself catapulted through the air by Brick's powerful arms, rocketed over Runch and over the wall, straight at Gynella, who jumped aside, swinging a sword of some kind. The sword missed as Daphne flew past.

Suddenly Broomy's astounded, gape-mouthed face loomed up, and Daphne laughed and thrust out her hands in an assassin's move she'd learned in her training on the Black Asteroid. Her hands were fanned to either side of Broomy's face as she flew at her, her thumbs stabbing toward two targets, Broom's eyes.

And Daphne struck, her thumbs driving deeply into Broomy's eye sockets, her palms striking the bone on either side of Broomy's head, knocking her backward, even as she dug her thumbs in deeply, through the eyes, through the thin layer of bone behind them, into the brain—all while catapulting through the air.

Then there was a crash. Broomy had fallen over onto her back, on the wooden floor of the back of Gynella's coliseum box, and Daphne was skidding over her, yanking her hands free of the gouting sockets, rolling to take up the impact.

She'd turned enough so that she took the impact on her right shoulder and slammed into the back wall, grunting, hearing a crunch and hoping it was wood and not bone. She lay a moment, gasping for breath, stunned.

She looked up to see Gynella standing over her with a blade—but then Gynella dived flat as machine-gun bullets peppered the coliseum box above Daphne.

Daphne was tempted to take Gynella on, then and there, but she didn't want to waste an opportunity for escape when there were hundreds of Psychos about to charge down and tear her to pieces if she gave them a chance. She forced herself to jump up, ignoring the pain in her shoulder, and leapt over the slashing blade from the prostrate Gynella. Daphne saw that Presta was shot dead, lying cozily beside Broomy. A glance at Broomy made it clear—she was stone dead.

"Told you so, slime-bag!" Daphne said, jumping over the bodies and then vaulting the wall.

Brick was slamming his fists into Runch's rib cage, when Daphne came down beside him. Runch's rocket launcher lay on the ground broken; there was blood on it, and Runch's head had been cracked open—it appeared that Brick had torn the launcher from Runch's grasp and smashed it over his head.

Two berserk punches, and Runch's ribs cracked like thin slats under a steel mallet, stabbing into his lungs. Runch fell, choking on blood, dying.

Gynella was shouting orders, up above, and

Psychos were beginning to pour down onto the field to "eliminate these disrespectful scum!" as Gynella put it.

Again Daphne thought she was done for—then she saw the outrunner racing up to them, Roland driving and Mordecai in the back firing machine-gun rounds at the Psychos. There was a shield on the outrunner, taking gunshots from the soldiers, but it wouldn't last long.

The outrunner slowed, and Mordecai yelled, "Jump on! Any place you can!"

She and Brick both jumped on, Daphne close to Roland, Brick clinging at the back, and the outrunner gunned toward the gates—which were broken, wisping smoke, blasted from outside by machine-gun rounds and Roland's grenades.

Bullets zinged into their shields, and a line of four beefy, vault-masked Psychos ran to block their way out of the coliseum, all of them armed with combat rifles.

Daphne heard a screech, looked up to see Bloodwing flying above the outrunner, darting down at the Psycho soldiers, clawing at their eyes, distracting them, then flapping up out of the firing line as Mordecai unloosed a whole belt of machine-gun slugs, hitting the middle two soldiers squarely, killing one, knocking down another. A third was hit glancingly by the outrunner, sent spinning bloodily as Roland accelerated through their broken ranks and out the gate, onto the barren valley floor. Bullets slashed the air above them and hissed into their failing shield. Then Roland cut left, and right, and left again, around a curve in the valley and out of range.

"Roland," Brick said, his voice grating, "I'm feeling kind of sad."

"Why, Brick?"

"Because I think I have to kill you."

"Yeah? Why you got to kill me, Brick?" They were seated on flat rocks around a fire, far out in the wastelands, southwest of the coliseum, in an old nomad's camp atop a hill.

"Because," Brick explained, "you shot that Goliath with that sniper gun." He shook his head in hurt disbelief. "But I could've killed that idiot Goliath *easy*!"

"Really? Even though you were stunned and still suffering from a concussion and lying on the ground, and he was about to spear you with a big sharp post?"

"That stuff? That's nothing! I was just about to jump up and grab that thing and shove it up his ass!"

Roland nodded gravely. "You know, I should've realized that. I was thinking about the girl, see. Mordecai's kind of sweet on her. I had to slow that guy down, give you a chance to protect Daphne till we could get in there. I'm sorry I messed up your action, Brick."

Brick scratched his head. "Well. I guess you were trying to help. But . . . I think I'm still gonna have to kill you. Sometime."

"Can it wait till later? Right now we should probably stick together, you know?"

Brick jabbed an accusing finger at him. "You didn't say *stick together* when you ran out on us! And sabotaged my outrunner!"

"Oh, that. Well. That was ill-advised. Another bad decision. Dumb. I shouldn't've done it."

"See, that's another reason. Got to kill you."

"Okay, but, like I say . . . a little later on?"

Brick scratched his chin this time. "I guess so. I'm tired now anyhow. Gonna take a nap."

Brick turned away, yawned and stretched, then lay down by the fire, head pillowed on an arm, and was snoring before his eyes had quite closed. His snores made the flames in the fire flap back and forth.

Roland turned to look for Mordecai, who was supposed to be standing watch. There he was, on the edge of the camp, standing between two mono-lithic boulders with Daphne. The two of them were gazing out at the rugged land spread below, talking in low voices.

Roland smiled and shook his head. He hoped that woman didn't get Mordecai killed—or maybe lose her temper and kill him herself. She'd killed enough people in her time.

But she probably wouldn't kill Mordecai—unless someone paid her a whole lot of money to do it.

"Mordecai!" Roland called. "You keeping your eyes peeled?"

"Yeah, yeah, we're watching. Nothing down there but some skags crapping out somebody's bones."

It was a good spot for a camp—the fire was under a lean-to of scavenged metal scraps and surrounded by a tall ring of boulders. It'd be hard to see from below.

They'd driven for five hours to get there, changing course, cutting across stony areas where they left no tracks, stopping from time to time to take turns driving, clinging to the outrunner. A hard ride. With any luck they were safe for now. But they couldn't count on luck—especially with Gynella after them.

Think about it in the morning. And think hard if you want to live.

Roland lay down near the fire, opposite Brick. Pretty soon their snores were wrestling for the flames.

Smartun knew Gynella was in a bad mood that morning, before she even looked up at him. It was the hunch of her shoulders, the tension in her hands as she clicked her long, polished, perfectly manicured nails on the desk beside her monitor.

"They got away. That woman who murdered my husband. Brick, who killed so many of our people. Roland and Mordecai. They got away. And they killed my Goliath! They killed my poor old Runch too! I valued him; he was so very intimidating. They killed two of my women's cadre. That dark little witch of an assassin got past me. I almost had a chance to stick my knife right up her birthing parts, but she was too fast, and I missed."

"It was all quite unexpected, my General Goddess. We were unprepared. It appears Roland or his partner sniped the Goliath, then surprised us by driving in and scooping up the prisoners. Introducing surprise and chaos, with boldness—a very effective tactical combination. Especially when so many of our forces are . . . easily confused."

"Yes." She made herself a drink, grimly pouring the liquor into the glass as if imagining drowning someone in it. "I had guards, of course, watching the outside approach to the gate. But what were they doing? They were looking in at the entertainment, moronically ogling the fight."

Smartun was tempted to say, *When you recruit morons, you should expect them to act moronically.* But instead, he sighed and remarked, "Human nature, I'm afraid."

"Or subhuman nature. They paid for it—I had them both set on fire and dragged behind outriders. Took them quite a long time to die."

Smartun admired her ease, her casualness, when she described the punishment. *My Goddess . . .*

Still, he was reminded that even he must be careful. The General Goddess would be merciless in dealing with him if he made a serious error—and he would have it no other way.

"You will need a new bodyguard."

He was about to suggest himself, but she cut him off with an impatient wave and said, "I have a Badass Psycho who'll take the job. Quite a frightening grotesque, is that one. Name of Spung."

"Spung? The one with the especially bad smell?"

"Yes. But I had him strapped down and washed with firehoses. We'll have to do that once a week. He has a tendency to soil himself." She sighed. "I can't wait till I can turn those gems into money and hire some real professionals from off-planet."

She looked moodily at her monitor, and he saw it bore a surveillance image of Roland, driving the outrunner. "He just kicked down the door, thrust himself into the arena. And took them away from me." She put on an expression of rueful admiration. "Really very impressive."

Smartun frowned. Again, Gynella demonstrated an unhealthy obsession with Roland.

"He's done huge damage to morale, ma'am," Smartun said. "We had our soldiers . . . *you* had the soldiers . . . convinced you were invincible, that you would always lead them to victory. We need to do something to restore confidence—can I make a suggestion?"

"Well?"

"Announce that you allowed the attack on the coliseum to happen, to test our competence. When it was found wanting, you executed two men as an example. Now you will select a special task force to find and kill Roland and his companions. And whoever succeeds at that will be specially rewarded. Who fails at it will be punished."

She smiled, although her eyes had a wicked glint. "I like the way you think."

SEVENTEEN

"I'm not going to cling to that outrunner anymore," Daphne said. "I'd rather walk."

"Hey, you can drive, I'll cling!" Mordecai said, grinning at her.

They had just had their meager breakfast of smoked skag meat and protein bars, Mordecai giving half of his to Bloodwing, and they were all standing between the two highest boulders, looking out over the rolling badlands to the north. Brick was yawning and scratching his stomach, blinking around him; there were bruises from shackles around his neck, welts and contusions on his arms, and scabs on his head where he'd been scored by the bullet.

Roland was peering through the scope of the sniper rifle, scanning the horizon. "Looks like we might have a chance to get a second ride—an outrider anyhow." He could just see the roostertail of dust and enough of the shape to be pretty sure it was an outrider. He lowered the rifle and pointed. "See it?

Mordecai squinted, then nodded. "Outrider. Looks like they'll pass about a quarter-klick west of here unless they change course."

"You see any more of 'em, Roland?" Daphne asked.

Roland raised the scope to his eye. "Yeah. A second one. They probably sent out parties of outriders, to look for us in different places. We gotta take one of 'em down and get the other outrunner intact."

"How do we do that and make sure the idiots driving it aren't intact with it?" Daphne wondered.

"You lure them over here," Brick said. "I smash one, the other you snipe. Might work."

Everyone looked at Brick with surprise.

They'd been searching for Roland and Brick and the others all night and all morning. Harmus the Bruiser was going bleary, staring at the wastelands, trying to locate smoke from a fire or a sign of that outrunner that had surprised them all in the coliseum. Sometimes, when he saw a rock shaped even vaguely like an outrunner, it seemed to turn into one for a moment.

But no sign of Roland. The tracks had led them nowhere.

He drove around a thick greenish growth and a boulder and looked down at the picture on his dash again. They'd all been given printout photos of Roland to paste onto their dashboards. "Bring me the head of Roland the Mercenary," Gynella had said.

Harmus had an electric saw in the back of the outrider for the head-bringing part. He was really, *really* looking forward to that.

He sure enjoyed cutting off a guy's head. Especially if the guy was still alive.

Why hadn't they let him study that, back when he was a boy in school, on the homeworld? He'd have gotten an A on every test. Whipped that head right off.

He sighed. Cutting off Roland's head might be easier said than done. Harmus thought about finding some guy who looked kind of like Roland, killing the dumb sucker, mutilating his face a bit, and bringing the head back to her.

But it wouldn't fool her long. And then she might set him on fire and drag him behind an outrider . . .

One of the Midget Psychos chortled, and he glanced at him in irritation. On either side of him were two of the stunted Psychos, irritating little assbiters who clung to hand-holds on the sides of the outrider, leaning out, shouting muffled curses through their white and red vault masks. Both bore shotguns strapped across their backs; the one on the left was an Angry Little Shotgunner, as the expression went, and the other was a Fuming Stunted Shotgunner.

Driving parallel about a dozen meters to Harmus's left was Kenzo, a vicious medium-sized Psycho with his mask pushed back on his head, his eyes in blue goggles; he wore skag-leather coveralls. Kenzo claimed to eat only the entrails of his enemies. Seemed unlikely to Harmus. You really did need a side dish.

The outrider bumped and jittered over the gravel and sand.

There was a big outcropping of rock up ahead, about thirty meters away, piled-up blue boulders, and beyond it rose a hilltop. A man stepped into view on the outcropping. The man waved to Harmus.

"Hey, assholes!" yelled the big, dark man standing on the outcropping. He made an obscene gesture.

Harmus stared. He looked at the picture pasted to his dash; he looked at the big man on the rock.

He could hardly believe his luck. He'd been driving for hours, looking for any signs of that guy. And there he was!

Harmus grinned and gunned the outrider

toward the outcropping—and suddenly Roland was no longer there.

He thought of those rocks that had seemed to be outrunners. Had he hallucinated this guy? He hadn't had any narcojuice all day. Maybe he was having a flashback. No, he'd been there!

He slowed the vehicle when they came abreast of the outcropping, looking for Roland, didn't see him. But there—tracks! Leading from the rock toward that hill.

He angled the car toward the hill and spotted Roland, just climbing up the hill, emerging from behind a boulder. He reached up, grabbed the machine gun, fired a long burst, hoping to weaken Roland's shield or maybe get a lucky shot through. Then he lost sight of him again. But he was there. He had him!

He glanced over at Kenzo, who was looking at him in puzzlement from the other outrider. He pointed at the hill and yelled, "Target up there!"

Then he urged the car faster, toward the hill, yelling at the Midgets, "Get ready to jump off and use those shotguns! Get up that hill and smoke him out! We're gonna—"

He broke off, as a shadow fell over him. He looked up in time to see a boulder, at least a hundred kilos, flying his way. What the hell? A meteor? Then he saw the big guy standing on the hilltop—the other one, Brick, arms still raised, having thrown that rock. Which was about to hit him.

He veered the vehicle hard right, and the boulder struck, glancingly, smashing into the Psycho Midget on the left side, turning him into red Midget jam.

The impact on the side of the vehicle combined with the sharp turn, and the outrider flipped over. Harmus felt himself flung into the air. He turned end over end, fell onto the ground, facedown, hard, his shield going out when the unit cracked on a rock.

The wind knocked out of him, he lay there, gasping, looking around, and saw his outrider had overturned on the other Midget, who was mangled under it.

There was still Kenzo, who was gunning toward the hill. A long burst from a combat rifle weakened Kenzo's shield—Harmus could see the bullets sparking on the shield, the long accurate burst draining its power. Then came a distinctive sound—*crack-zing, crack-zing*—a sniper rifle. Kenzo's head snapped back. Shot clean through. The outrunner spun out of control and stopped in a cloud of dust.

Kenzo was slumped over the steering wheel. Even from there it was obvious he was dead.

Harmus was unarmed, unless he could find one of the Midget's shotguns. He was bruised, and he suspected his left arm might be—he bit back a shriek of pain as he tried to use it—broken.

So he lay still, playing dead, watching with slitted eyes for the enemy. Maybe he would get his chance . . .

There they came, three men, looking pretty pleased with themselves, running from that hill, Roland, then Mordecai—and Brick. Harmus recognized all three. Mordecai had the sniper rifle.

A fourth one came down, sauntering after them. The woman. He'd almost had a piece of that woman in the coliseum. If he lived, he'd . . .

He closed his eyes when they glanced toward him.

He heard them talking loudly, not more than thirty meters away, from Kenzo's idling outrunner. He cracked his eyes open. Roland was lifting Kenzo's body out of the way, shoving it aside. "Good shooting, Mordecai!" Roland said. "Two right in the forehead! Moving target too!"

"Good scope on that rifle!"

"Don't be modest," the woman said. "That was a good shot!"

"What about me, I got three of them with one rock!" Brick rumbled.

"That was impressive!" the woman said. "Good arm!"

"Okay, we got two vehicles now." Probably Roland's voice. "Question is, which way we go from here?"

"Who gets this one?" another asked, likely Mordecai.

"More your size," Roland said. "There's a spot just big enough for Daphne to sit comfortably, behind there . . ."

Mordecai clambered into the vehicle, the woman behind, and drove it toward the hill. Roland and Brick trudged after them.

Harmus waited, his left arm throbbing miserably. Time passed. A rakk squawked from the sky.

At last he risked looking up and saw an outrunner take off from behind a boulder at the base of the hill, the outrider following. They cut southwest across the desert. A rakk or a trash feeder—some kind of flying creature, anyhow—flew along, right above the outrider, as if going with it.

Harmus felt a mix of relief and frustration, seeing them go. At least he knew what direction they'd gone.

Another rakk squawked. Better get moving.

He forced himself to his knees, groaning with pain. He managed to get to his feet, feeling dizzy, then turned toward the overturned outrider. Could he flip it back over? Not likely. He could scavenge a shotgun, maybe use the outrider's ECHO to call for help. He heard a whooshing sound from above looked up to see a forager rakk diving right at him, its wings extended for the dive.

"No!" And he lurched quickly toward the

shotgun lying by the outrider. But the rakk struck, the rasping fold of its weirdly pursed mouth snapping at him, slashing, and he felt a cruel blow to the side of his head; he spun and fell onto his right side.

He lay there shaking with pain; his broken arm seemed to scream from inside. He had to get up, get to the outrider. The rakk was calling to others, circling overhead. They were coming down at him now.

He forced himself to stand, to stagger toward the shotgun.

But it was too late. Something moved between him and the weapon. A skag. And another. And two more.

He was caught between skags and rakks, as the local expression went, and he didn't have long to live.

But it wasn't in him to just lie down and die. He tried to run, but the skag's long tongue whipped out, knocked his feet out from under him.

And then it leapt upon him—and began feeding, tearing into him with great hungry snaps of its jaws.

"Man, I'm hungry!" Brick said, from the turret behind Roland. They were driving southwest, toward the Eridian Promontory. It rose suddenly beyond the rolling, ravine-slashed lowlands, a steep wall of crags capped in ice and snow, starting to take on the tint of sunset at their peaks.

"You're always hungry," Roland said.

"It's getting dark!"

"No kidding."

"So we should camp!"

Roland ground his teeth. "Brick, we've got a big part of a continent to cross to get to the crystalisk den—wait, what's that?" Roland slowed the outrunner. He'd noticed a sharp drop-off, up ahead, and the twinkle of lights beyond it.

He stopped the vehicle, and they got out; the outrider caught up with them, screeched to a half-spin stop, dust billowing around it. Mordecai and Daphne got out, their movements in easy coordination with each other. They walked together over to the outrunner, and Roland thought they already looked like a couple.

"We run into a canyon?" Mordecai asked.

"We almost ran into it, anyhow," Roland said. He and the others walked over to the cliff edge and—keeping back enough so they wouldn't be spotted—looked down at a wide canyon, not terribly deep, with a flat bottom. Purple shadows seemed to spread like slowly oozing oil to fill the canyon near the farther wall, about half a kilometer away. Nearer was a string of campfires, streamers of smoke, temporary huts and tents—and every fifty meters or so, raised up by poles, Gynella's banners waved gently in the sluggish wind.

"Must be most of her Second Division," Daphne said. "And about half her First."

Mordecai pointed. "Look there—outriders, coming in from the south, and more going out. Lots of patrols."

"Same up north," Roland said, squinting in that direction.

"How far do we go to get past them?" Daphne asked. "If we go far enough south . . ."

Roland shook his head. "It becomes impassible too far down that way. Too far north, there's the Trash Coast. Dakes said Gynella's army has over-run that whole area . . ."

Brick scratched his head in puzzlement. "Why go around them? We find a way down there, and then we kill our way through!"

Roland smiled. "That your solution to everything, Brick?"

Brick looked at him. "On this planet it is."

Roland nodded. "Good point."

Brick stared sullenly at the encampment of Psycho soldiers. "I want to kill Gynella's soldiers. They chained me. And they kicked me." He sniffed and clasped the mummified dog paw around his neck. "They offended me."

Mordecai pointed out to the east, back the way they'd come. "Looks like you'll get your chance, sooner than you expected to, Brick."

Roland looked east and saw two outriders coming straight toward them, full bore.

"If we jumped outta the way, last minute, do

you think they'd keep going and fly off the cliff?" Mordecai suggested.

"Sadly, I do not," Roland said. "They're already slowing down. Let's get to our guns."

Brick was already trotting toward the turret on the outrunner. He vaulted up to it, swung it around to face the onrushing outriders, as Roland got to the vehicle and snatched up his combat rifle. He leveled it at the oncoming outriders, guessing they were a patrol and wondering if they'd already alerted the army in the canyon bottom to their presence out there.

Mordecai had the sniper rifle in hand, was standing by his own outrider, Daphne beside him. He laid the sniper rifle across the big skag skull on the left front fender of the outrider, put his eye to the scope . . . and straightened up just as Brick fired his first rounds.

"Don't shoot!" Mordecai yelled. "It's Dakes!"

Brick's bullets hadn't quite nailed the outrider, strafing the ground to one side of it. The outriders swerved—but Brick stepped away from the gun and waved his arms.

Dakes saw the greeting and swung around again, heading their way. Another twenty seconds, and the outriders were idling, engines chugging, beside Roland's outrunner. Gong had driven one of the outriders, with Lucky on the running board, holding on; Dakes drove the other. They shut off the engines and climbed out, Dakes coughing in the dust of their passage, blowing past them.

"How'd you find us?" Roland asked.

Dakes grinned. "First of all, I'm the best tracker this rock has ever seen. Second—more important—you told us kinda generally where you were going. I looked at some maps and worked out where you'd most likely be headed. We spotted a wreck you left back there. Then we hit your tracks again."

"I'm glad you don't work for Gynella. How about the other settlers—they okay?"

Dakes winced. "Couple more guys dead. A platoon of Gynellans came into Jawbone Ridge. They started searching through the place, looking for the 'rebels' from Bloodrust Corners. There was a short firefight when they found some of our guys—a bunch of us left to draw them away from our families. We managed to shake the platoon in the badlands, but we're kinda worried if we go back, they'll track us back to our people. Long as they're out looking for us . . . well . . . our families are safe. Safe as anyone is, anyhow, in a place like Jawbone Ridge."

"Where's Glory?" Mordecai asked.

Lucky was eyeing Brick suspiciously, but at the mention of Glory he glared warningly at Mordecai. "Glory's back there, looking after them. We're in radio contact. That's all you need to know."

Mordecai chuckled. "Take it easy, kid."

"I'm guessing, Dakes," Roland said, "you figure we'll rid you of that platoon?"

"We could do it ourselves, probably," Dakes said. "I've got another ten men waiting for us, about a kilometer back. We got some vehicles. Only, we're low on ammo, and they've got us out-gunned. And I should mention, we think they're on our trail again. Thing is, they could be here in an hour."

Roland sighed. "We don't want to get in a fight right here if we don't have to—it'll bring that army over there down on us."

Dakes swallowed. "What army?"

Roland hooked a thumb toward the canyon. "They're down there. A lot of 'em. And they're patrolling north and south. And there aren't a lot of ways to get through to where we're going. We were just trying to figure that out. Maybe we could help each other on this. We take care of that platoon, rearm you guys, and you help us create a little diversion to draw that army off, out of our way. Might work for you too, make them think the real trouble is based out here."

"Then they'll follow us back to Jawbone!"

"No. I'll see they don't. Once we get past them, we'll get their attention. They can follow us. But they won't catch us. Not the way I've got it figured."

"Okay," Dakes said. "You've got a deal."

Lucky shook his head. "I think it's a crazy damn plan. And it's liable to get us all killed."

Gong grunted in agreement. "Sure—but if it involves killing Gynella's bunch, me, I'm for it."

"You know, I think I'm gonna like this guy," Brick said, nodding to Gong.

EIGHTEEN

The moon was up, as if it were watching Smartun inspecting the troops. An inspection out in this canyon encampment mostly meant stepping over snoring drunks, edging past grumbling bloody Psychos squatting by campfires, and trying not to step on sleeping Midgets. He had only just arrived from the Devil's Footstool, and few of the men knew he was commander there—he caught more than a few muttered invectives as he pressed through. Luckily he had Skenk with him as an enforcer, carrying a large and highly effective Eridian energy rifle.

Smartun heard the rumble of an engine and turned to see Fwah Grass, alone on her outrider, tooling along the outskirts of the encampment. She made a kind of haphazard salute and pulled up, parked, and strode over to him. One of the few members of the women's cadre left alive, she was an obese, cocoa-colored woman in black leather, with a triple white Mohawk, eyes outlined in silver eyeliner, mouth glimmering fluorescently—using a glowing lipstick of crushed Eridium crystals had made her mutate sharp tusks, which curved down from the sides of her mouth past her jawline. Smartun had once seen her sink those tusks into a man's chest so deeply she was able to crunch through the ribs and wrench his heart out, all in one motion. Still, she had more sophistication than many of the bandits—on her home planet she had been in law enforcement, till she'd been caught robbing narcojuice dealers. Like a lot of other prisoners, she had been sent to Pandora as part of a convict work detail, before the planet was mostly left to rot.

"Hail Gynella!" she called, stopping in front of him, hands on her wide hips.

Smartun blinked. *Hail Gynella?* When had that started?

"You are supposed to say 'Hail Gynella' back, when so challenged," Fwah said. She spoke slowly, with exacting care, each syllable sharply pronounced, because otherwise her tusks gave her a terrible lisp. "It's a new rule."

"Okay, hail Gynella," Smartun said, nodding. "Really, it ought to be something better than that. Perhaps I'll suggest 'All glory to Gynella.' So, Fwah, you're still acting as if you have a message.

You have something more to tell me about besides a new greeting?"

"Eight of the outriders sent to find Roland and the other rebels have failed. They are being ordered to report to you. Gynella wishes you to kill one man from each outrider, as an example. They may be fire-circled, if you like. I do like a good fire-circling, myself. I'll be happy to take charge of that. I've always enjoyed being a party planner."

Smartun grimaced. He'd rather just shoot them and get it over with. A "fire circle" involved throwing a man into a bonfire with a circle of men around it pushing him back in every time he tried to run out. The screams were rough on Smartun's nerves.

"Fine," he said. "You take charge of it. She could have radioed the command to me."

"She's maintaining as close to radio silence as possible—there's someone in orbit, listening in. People she doesn't want knowing anything about her activities."

"I see." Smartun guessed that would be the Dahl Corporation—specifically Mince Feldsrum and his men. She must be worried they were closing in on her. "Anything else?"

"Yes. Drone surveillance suggests rebel bands moving to the east of here. More than one."

Smartun rubbed his hands together. "Now *that* is information I can use. Those rebel bands just might be linked up to Roland's bunch. If we take care of those slinking scumbags, I'll be freed up to swing the Hatchet Legion against New Haven. There's a platoon out that way—I'll radio them to find these rebels and deal with them. They've got some Eridian weaponry with them—they should be able to deal with Roland."

Roland drove the outrunner hard, leading the three other vehicles across the dusty plains, under a bright silvering of moonlight, and they got to the cold camp of the other fighting men from Bloodrust Corners just a few minutes ahead of Gynella's search platoon.

The cold camp was in the moon shadow of a landmark. The Jut was a fang-like spike of crystalline rock, thirty meters high, sixty around the base, pitted by weather and marred by dust, in the midst of a veldt-like plain. There were rumors of a great cavern underneath it, where fabulous Eridium deposits could be found, but no one had survived out there long enough to dig for it. A shadowy form could be seen within it, a vague humanoid silhouette, like a man frozen in ice—but most people thought it was just a man-shaped flaw in the crystal. It did make viewers uneasy, especially when the moon shone, as tonight, and the shadowy shape seemed to shift a little, as if restless.

Many battles had been fought in close proximity

to the Jut; many men had died. It was known to be an unhealthy place to linger. The area around it was littered with human bones, burned-up old wrecks, blast craters, and rusted weapons.

"There's a story," Mordecai told Daphne, as they climbed out of their outrider, Bloodwing cawing on his shoulder, "that when people first settled this planet, the Jut was much smaller. Every time someone gets killed near it—anyway, this is the claim—it gets a little bigger. Like something in there is feeding."

"What a lotta yokel superstition," Daphne scoffed. But she looked at the Jut nervously.

"That big guy's Scobold," Roland told them as they walked up to the camp. Five outrunners were parked in a row, as a barrier around the cold camp. "He's your kinda people."

Scobold was a stout, red-faced old miner who'd killed two Psycho Midgets at once with his bare hands at the battle of Bloodrust Corners—he'd taken their necks in his two hands as they'd rushed him, and he'd squeezed till they stopped moving. Now he stumped out to meet Dakes. "They're coming. About a klick east of here. You can just make 'em out in the moonlight from the top of the Jut. They're coming in a big ol' dump truck and one outrider. Most of 'em in the back of the truck."

Brick scratched his jaw. "A dump truck? Soldiers in back of a dump truck?"

"It's fitting," Mordecai said, scratching under Bloodwing's beak. "They're trash, more than they're soldiers."

The men laughed at that, and Dakes explained, "See, we sabotaged their outriders, many as we could when we lit out from Jawbone. Gave us a good head start. So they scrounged that thing up, we figure, from the old mining site."

"A dump truck." Roland was getting an idea. "That could be valuable. Nuclear-powered, Dakes?"

"Some kinda isotope power, yeah."

Roland nodded. "We got to try to get that thing intact, Brick."

"Sure! I'd like to have one of those. I could dump stuff on people." Brick looked thoughtful. "And dump people on stuff."

"Okay, I need Brick with me, two volunteers from the Bloodrusters, and Mordecai on the Jut with the sniper rifle."

"What about me?" Daphne demanded.

"You? You hang back in front of the Jut. You can be the lure. If they get past us, you can kill 'em all. There's only ten of 'em."

Roland was driving the outrunner; Brick was at the turret. Coming at them about a hundred meters out, limned in moonlight and the headlight glare of the truck, was an outrider, with a Psycho soldier driving and two others clinging to its hand-hold positions, and the dump truck itself, rumbling along more slowly, a few truck lengths behind.

"That's a self-directed dump truck!" Roland shouted, yelling over the noise of the outrunner's engine. He'd noticed there was no driver in the cab of the oncoming six-wheeled truck.

"Always wondered why they got a steering wheel and all that if it's self-driving."

"It's got a place for a driver so it can be operated manually if need be."

"I saw 'em using that one at the mine, but I never figured out how you tell it where to go!" Brick said.

"I'll show you—when we get hold of it! Now get that machine gun rocking! Time is bullets!"

Brick shouted at the enemy, "Brick is here, bitch, and I'm bringin' the pain!" and he fired the machine gun, slamming bullets into the two men clinging to the oncoming outrider.

One of the platoon Psychos had a strong shield that held up, but the other one was knocked off the outrider. He was still alive, rolling, his shield sparking, and the dump truck automatically tried to veer around him—but ended up crunching him under its right front wheel.

There was a humming sound, like a supersonic insect flying past—Roland knew what it was. Another supersonic hum, and Mordecai's sniper shots, using the scope's night-vision setting, took out the driver, two quick shots—one to weaken his shield, the other to penetrate, blowing his brains out the back of his head. Roland had to swerve to avoid the fiery outrider as it spun out of control.

Bullets splashed his outrunner's shield, then, as platoon Psycho soldiers in the back of the dump truck fired at him over the front top of the big chunky steel truck's dump box. An Eridian rifle spat fireballs at the outrunner, and combat rifles chattered. Sparks flew from its chassis, and Roland ducked down in time to miss a spinning fireball that exploded at the base of the turret. Flames singed Brick, but he ignored them, firing steadily at the top of the dump truck to suppress the enemy's fire.

Roland accelerated, weaving a little as an evasive maneuver, and then they roared past the dump truck.

"Hold on!" he yelled, turning the outrunner as tightly as he could without flipping it.

Brick had his powerful grip on the machine gun, and he spun it around before Roland got the vehicle turned, strafing the back of the dump truck to keep the seven men in back from jumping up and firing.

I hope this works, Roland thought, as he accelerated to pull parallel with the truck, his right front wheel just a hand's breadth from one of the truck's rear wheels. He was thinking there was a factor he hadn't quite worked into the plan. One problem was that they were getting close to the Jut . . . and the truck was aimed right for it.

"Closer!" Brick shouted, firing a long burst of rounds into the back of the truck—most of the bullets *spang*ed off the tailgate top.

Roland nudged the accelerator a little, and the outrunner surged, bringing Brick closer to the speeding dump truck.

"Now!" Brick yelled.

Roland, steering with one hand now, already had the grenade ready. He tossed it into the back of the dump truck. A man screamed, grenade fragments clattered and sparked, as the explosion sent one of the platoon Psychos flying out of the back of the truck, a spinning wheel of blood, gone into the plume of moonlit dust.

Roland accelerated a little more, and Brick made his move, leaping up onto the back of the truck, getting a booted foot into place, his hands clamping the edges, and vaulting into the back, howling as he came to chill the disoriented survivors of the blast.

Up ahead, the Jut was . . . too close. He was surprised to see Daphne had taken him literally, was standing there with a pistol in each hand, in front of the Jut. Which was closer, closer . . .

"Oh no," Roland said, realizing there wasn't

time for Brick to climb up front before the truck crashed head-on into the looming Jut. The driver's-side window was open, as if inviting him to risk suicide. Swearing, he switched off the outrunner's engine—it kept going on momentum, starting to slow as he clambered, struggling with wind pressure, onto the front of the vehicle and leapt onto the side of the truck at the door. The metal frame of the door struck him in the side of the face, but his hands closed over the rim of the window, and, using all his strength against wind and momentum, he pulled himself through the window. He was halfway in, legs sticking out in the open air. The emergency manual button was right where he'd hoped it would be, on the dash to the right of the steering wheel. He slapped the button, then immediately grabbed the wheel and turned it left—a little too sharply.

The truck spun, its rear end swinging right, and Roland struggled to keep from falling off. Then the dump truck steadied and started off, past the Jut, crunching over a pile of old bones.

Roland climbed in the rest of the way, got into the driver's seat, found the brake, and stopped the dump truck.

He glanced over at the Jut, now to their right. They'd missed it by a few meters.

Heart pounding, mouth dry and metallic-tasting, he sat there, breathing hard for half a minute. Then he opened the door and climbed out, rubbing the aching bruise on his right cheek.

He saw Brick climb out the back, blood on his fists. Brick walked over to Roland.

"Fun, Roland. That was fun."

"If you say so."

Roland reached into the cab and threw the dump switch—the box tilted up on humming hydraulics, the tailgate opened, and the bodies of six assorted dead Psychos tumbled out into a pile on the ground.

NINETEEN

"**E**veryone know what they're supposed to do?" Roland asked.

Everyone nodded. Even Lucky.

It was about an hour before dawn. After a chilly, uncomfortable night without a fire, enduring the smell of rotting bodies carried sharply to them by a wind from the southeast, Roland had brought his sixteen companions to a cut in the canyon wall north of the overlook where they'd first seen the army encampment.

He'd found the old streambed, scouting during the night, following the canyon north. It cut through the wall of the canyon, but the stream was seasonal, and it was dry now. They'd have to watch out for crabworms or scythids in a streambed, but it was a straight line to Gynella's soldiers. Beyond the streambed, the ground rose and merged with the side of a butte. There was no getting past that butte to the north—not without going a long way around it. This was as far north as they could go. With luck it would be enough to misdirect the Gynellan commanders.

Roland climbed up into the cab of the truck, getting behind the wheel. Mordecai was waiting in the passenger seat, his hands clasping the barrel of a big Hyperion auto shotgun, its butt propped on the floor between his boots. "Where's Bloodwing?"

"I made it stay with Daphne. It wasn't pleased. But I think it kind of likes her."

"This whole plan—I must be crazy," Roland muttered, settling into his seat.

Mordecai nodded gravely. "I was thinking the same thing. About you, I mean, not me. You must be crazy. But fuck it, let's do this thing."

"That's the spirit. Why be safe when you can be crazy? If the sun was up, I'd say we were burning daylight. So . . ." He slammed the truck's door shut.

He wanted to strike while it was still dark. There would be sentries and soldiers awake but not many, and after a long night's watch the defense would be bleary and slow to react.

He called Daphne on the ECHO they'd found on one of the platoon Psychos. She had her own communicator, and they'd agreed on a bandwidth Gynella wasn't likely to use. "You guys all deployed up there?"

"We're in place," she replied.

"We're moving out."

He leaned out the window. "You guys ready?"

Someone knocked on the roof of the truck to signal readiness. They were ready, and they'd gotten eight good weapons from the dead platoon Psychos—the other two weapons had been wrecked by the grenade.

They'd covered the bloody bed of the truck's box with sand, but it must still have stunk of death back there. He was glad he didn't have to belly down on that truck bed like those guys in back.

But if he were back there, it'd be safer than where he was sitting. Since the dump truck had been readied for Pandora, it'd been given bulletproof glass—but no glass is bulletproof if you hit it hard enough.

"Really it should be you with that sniper rifle up on the rim," Roland said, starting the truck.

Mordecai shrugged. "Daphne seems to be as good . . . well, nobody's *as good*, but almost as good as I am with a weapon."

Roland laughed and put the truck into gear, slammed on the accelerator, and they were rolling. He had the truck on manual and drove it himself—the time would come for the self-drive.

"They're going to see those headlights," Mordecai pointed out.

"I think it's okay for a while—we're a

quarter-klick from the canyon. I'll turn 'em off in a minute, but it's damn dark down here, I don't want to drive in a hole."

Up ahead, something grotesque reared up in the headlights—the clacking pincers of crabworms, three of them, pretty damn big too—but Roland simply put the truck in a higher gear and stamped on the accelerator, and the truck took care of them, the enormous vehicle smashing over the crab-worms, crushing them into pulp.

Another minute, and Roland switched off the headlights. Up ahead he could see the outline of sentries against the firelight beyond them. At this distance he could just make out a couple of weapons, in the sentries' hands—and was that a rocket launcher? He'd try to nail that guy fast—the rocket launcher just might be able to stop the dump truck, thick and heavy though its metal chassis was.

Bumping over rocks and lumpy ground, the men in the back of the truck cursing, the dump truck roared toward the enemy lines.

Bullets cracked into the windshield; it chipped, but the armor glass held up, for now.

"Too bad this truck hasn't got a real shield," Mordecai muttered, rolling down his window. He shoved the shotgun muzzle out, checked the load, angled it toward the enemy. He wouldn't be able to shoot directly ahead, but he could cover their right side pretty well.

Roland heard the familiar deep cough of a rocket launcher, tensed to try to evade the missile, but he saw it rocketing too high, going over the top of the truck. So the launcher had done him a favor—now he had to reload, as Roland accelerated and ran him down, crushing two other sentries in the process. One of the sentries, a tall Psycho, was flipped up by the impact, back broken, and ended lying across the hood like the wild prey of some sportsman coming back from a hunt.

Bullets slapped into the dead Psycho on the hood, as Roland plowed under another group of Psychos and turned the vehicle to the left, so they were running down the middle of the canyon—and right down the middle of the encampment.

Pulse banging like an alarm bell, Roland shouted, "Tailgate going down!" out the window, to the guys in back. He hit the switch that lowered the tailgate, and Dakes, Lucky, Brick, Gong, and Scobold, lying on their bellies with their automatic weapons pointed out the back, opened fire at the Psychos trying to fire at the truck. They had good shields cadged from the dead platoon, and they were hard to hit, lying down in the back of the swerving, bouncing truck.

Roland rolled up his side window, just in time for the bulletproof glass to deflect a spatter of shotgun pellets, as Mordecai blasted his own shotgun through the face of a Bruiser trying to leap onto the truck, Mordecai's second shot shooting the top of a Midget's skull off.

A spurt of machine-gun fire ripped through the Psycho carcass on the hood, cutting it in half; one part fell to the right, the other to the left. Bullets hammered into the windshield, and now it began to crack . . .

But the truck raged onward, engine roaring, wheels spraying mud and blood. The dump truck's six big wheels crunched over still-sleeping Psychos. Sentries and furious Gynellan soldiers behind them fired at the dump truck; bullets ricocheted from the metal, thumped into the solid-synthetic wheels, doing no appreciable damage. Bullets ricocheted around in the back of the dump box, but the shields worn by Brick and the others held, and they fired effectively on the Psychos behind them, bullets breaking the bones, bursting the brains, gouging into the guts of the unprepared soldiers.

Engine roaring, shotgun booming, rifles rattling, the dump truck crushed its way through the camp, leaving red puddles of men garnished with bone fragments and mashed entrails; it smashed mortar emplacements and sent the dozens of Psychos running in a panic of confusion. Men shouted and argued and screamed and bellowed in their wake.

It was the panic, the bewilderment, that best worked to their advantage. The waves parted for them—waves of men getting out of the way. Bullets came their way, but so far ineffectively. Mordecai had to draw his weapon back in, though, as two rounds came through the window, one of them hitting him in the right shoulder, the other striking the right side of Roland's seat.

Adding to the panic was the fire from up on the promontory overlooking the canyon, where Daphne was raining deadly sniper fire down, often able to hit nearby ammo boxes and barrels of fuel, exploding them, killing the enemy and keeping the Psychos back from Roland and Mordecai. Half a dozen other Bloodrust gunmen were ranged along the top of the cliff, firing into the canyon, spread out to give the impression that there were more of them than there were.

Roland jerked the wheel to the right to slam the right front fender into a Psycho trying to run up to them with a grenade. The grenade exploded—under the fallen soldier. It rained body parts on the truck. Mordecai had to toss a bloody hand out the window.

Mordecai rolled up the window, shouting over the boom and rattle, "I'm almost outta ammo!"

Another punishing spurt of machine-gun rounds thudded and rattled over the truck. Roland spotted the source, a turret gun on an outrider, and he jerked the wheel toward it, accelerated over a campfire, so that sparks and flame mushroomed around the truck, and then rolled right over the outrider, turret, gunman, and all, crushing them under the truck's six big wheels.

"Ha!" he shouted, swept away in vengeful glee. "This big hunk of steel really digs in and gets it done! I shoulda been a dump-truck driver—I *like* it! And there goes a Badass, his bad ass going under the wheels! Uppin' the kill count!" He took particular pleasure in knocking down and running over the poles holding up Gynella's banners.

Roland heard a groan from Mordecai as they bumped over a big rock, and the whole truck shuddered. He glanced over, saw that Mordecai was trying to stanch the wound in his shoulder. "You're hit, huh? There's Dr. Zed in that glove compartment!"

"Better save it for something worse—look out!"

Mordecai pointed, and Roland saw, not far up ahead, a big one-armed Psycho, one of the biggest Roland had ever seen, a muscle-ripped specimen with high spiky Mohawks and a white and red vault mask, aiming a rocket launcher square at them. Roland couldn't turn—that would present a better target, at this range. All he could do was accelerate, but the front end ran square into the flashing rocket, and the truck rocked like a junk heap in an earthquake, Roland's teeth clacking together, his stomach lurching, the grille of the truck consumed by a ball of flame. They drove through flame and smoke, and then the Psycho with the launcher was there, bashed by the flaming front end of the dump truck, knocked onto his back, first the front right wheel, then the two right rear wheels of the multiton six-wheeled dump truck rolling, thumping, bumping over him—by the end he was a human tire track, mere roadkill.

The front end of the truck was smoking, on fire, with scrap metal twisted up like horns, but the engine was still intact, and the dump truck rolled on and rolled over two more Psychos, and the men in the back kept up their fire—and then a big Bruiser leapt onto the left side, pounding at the driver's-side window, cracking it.

Roland had been about to start the second half of his planned run, a turn back the way they'd come, so now he swung hard into a sharp leftward U-turn, hoping to jolt the Bruiser off. The wrenching turn flung the Bruiser back so that he had to flail to keep a hand-hold. One more punch, and he'd punch right through that window, Roland realized. He turned to Mordecai, who was already offering him the shotgun. There was blood on it, but it was ready to fire, and as the Bruiser, cocked his right fist to smash the window, Roland turned the shotgun so it angled left across his body, pressed the muzzle against the badly cracked armor glass, and, with the butt in the crook of his right arm while his other hand operated the wheel, squeezed the trigger. The shotgun blasted through the glass and right into the driving fist of the Bruiser, shattering knuckles and fingers, the load flying back into the Bruiser's face. He screamed and fell away.

Coughing from gunsmoke, Roland kept the auto shotgun aimed out the side window—there were three shots left in it.

They were driving back through the rut they'd cut through the Psycho army encampment, a road of blood, guts, and wreckage—more than once the wheels of the dump truck spun in slick human remains, and he almost lost control.

He angled to the right, off the truck's blood-soaked rut, to get more traction, and ran into a cluster of tents, one of them getting stuck on the twisted metal at the front, a man tangled inside the tent dragged along and then pulled shrieking under the wheels.

"Ooh, that's gotta hurt," Roland murmured.

"Wait—what the fuck is Brick doing?" Mordecai demanded. "Look at that lunatic!"

Brick was leaping from the cab roof onto what remained of the hood, then down onto the ground to the truck's right. Roland slowed to give Brick time to get back to them. He hoped to the Angel that Brick knew what he was doing.

Brick had no weapon on him that Roland could see, but the big warrior laid out two Psychos with two swipes of his big, mailed fists and then grabbed a three-meter metal pole from which flew one of Gynella's banners. He used the pole as a pike staff, swinging it to bash heads in, stabbing the upper end, flag and all, through the middle of a large, big-bellied Psycho. Then he rushed past his screaming victims and into a tent—he emerged almost immediately with a box in his arms. *DR. ZED* was stenciled on the side of the crate. So that was it—someone was hurt in the back.

The truck was only just moving, and Roland saw two Midgets running at it with firebombs in their hands, on the left. "I'll toast your balls and eat 'em!" one of them shrilled.

Roland squeezed off his last shotgun rounds, aiming at the firebombs—and the bombs exploded, covering the Psycho Midgets in flaming liquid. They fell to the ground, rolling and babbling.

Another hailstorm of bullets rocketed into the windshield, and its cracks spread; it wasn't going to last—but there, up ahead, was the cut into the dry riverbed. Roland accelerated, going at it full bore, crashing through a group of sentries, then over a Scorpio. As the windshield flew apart under a shotgun blast, they jounced up onto the rising riverbed and headed east, with Gynella's army behind them. But Roland had known there'd be pursuit.

He tapped the screen on the dash for rearview

and saw a digital image of two outriders in the gray dawn light, rushing after him. One of them was firing a machine gun. He heard the bullets smacking *rat-a-tat* into the tailgate. The other was trying to get into position.

He activated his ECHO and spoke into it. "Daphne? You there?"

"I'm here. We're moving into position two as planned."

"That's what I wanted to hear—one of those outriders has a cannon turret!"

"On it!"

A quick series of unnerving detonations sounded from behind—the cannon, firing at them. The truck was hit, low on the right, and it sounded as if one of the wheels had been blown off. The dump truck fishtailed, and he fought for control of it, desperately trying to keep it from flipping over. He was so caught up in this he hardly noticed that he'd crushed two crabworms on his way.

The swerving made him a tough target to hit, and the next two cannon rounds missed.

"That's my girl!" Mordecai said.

Roland glanced at the rearview screen and saw the lead outrider spinning out of control, the driver leaning over, limp, his head a red mess. Daphne had nailed him with the sniper rifle. The outrider hit a rock, flipped over, burst into flame— and the other outrider crashed into it.

"Good work, Daphne!" Roland laughed. "All right . . . we're pulling over, and I'm gonna move to the next phase."

He slowed on reaching the gentle slope, on the right, that led up to the cliffside overlooking the canyon. He turned the truck around, aiming it at the encampment. It was almost two-thirds of a kilometer back. There was smoke rising thickly from the wreckage they'd left.

"Looks like we made an impression," Mordecai said dryly.

But he was pale and drawn, Roland noted. He'd lost some blood. "Use that Dr. Zed in the glove compartment—Brick got a whole case of the stuff. We can afford it, Mordecai."

"You talked me into it."

Roland pressed the switch to drop the tailgate, then said, "I'll be right back." He opened the door—blood-spattered broken glass fell off it when he pushed the door—and stepped down to the ground.

Brick was standing by the tailgate, frowning. "We lost that Dakes guy. Too bad."

Roland looked into the back. Scobald was applying medicine from the crate—he'd been shot in the upper left arm. Dakes was clearly dead, still lying in the belly-down rifleman position the men in back had used, shot through the top of his head.

Roland felt his gut twist at that, thinking about

how Glory would feel. Lucky, climbing out, had a chest wound, but it looked as if it was already healing thanks to the Dr. Zed that Brick had fetched.

"Hey, uh, Brick," Lucky said, uncomfortably. "I'm, uh . . . listen, thanks. Risked your ass getting that stuff for me."

Brick shrugged. "We already lost Dakes here. Needed to keep you around for the firepower."

Roland looked at Brick in surprise—clearly he was covering up, embarrassed he'd gone out of his way to save the young man's life. Not the kind of thing Brick was known for.

Brick turned away, his hand going to the mummified dog's paw around his neck.

Scobald and Lucky gently removed Dakes's body from the back of the truck.

Mordecai joined them, shaking his head on seeing Dakes. "I liked that guy. Even if he did call me a vagabond."

"You *are* a damn vagabond," Roland growled. "Yeah. He was a good guy. He'll be hard to replace." He felt maybe this was his fault—it had been a pretty cockamamie plan. But no one had forced Dakes to sign on for it.

Lucky sighed. "Yeah. I don't know how I'll tell Glory. Well . . . we'll carry him upslope; better get him strapped over an outrunner, take him out east and bury him. Gotta get out of here before the Gynellan bunch get organized again."

"They'll be here pretty soon," Mordecai said.

"Yeah—run up and get the outriders rolling," Roland said. "Have Brick drive my outrunner. I'll be right up. We all wanna book outta here fast as we can—we'll catch up to you."

The others, up above, were already on their way, he knew, in the settler's outrunners and the stolen outrider.

Roland turned back to the dump truck, and, humming tunelessly to himself, he climbed up into the cab and turned the engine on. He tapped the dash controls, activating the self-driving feature.

A woman's voice said, "Self-driving mode. Awaiting directional input. Mapping the area."

Using the local global positioning system, beamed from the Study Station in orbit, the screen on the dash lit up with the local coordinates. It showed the canyon from above, in simulation, and the streambed, including his own position.

"Beautiful," Roland murmured. "There I am, and there they are . . . okay." He tapped the screen's menu, designating the dump truck's destination, the center of the camp, and its course thereafter. He put it on a four-minute start delay, climbed out, taking the toolbox from under the seat. He got down on his hands and knees, looked under the truck, and flattened and crawled under, dragging the toolbox.

Roland found a small flashlight in the toolbox,

held it clamped in his teeth so he could see to use the autoscrew. Its gripper field quickly removed the bolts holding the powerplant cover—when the thick metal cover came off, it nearly pinned him to the ground.

He could hear the sound of vehicles coming, way down the riverbed to the west. Not much time . . .

He forced the heavy steel cover to one side, then wriggled out from under the truck, rolled, jumped up to look into the truck cab at the timer. He'd cut it close—only thirty seconds left.

Roland chuckled and ran up the slope toward the others. It was coming on dawn now, the gray light taking on golden tones.

Behind him, the dump truck started moving, picking up speed—it rammed the three oncoming outriders, crunching them under it, and kept going over the wreckage and the maimed Psycho soldiers.

Roland rushed to the cliff edge, got there in time to look down on a satisfying sight: the dump truck was smashing through more Psycho troops, driving in the circles he'd programmed, over and over, crunching equipment and bones.

And then some idiot, as he'd hoped, threw a grenade under the truck. The grenade exploded, blowing through the unprotected powerplant— the subsequent explosion was almost blinding. He walked quickly away, wanting to get gone before the radioactive dust pattered down on the area. It was mostly just a "dirty bomb" effect, but it was nasty—the entire truck had been turned into one big hand grenade.

Must be one big ugly mess down there.

"Well," he said, climbing into the outrunner, with Brick at the wheel. "I do warn them, pretty often, and they just don't listen to me."

"What warning?" Brick asked, turning the outrunner east.

"Mess with the bull, and you get the horns."

TWENTY

"*Devastated*, you said?" Gynella asked, walking up to the cliff's edge. She had come in person to survey the damage. Now she and Smartun stood on the edge of the cliff—her new, hulking bodyguard, the Badass Psycho, Spung, looming behind her. The three of them looked down on the encampment from the spot where the snipers had been posted when the truck had begun smashing its way through the camp.

"As you see," Smartun said glumly, as they stared down at the wrecked camp, the bodies, the tire tracks thick with blood, and the crater in the midst of it all. "Devastation." He licked his lips. "We lost about half the division. A great many were maimed—we didn't have enough Zed to go around. We had to put most of them down." He sighed. "Fwah volunteered for that, of course." His heart banged as he went on. "I . . . submit myself to your judgment. I ask only the mercy of a . . . a relatively quick death."

"All in good time," Gynella said absently, clicking her long nails together. She looked positively inscrutable at that moment, as she gazed down on the scene of devastation. "And you think he set that truck up to explode, on purpose, in that way?"

"I suspect it."

She shook her head and smiled thinly. "He is quite a tactician. But then, he simply took advantage of one of our consistent weaknesses. We're poor on defense. You should have had men posted up here, overlooking the camp, watching these plains."

"I did have outriders patrolling up here. And I called in a platoon to come back this way—they were tracking some rebels anyway, and . . . well, they killed the platoon. And took the truck from them."

"But no sentries up here. In the obvious place."

Smartun swallowed. He hoped she'd kill him herself. That would almost be a pleasure, to be killed by the love of his life, the person who was all meaning in his life. "I did ask someone . . ." He shrugged. He'd asked Skenk to post sentries there but had failed to make certain he'd done so. Skenk had a tendency to wander off, find some narco-juice, and forget his orders. "I won't make excuses by blaming it on someone else. Do as you will. I have failed you." He knelt before her. "You would honor me if you would execute me yourself. I don't deserve it, but if I have served you well at all . . . up to now . . . perhaps, then, my . . ." His voice was hoarse. He had let her down. "My General . . . my Goddess . . ."

She made an imperious little *hmph* sound. "Enough! Get up. On your feet."

He stood up, thinking she meant to allow him to be killed standing up. He ducked his head, waiting for the death blow. At least it was by her beautiful hands . . .

She sighed, and when he looked up at her she was rolling her eyes. "As for killing you for your failure, I'll take the matter into consideration. You may have a chance to redeem yourself. *If* you can repair this problem with our defenses and bring this man Roland to me. The others—kill them. But Roland I want alive."

Smartun blinked. "Him? *Alive?* Are you sure?"

"Yes. I'll give you access to the tools you'll need. One thing you should know is that I set one of our spies in Fyrestone to see what he could find out about Roland's activities there. It seems that before heading out this way Roland made some kind of deal with a former Dahl mining engineer name of Skelton Dabbits. This Dabbits was spending a lot of money on narcojuice, stoned out of his head, and babbling about how a man could get rich on crystalisks out past the Eridian Promontory, if he only knew just where to go. It could be that's exactly where Roland and his rebel scum are headed. So here is what I propose . . ."

They gathered at the Jut, ate a sparse breakfast of canned supplies, and looked out across the desert to the west. Roland was restless—he wanted to send these men back to Jawbone quickly. From there they could make plans to retake Bloodrust Corners—when the right time came to retake it. He hoped they didn't jump the gun.

He planned to take his own crew and head south and then west across the canyon. With luck Gynella's army would now be gathering its remaining strength farther north, thinking to retaliate against a band of organized rebels that didn't really exist anymore. It ought to be possible to get across the canyon.

"Why don't you come with us?" Gong suggested, striding up to Roland. "Lucky went to spy on Bloodrust Corners, a few days before we came out. There's only a skeleton force there. Maybe forty men. We could take them by surprise."

Roland shook his head. "Gynella would only send more forces to retake it, and you'd be in the same spot you were in before. No, what needs to happen is to get rid of her . . . and her little mind-control system."

"What mind-control system?"

"Just something I heard about. But I've gone too far off mission already. If I get a chance . . ." He shrugged. "You need to head back to Jawbone, and we'll keep Gynella's attention on us while you do that."

"You sure got a one-track mind. You could make more money helping us mine glam gems. But—" Gong stuck out his hand. "It's been interesting. Thanks." They shook hands, and Gong went to round up the others. "All right, let's move out! Gynella'll send some of those bums out after us right quick! Let's go!"

Mordecai, Brick, and Daphne strolled over to Roland. Bloodwing flapped down from somewhere above and settled on Mordecai's shoulder. Roland noticed Mordecai looked freshly shaven, his small beard perfectly clipped. He never missed a chance to spruce up. Roland was a little envious—he was feeling grubby. He'd kind of have liked to go to New Haven and sit in a hot bath for a few hours himself.

He shook his head. *Getting soft.*

"Okay. Let's head out, south and west. We're burning daylight, standing around here."

They found a place, a few kilometers south, where the canyon wall had collapsed in a landslide. It was steep, but Roland drove the outrunner down the scree, a natural ramp down to the canyon floor, the outrider coming close behind. To the north, they could make out one of Gynella's outriders, parked beside Gynella's banner. Three sentries, rifles in their hands, stood close to the outrider, looking their way. That was the outer southern perimeter of Gynella's encampment, probably swelling with reinforcements about now.

Good. Let them see him—that'd turn their attention his way and away from the Bloodrust men, who were heading east. By the time the Psychos got orders to pursue, he'd have plenty of head start, and he could disappear into the Eridian Promontory, back on mission to hunt down those Eridium-rich crystalisks.

A stream flowed into the canyon across the way, its ravine heading due west. They drove up the shallow stream, the wheels of the two vehicles spraying water as they went. They passed a small troupe of skags and had to shoot a couple of too-inquisitive rakks swooping near them but encountered no other trouble, not all that day. Late that afternoon they emerged from a gulley, on the north side, that led up to the rolling hills below the promontory; they drove through the hills on an old mining road, seeing no one, nothing but a few scythids. The peacefulness of the trip seemed unnatural, even eerie, to Roland.

That night they camped in the mouth of a

shallow cave in the side of a boulder-strewn hill, their only companions the bones of men long dead, piled at the back, much marked by the teeth of animals. Sitting by the fire, across from the snoring Brick—Bloodwing had chosen to roost on Brick's upraised knee, as if it were a bird perch—and waiting for Daphne and Mordecai to finish their watch outside, Roland wondered who they'd been, what the dead men had hoped to find on this sere, ferocious world. And Roland suspected someone would wonder the same about him, some day, when they found his bones, desiccated in the wastelands of Pandora.

The next morning they drove west through the rugged hills hugging the serrated crags of the Eridian Promontory.

They came to an old dirt road, half overgrown with shrubbery, crossing their path, and Roland signaled to Mordecai to slow up and draw back.

The outrider and the outrunner slowed and backed up. They stopped, and Mordecai got out and walked over to him, Bloodwing on his shoulder. "What's up?"

Roland said, "Way down that road, to the right—I saw someone coming around a bend. Looked like some kind of truck. You guys take the vehicles out of sight behind those rocks there. I'm gonna check it out. Might be useful, at least to know about. Could be Gynella's dumbasses looking for us."

As they moved the vehicles, Roland took his combat rifle and ran up into a crotch between two hills, then headed due west, over the top of a low hill on which grew a thicket of blue and red cactus-like growths. He slipped between the man-high flora and, hunkering down under cover, looked out over the road. The truck had stopped, just short of the trail Roland had been following in the outrunner; three confused-looking bandits, none of them wearing Gynellan livery, were standing around the hood of the truck's engine, staring at the smoking grille, arguing about how to fix it.

Chained down onto the long flatbed of the truck was a big shipping container; the metal container had a rust hole in the side, and through the rust hole he could see Eridium crystals. It looked like a whole shipping container of Eridium crystals.

Pretty tempting. If he took out these asshole bandits, there might be enough Eridium in that container to make it unnecessary to go after the crystalisks. And if he took that truck, he'd have the stuff already loaded, solving the problem that had been nagging at the back of his mind: how to get the Eridium back to Fyrestone. Plus he would be able to look in on the Bloodrust settlers. It bothered him, leaving them to their own devices back there.

It did occur to him that this truck stopping here

was a little too handy, a little too enticing, a little too coincidental . . .

But what did paranoia get you on this planet? Well, sure, it got you a longer life, maybe—but you lived cowering in a hole. A man had to take some chances.

He glanced up at the sky, looking for one of those camouflaged drones of Gynella's. He did see a couple of rakks off to the east. But you always saw those somewhere in the Pandoran sky.

He ought to get Brick and the others over there. But Brick might do something rash and wreck the truck, which might end up with the Eridium blown to flinders. Hell, there were just three bandits down there. Two of them didn't even have their guns in their hands.

When had he needed help taking down three clueless bandits?

"Fuck it," he muttered. He slipped down the hillside toward the truck, quietly as he could, using outcroppings of red stone as cover, keeping his head down. He got near the bottom of the hill, crouched behind an outcropping. He jumped up, looking for a target—the bandits were gone. But he heard a whirring above him, looked up to see a rakk, hovering with rapidly flapping wings. Only it *wasn't* a rakk; it was a machine camouflaged as a rakk, with a glittering camera eye instead of a mouth, and it was firing two small missiles at him from its undercarriage. He turned to run, but the missiles weren't aimed directly at him. They struck the ground at his feet, stuck there like arrows in the dirt, and spewed a green smoke that swirled chokingly around him.

He tried to hold his breath—a second too late. He'd already inhaled, just once. And once was enough.

Mordecai shook his head. "I don't like this. He's been gone too long by half, man. Something's off."

On his shoulder Bloodwing squawked in agreement.

Brick shrugged. "Maybe had to pee or something."

"I gotta pee myself," Daphne muttered.

Mordecai muttered an order to Bloodwing, and the creature lofted into the air, flapping up, circling around, spying out the situation. Mordecai noticed a rakk, gleaming oddly at its snout, flying overhead, coming from the direction Roland had gone.

"Uh-oh."

Bloodwing flapped down, alighting, and made the rough, low, warbling distinct sound in his throat that meant *enemies near.*

"Angel fire!" Mordecai ran back to the outrider, where Daphne waited. He shouted at Brick at the turret of the outrunner. "Brick—shitheads are coming! Let's get under cover till I can locate Roland. I think Gynella's set us up for a trap! Go!"

"So let's hit 'em head-on and kill 'em! I was getting bored anyway!"

Mordecai stared at him. "Brick, the word is *trap*, man! They'll be prepared for that, dammit! Come on—get in that driver's seat and follow me. Just trust me!"

Grumbling, Brick climbed into the outrunner driver's seat as Mordecai jumped in beside Daphne. He started the outrider and did a three-point turn, headed back east on the trail.

Almost immediately, Mordecai whipped the outrider to the right, between two low hills, driving along the side of the hill with his left wheels higher than his right, afraid they might flip over. Brick came along close behind, still bellowing that they should turn around and fight.

Mordecai heard the deep cough of a rocket launcher and accelerated, risking losing control at this awkward angle on the hillside, so that the two vehicles—with Brick accelerating to keep up—just barely outran the rocket fired from a hilltop somewhere behind them.

The explosion just behind Brick sent broken rocks pattering down on him, but he got through intact, following Mordecai so close he bumped the outrider a couple of times.

They got through to a little gulley and bumped

over rocky ground to the west. Mordecai was planning to hide the vehicles and sneak overland to try to help Roland.

He spotted something up ahead—a triangle-shaped opening of a cave, and in front of it were two moderately large skags. To the right of the cave was a large boulder.

The entrance of the cave, which was doing service as a skag den, was just big enough. He hoped Brick was willing to follow his lead.

He stopped the outrider. Brick rear-ended them, but not badly, just whiplashing the vehicle a little as he skidded to a stop close behind.

Mordecai spoke a command to Bloodwing, which leapt into the air. It rose up, and up, and then headed for the rakk drone, to knock it down.

Mordecai just hoped they could get under cover before the soldiers following them had a clue what was going on.

He squinted at the sky and saw the fake rakk falling, spiraling down, knocked out of commission by Bloodwing. He whistled for Bloodwing, and as the creature flapped down to the outrunner, Mordecai shouted, "Brick! This way!"

And he drove right into the skag den. Brick drove into the cave behind them, scowling. "Phew! This place smells like old skag droppings. Lots of them."

"Mordecai!" Daphne gasped. "What the hell!"

"Get on that turret gun!" he shouted as they came to a stop in the stinking recess.

She climbed quickly up, got on the turret in time to blast a snarling mama skag, charging at them from the back of the cave, and two yipping whelps.

Mordecai climbed out and crawled over the two parked vehicles to join Brick, who was happily smashing the skull of a large skag at the mouth of the reeking cave. "Brick, that big rock, can you roll it over to block the entrance, shut us up in here?"

"You want to hide in a stinking hidey-hole?"

"Just for a few minutes! It's tactics, man!"

Brick growled and shook his head, but he went to the boulder, found two hand-holds, and rolled it to the left, the boulder making a grinding sound as it came as if complaining of being shifted. But it worked—the boulder mostly covered the entrance.

They were left in stinking near-darkness.

Mordecai lay down on his belly and peered out through the small opening left by the boulder covering the entrance. He was just in time to see an outrider drive by—and another. And two more. And then three more. And another two outriders, each with three Psycho soldiers on it. "Oh, by the Angel's backside—eight outriders. There's a big force around here, and they're looking for us."

But they'd gone right by. The skag cave had worked—for now. But . . . how was he going to get to Roland?

TWENTY-ONE

When Roland woke, his mouth tasted like rot, and his head rang like a cracked bell tumbling down a flight of stairs. He was lying on a metal slope.

He was chained flat on his back, faceup, on the trailer of the flatbed truck. The sky was darkening overhead; a cold, dry wind lashed his face. He had a sense of height, and, wincing with pain, he turned his head and saw they were high over the plains, going up a narrow road cut into the side of a cliff or maybe some kind of butte. He looked for landmarks in the misty distance, picked out a few, and worked out that he was probably on some access road going up onto the Devil's Footstool.

He tried his bonds, found there was very little slack, no real leverage possible. He couldn't break loose, not yet.

He turned his head and saw the rust hole in the

side of the container—he could see, up close, that the hole had been cut in and the "rust" painted on. And that the Eridium visible in it was just a few crystals. He could see past it from there. The container was empty. A lure in a trap.

He laughed out loud. At himself. "You idiot. You deserve this."

Really, he'd gotten into this because he wanted to go back and rejoin the Bloodrust miners. He'd been a fool, gotten himself emotionally caught up in their hopeless cause.

"Idiot," he said again. He closed his eyes and tried to rest. He had to wait for his chance.

They had taken him nonlethally, planned it that way, and they could have cut his throat while he was unconscious. They didn't intend to kill him—not yet. And that gave him time. Sure, he was chained down and about to be surrounded by hundreds of enemies.

But there was always a chance.

If you took armpit squeezings and fermented them, that, Roland figured, would approximate how this guy smelled.

Arms chained behind him, Roland was being shoved by a huge, reeking Badass Psycho whose name, he gathered, was Spung. The Psycho was clomping along behind Roland, giving him an unnecessary shove every so often, as they crossed the parade ground between the Psycho soldiers' barracks and Gynella's headquarters.

At the door to the headquarters stood two people. One was an unremarkable-looking medium-sized man in Gynellan livery, brown leather, with improvised epaulets on his shoulders made out of tire tread and screws—some kind of army commander. He was one of the few men Roland had seen in Gynella's army without a vault mask. Roland guessed the guy wasn't a Psycho at all.

The other one at the door was a tall, obese, dark-skinned woman in tight-fitting black leather, a shotgun in her hands; on her otherwise bald head were three white Mohawk fins. She wore no vault mask—it wouldn't have fit over the tusks that curved from her upper jaw down past her chin. She had on flaring red and blue eye makeup and seemed to have a coating of crystalline dust glued to her heavy lips.

"Smartun, Goddess said bring him from truck, so I bring him from truck," rumbled Spung.

The small man nodded, looking at Roland with cold hatred. "You take up your post here, Spung. Fwah . . ." He turned to the big woman. "Take him in . . ." He seemed to struggle to finish saying it. Clearly this "Smartun" didn't want Roland to go inside at all. "To *her*."

So that was what that vibe of personal hatred was about. Jealousy.

Fwah opened the door for Roland, winking at

him, and Spung gave him a particularly vicious shove to propel him through it. Roland staggered in, then turned toward the door.

"Spung," he said. "I can't promise you'll be the first one I kill. But you'll be one of the first. So don't get impatient. It's coming."

Spung blinked at him in confusion, shrugged, and walked lumberingly away.

Roland turned and saw Gynella herself standing in the open doorway to a room on the left. It must be her. She was a tall, voluptuous, powerful-looking woman with an intense expression and long flaxen hair; she wore a tight suit of armored skag leather. She was so striking he didn't at first notice the gangly, hollow-eyed man in a stained lab coat standing behind her.

"Vialle," Gynella said, "don't you have some lab work to do?"

Vialle sniffed and slipped past her into the wide hallway. He stopped to stare at Roland. "Gynella, this man . . . if he is not suitable for your purposes, can I have him? He is an interesting specimen. I would like to do a vivisection, perhaps, possibly some creative splicing."

"If I can't use him, you shall have him, Dr. Vialle," she promised. "Now just . . . go."

Vialle turned reluctantly away and walked, storklike, to a room marked "VIALLE LAB 1." He opened the door, stepped through, turned to close it, and gave Roland one last long, lingering look. "Yes. I think so," he muttered. "Vivisection. For you. You would find it a very . . . intimate experience." And he closed the door.

"Kind of a party animal, isn't he?" Roland said.

Gynella smiled thinly. "Come into my office."

"You going to take these chains off me?"

"Maybe, maybe not."

She walked into the office, and he followed her in—and stopped when she put a long slim blade to his neck. "This is what we use as a meat cutter on my home planet. I'm quite skilled with it. It has a very small, very efficient moving edge on it, like a microscopic chain saw. It's hard to see it, but it's there. It'll cut through flesh and bone easily and quietly . . ." She put her lips to his right ear, keeping the blade on his Adam's apple. He felt her breath tickling his ear when she said, "Quietly as a whisper."

He tried not to shiver—and wasn't entirely successful.

"Over there," she said, nodding toward a long chaise longue near a workstation and a portable bar.

He walked over to it. "You want me to sit on this thing? Waste of a comfortable seat, with these chains on me."

"You keep the chains on for now. It is a sign of our respect for you, if you like—you're quite a dangerous man."

He turned and sat awkwardly on the edge of the chaise. "So . . . big evening of executing me planned?"

"After what you did at my little coliseum show, I'm tempted!" she said, chuckling, sheathing her blade. She stepped over to a rifle leaning against a table to her right, keeping her eyes warningly on him the whole time. The only things on the table were two glasses and a pitcher of thick orange fluid—and the contact box that Mince Feldsrum had given him, taken off him while he was unconscious.

She picked the rifle up and pointed it at him. It was a great blunderbuss of an energy rifle—he could tell by the curving, almost organic lines on it that it was Eridian, but it was a weapon he hadn't seen before. "You have no shield now. This is the most powerful portable weapon we have. There's only one of these that I know of. It's an Eridian Remover. If I shoot you with it, it'll leave a blot where you were before. We'll sweep what's left into a dustpan. Do you believe me, Roland?"

"I do, yeah. You seem sincere. And that weapon looks . . . like it could do it."

"It could. And I won't hesitate to prove it if you make one wrong move in here. You're good, but I could probably kill you without this weapon, even if you had a gun and your hands free. Because I'm better. But I don't like to take unnecessary chances. I'd rather not have to kill you at all."

This surprised him. "Yeah?"

"Yes. You do have qualities I like. Qualities I need. I've been watching you for a while. I have people in Fyrestone. I have my drones, and I have files on you. I became especially interested in you when I saw footage of you in action around Bloodrust Corners. And then when you hit our coliseum . . . and you made a terrible mess in Goddess Canyon with that truck."

"Goddess Canyon, that what you're calling it? Going to name everything on the planet after you?"

"Once it belongs to me, why not? I will, however, name a mountain after my late husband. He was murdered by that horrendous little assassin you have been running around with. Daphne Kuller. Where is she?"

"You don't know?"

"The cowardly backshooters you ran around with gave us the slip. But we'll find them."

"I really don't know where they are. We were prospecting for Eridium——they probably went on into the mountains to do that. I don't know."

"Yes, they probably abandoned you. Because they're cowards. But you, you're no coward—you went after the bait alone. Smartun was in charge of that operation. He didn't think you'd fall for it, but I see everyone's weakness. And I see yours."

"Yeah. I got chains locking my arms behind me."

"Your weakness is hotheadedness, opportun- ism—you're bold to a fault. But your strengths are much more impressive. You have a talent for tactics. You fight creatively. You're resourceful. You're fairly bright . . ."

"Oh. Thanks."

"And you emanate power. In the way my hus- band did. They couldn't kill him fairly, you know. They had to send a sneak to shoot a dart into him. It had to be done the cowardly way."

"Like the way you took me down?"

She shrugged apologetically. "I was trying to save your life. Now, who gave you this?" She picked up the contact box. "We found this on you—did you take it off Feldsrum? Or did he give it to you?"

"I found it."

"I don't think that's true. No matter." She put it down. "Turn around. I am going to remove your chains."

He stood up and turned around. Half expecting to be shot in the back.

She walked over to the workstation, and out of the corner of his eye he could see her put the pitcher of orange-colored fluid on the desk. "Be very careful what you do, now," she said. "I'm faster than you—and I have that knife ready to slice you apart." She went to a desk drawer, drew out a remote control, and pointed it at his chains.

They fell off his arms, clattering to the floor.

With enormous relief, he stretched and rubbed his wrists. "Can I turn around?"

She stepped back from him and retrieved the rifle. "Go ahead."

He turned. "You know that big guy who shoved me into this building? The one who smells like he's never been near water?"

"You're smelling a bit ripe yourself. What about him?"

"I'm going to kill him. Whether or not I decide to work for you."

"I haven't made an offer yet."

"Isn't that what you're getting at?"

She nodded. "Once I've prepared you to obey me. There's only one way I can be sure I could trust you. How are you feeling? You had a rough ride getting here."

"I feel like death warmed over."

"So have a drink." She poured two glasses of the orange fluid and sipped some. "It's vitalizing."

He was damned thirsty and hungry, and seeing as she'd drunk from the same pitcher . . .

He picked up the glass and drank deeply. It had surprisingly little taste; just a mild sourness.

But he started to feel better almost immediately. Strength rippled through him; the pain in his arms ebbed away. "You should bottle that."

"Now, behind you is a small door. There's a

shower in there. Go on in, shower, clean up. Then come back out here. There's no back way out of there, no window. I'll be watching the door. Don't get cute."

"No clean clothes?"

"There's a pilot's jumpsuit if you want it. Or just put on the robe."

Under the influence of the drink, he found he was looking at her curves, her legs, her eyes . . .

This, he thought, *is crazy.*

But Roland went into the back room, undressed, and showered. A hot shower and soap—it felt unbelievably good.

He toweled off after, with a clean white towel, and looked at the clothes on the two hooks. A clean white jumpsuit; a black bathrobe of some soft, thick fabric.

Don't be a chump, he thought. He should put on the jumpsuit, step through the door, look for a chance to take that gun from her.

But he put on the robe.

He took a deep breath and went through the door into the other room. She was wearing a robe herself. And nothing else—except a circular pendant around her neck.

She put her hand to the pendant. "In fact," she said, "there *was* something else in that drink. In your glass. The interior glass itself was treated— with a certain drug. We usually give it by injection, but . . . this is a new formula, a thin spray of Sus-Drug. Just perfected today. Should be powerful, and safe—it won't hurt you. Quite the contrary. It's not fully activated until I use this device."

She pointed a hand at him—so that her robe fell open—and with the other hand twisted the dial on the pendant.

Ecstasy struck Roland like a bolt of lightning, so powerful it drove him to his knees. He groaned. "This . . . isn't . . . fair."

"Oh, but it's lovely, isn't it? Doesn't it feel good?" Her voice sounded impossibly sweet.

She turned the dial a little more, and he groaned and had to struggle to keep from crawling to her on his hands and knees.

No, Gynella, he thought. *I am not going to let you do this to me.*

"I need a new general," she said, her voice reverberating through him. "And if you will obey me, if you will be completely loyal to me, to the death, you can be that man. I must either kill you or recruit you. A man like you could double my progress on this planet. I give you the gift of ecstasy . . . and more. Something I've given to no other man on this world. Something I've given to no one since my husband was murdered."

"Oh . . . I can't bear this."

No. Don't crawl to her. Stand up!

Shaking, he forced himself to stand.

"Impressive," she said. "Now, go to the lounge. Lie down. I'll join you. And I have my knife strapped to my wrist. If you give me trouble, I'll carve you up. But I don't think you will. I have made my mark within your brain—I have put my brand there. I have seared myself into you! You are mine, Roland. You are now mine, forever."

TWENTY-TWO

The morning light was veiled in dust—a dust storm roiled the horizon to the north. Mordecai hoped it wouldn't swing their way.

"First that Roland shoots the Goliath in the head, just as I was about to kill him!" Brick complained. "Then you—you make me hide in a skag hole!" He scratched under his left arm. "I've been itching ever since! No man takes away my kill! No man makes me hide!"

"Take it easy, Brick," Mordecai said, looking across the plains with the scope of the sniper rifle. They were on a hilltop, about ten klicks north of the skag cave. Daphne was sitting on a rock nearby, looking balefully off into the distance. Bloodwing circled high overhead. "You'll get your chance to kill lots of big ugly bastards before this is through. If you still feeling like killing me and Roland after that, then . . . fine."

"Okay, just so you know!"

"Fine, good." He sighed, lowering the rifle. "I can't see much. Damn dust storm."

Daphne cleared her throat. "Mordecai. Can we talk?"

"Sure." He smiled at her, hoping for a smile in return. But she just looked pensively at the ground. That scary calculating look she got in her eyes sometimes was there now. They'd kissed a couple of times, but it hadn't been the right moment for anything more. She was a strong woman, stronger than most men. No way she was going to just melt in his embrace, not that easily. Anyway, skag caves and campsites with Brick snoring nearby were not ideal romantic settings.

"I just think," she began slowly, "that we ought to be realistic about this. Roland's probably dead."

"Couldn't find his body. They'd never bury him. And those missile canisters—they smelled of chemicals. Word is she uses a knockout gas to get her recruits to where she can, I don't know, brainwash them or whatever she does."

"She'd never recruit him. After what happened in that canyon . . ."

"Right—she'll take him to a coliseum, make sure he can't get away, and feed him to some Goliath. But that gives us time to go after him."

She shook her head slowly in disbelief. "You don't seem like the suicide-mission kind."

"I am!" Brick put in. "I like suicide missions!" He scratched his head. "Or is that homicide missions?"

"I don't know, as it's suicide," Mordecai said. "The General's forces are pretty badly reduced. Must be demoralized. If we can track them back, we might slip in, get him out . . ."

"'We'? Why should I do that?" Daphne asked. "I kind of liked Roland. But first of all, by the time we get there, he'll be dead. Second, even if he isn't, there's no money in it for us. I might go out of my way to save your ass . . . I got kind of used to your face. So maybe."

"Heartwarming."

"But nobody else. I'm a professional assassin, not a rebel, not a hero in some stupid cause. I risk my life all the time. But I'll never throw it away, Mordecai."

He nodded. "I gotcha. Well. You could take the outrider, head back to, say, Jawbone. I'll meet you back there."

She snorted. "You'll never make it back alive."

He looked out at the swirling dust to the north. She was probably right. The chance of success was small. But once he partnered with a guy, he saw it through to the end of the mission. That was his code. And he was pretty sure if their positions were reversed, Roland would be there for him.

"See you in Jawbone," he said.

• • •

Roland woke from a sleep where dreams were mixed up with remembrance. The fight at Bloodrust Corners. The kids running by—him wondering what it would be like to have a child of his own. Memories of a woman, a strong, sensitive woman, who just might be waiting for him on the planet Xanthus. Dreams of Gynella. In one dream she'd made him carry her on his back, across the plains.

She had ridden him last night. Most of the time she'd straddled him, used him. Even when he was on top he felt as if she was in control. But he'd surrendered to it, gone with it, because she was like a living landscape of sweet touch, and he felt as if he wanted to melt into it and die . . .

He sat up on the chaise and looked around. He was alone, naked, a little sore, his head throbbing. Hungry. And he could smell food. There was a bowl of something that smelled savory on the desk, and he figured it was for him. Some sort of stew. Beside it was a spoon.

The stuff was good, rich and meaty and hot. First good meal he'd had in months. He ate hungrily, felt strength and alertness return.

He put down the bowl . . . and then the craving hit him.

He craved *her*. Just to fall to his knees before her. To feel her benediction.

And it made him angry. Roland's fists balled with anger as he thought about it. The anger swept away the craving.

No. This is one soldier you can't have, Gynella. Never again.

She'd primed him with that drug. It was probably still active in him. He couldn't let her get near him. He might buckle under to her again, maybe for good, if she sent that vibrating singing through him one more time.

He went into the back room and found his clothes, his boots, everything cleaned up and ready for him. Everything but a weapon.

Roland dressed, then returned to the office and did a thorough search, assured himself that there were no weapons in the room.

None. That was no surprise.

He tried the door to the hall. It was locked, of course. She wasn't sure of him yet.

Last night, in her arms, he'd told her he'd be her new general, he'd help her conquer the world. He'd almost meant it, then.

Today the memory sickened him.

She was beautiful. They had both arched their backs in ecstasy; they'd both climaxed more than once. But he was no one's slave. And there was only one way to make sure.

Once he killed her, he'd never make it out of there. All those Gynella fanatics—too many of them. He could only kill so many. They'd drag him down and tear him to pieces. He'd be lying in pieces on the Devil's Footstool, in the dirt, and the trash feeders would come down . . .

But his gaze stopped, as he looked around the room, fixing on one object on the table.

He walked over to it and picked up the small metallic box that Feldsrum had given him. She'd forgotten it. Or maybe it didn't work.

He found the activation stud on a corner of the contact box and pressed it. A crackling noise came from the box.

Then a voice seemed to come out of the air itself. "Who's that? This is Dahl three-one-one on tight-frequency reserve. Identify yourself!"

"Roland here. That Feldsrum?"

"Ah, at last! I'd almost given up on you! We were just trying to arrange for another twenty specialists to come in and . . . take care of the Gynella problem. But it's all rather embarrassing. If you are willing to accept our offer . . ."

"I am. There's something I need. You in orbit?"

"We are."

"Can you pinpoint my transmission? Locate me?"

"We can. But I'm not sending my personnel down there."

"That won't be necessary. There's something else I want you to send. And I need it fast."

• • •

Smartun hadn't slept all night. He had gotten up from his bunk in the small officers' quarters building and gone out into the moonlight, to pace back and forth on the parade ground, hands in his pockets, under the puzzled gaze of the sentries.

Every so often he'd looked toward the headquarters building, hoping to see her sending Roland out, preferably in chains.

But he never came.

Now it was morning, and he was exhausted, but he stood in the middle of the parade ground, alone, arms at his side, staring at that door.

She'd kept him there overnight. Perhaps she'd given him to Dr. Vialle. Her bodyguard was there, squatting against the wall outside, sleeping still. He wouldn't know . . .

But there—Fwah was coming out now, yawning, scratching her ass. She slept in a storeroom, near the office, in case she was needed. She was part of Gynella's personal guard.

Smartun strode over to her, breathless. She seemed startled when he stalked up to her. "Fwah!"

"What? What did I do?"

"Listen—where's Roland? Did Vialle get him?

"No. No—*she* got him." She tittered nastily. "I could hear them going at it. They shook the whole building sometimes. I guess she was tired of waiting. I heard her say once there was no man here who was her match in bed. She had to import one."

A white light burst behind Smartun's eyes. "She said that . . ."

"Oh yeah. You were thinking that you . . . ?" She chuckled. "No disrespect, commander, but she'd-a broken your back, that woman, if she took you into her bed. But say, you and me, now . . ."

He shook his head impatiently. "He must die. You know that, don't you? He cannot be trusted. At the first chance, he will betray her! I saw that she was becoming obsessed with him. She watched the footage of him in action, over and over. She's not thinking rationally! He should be her slave—but she's become his!"

"Gynella? The General Goddess? She's no one's slave, Smartun. Hell, you know that."

"She must not trust him! He'll wait his chance—and kill her. He slaughtered half a division, him and his rebels! He's filled with hate for all of us!"

She ran a thoughtful finger down one of her tusks. "You could be right. But you'd need an excuse to kill him. A good reason. Maybe . . . make it look like he's plottin' against her, like. You know?"

"Yes. You'll help me with that, to protect the General Goddess from him . . . won't you?"

"On one condition."

"What's that?"

Her eyes shone, and she licked her crystalline lips, making them shine. "*I* get to kill him!"

"Just so long as you get it done. But you'd better not take him on face-to-face unless he's got no shield and no weapon."

"Oh, of course not—I'll step up behind him, stick a gun against the back of his head . . . and blow it right off!"

Roland was pacing, himself, back and forth in the locked office. He'd tried kicking the door down. But it was specially reinforced. He swore to himself that he'd snap that pendant off the queen bitch's neck, first time he got within reach, before he'd let her use it on him—even if that risked her using that special offworld "meat cutter." He didn't want anyone tinkering in his brain, turning him into a puppet.

He looked at the table, thought about breaking it up, using it to make tools, and then—

The door was clicking; the door was unlocking.

He positioned himself close to the door, but not too close, and waited. The door swung outward, and there was Spung, with a shotgun in one hand, hulking and reeking in the hallway. He was so tall he had to stoop under the ceiling, leaning a little toward Roland. That could be useful.

Roland noticed Spung was wearing a shield too.

And the shield was flickering a little. Which didn't mean much of anything. But it might seem to mean something. Because he'd noticed something else about Spung.

Spung was stupid.

"You come with me," Spung rumbled. "She wants you outside."

"Does she? Sounds good, bro. Hey—what's wrong with your shield there?" Roland frowned and pointed at the shield. "See that? That a Hyperion shield? Yeah, those'll flicker and go out—it's the weather. Too much moisture in the air. But you can fix that."

"Fix it? How?"

"Reboot it, man. Just turn it off and then on. A quick reset. Click off, click on. Like that."

"Like this?" Spung clicked the shield off—

And Roland struck, straight-arming up at the bridge of Spung's nose. He had only one shot at this, and he made it good. He slammed the heel of his hand in an ancient martial-arts move, with all his speed and strength, into that nose. And Spung was leaning toward him because of the ceiling—the perfect angle.

He felt the cartilage crunch and the bone, at the top of the nose, shatter and turn into shards . . .

To stab back, into Spung's brain.

He didn't know if it would work—he'd only pulled off that move once before.

Spung stared at Roland in astonishment, the big Psycho rocking on the balls of his feet, mouth gaping open. Blood gushed from his nose and trickled from the corners of his mouth. "You . . ."

"Yes?" Roland asked, curious.

"Can't . . ."

"I can't what?"

"Kill me . . . like . . ."

Then Spung fell over backward, hit the floor with a thud that shook the building.

"I can't kill you like that?" Roland asked, bending to grab Spung's ankles. "If it's done just right, I bet I can."

He looked around, saw no one else in the hall, and dragged the deadweight of the big Psycho through the door. Spung barely fit. Roland had to jerk the body hard to get the arms through the door, breaking one of them. He dragged Spung back into the shower room, dumped him under the shower spigot. He started the shower. "Your one and only shower, Spung. Everyone should have at least one." He hoped the sound of the shower would deceive Gynella a short while, if she came in. He closed the back room's door, hustled to the shotgun on the floor, picked it up, and looked around. Still no one around. That couldn't last.

He crossed to the door of Vialle's lab and found it unlocked. He opened it quietly as possible, and saw Vialle inside, leaning over a bandit strapped to a gurney.

It was a Midget Psycho, strapped on his back, naked, without his mask, chattering mindlessly, struggling with his bonds. Vialle was crooning to the Psycho, leaning over him with a syringe. Around Vialle's neck was a pendant. Did Gynella even know Vialle had one of those?

Didn't matter. He wouldn't have it much longer.

Roland strode over to Vialle and snapped the pendant from the chain with his left hand, tossed it onto a shiny metal table; with his right hand he grabbed Vialle's wrist. "Drop the syringe, Dr. Screwloose."

He squeezed Vialle's wrist till it was close to breaking. Vialle squeaked and dropped the syringe—it fell to the table right by the Midget's hand.

"Hee-*heeeeeee*!" the Psycho Midget tittered. "Now I gots it!"

"What do you imagine will happen to you," Vialle began, "when she finds out—"

"What's going to happen to *you*," Roland wondered aloud, twisting Vialle's arm behind his back, "if you don't tell me where the rest of the drug is? You know the drug I mean. The SusDrug. Your pretty princess told me about it last night—where is it?"

"She will remove your skin from your body and drag you behind an outrider and—" The rest was lost in a long squeal as Roland cracked his arm, beginning to break it. With his left hand he pressed Vialle down over the Midget on the gurney, so that Vialle's head was close to the Midget's right hand. The hand that held the syringe.

The Midget slammed the syringe into Vialle's ear, right through the eardrum. And pressed the plunger.

Blood spurted out along the syringe, and Vialle screamed.

"It's in the steel outbuilding, behind the headquarters! There are barrels of it, they—*take it away, don't, don't do it!*"

Roland let go of Vialle, who pulled away from the Midget, snatched the syringe from his ear, then bent double in agony, moaning.

Roland looked at the pendant on the table, then he looked at Vialle. He picked up the pendant thoughtfully.

Vialle looked up at him. "No! Don't touch that! I've been injected!"

"I took some orally last night, Doctor. How long's the stuff last?"

"Orally? Only a few hours, four at most. She wanted to give you the shot this morning, for the five-day release—oh my." He realized he'd revealed that the pendant wouldn't affect Roland unless he got a booster shot.

Roland grinned at him. "You know what? I believe you! Let's see what that stuff does to you . . . when you get a big dose shot right into the ear, eh, Doc?"

"No! It's a new serum, I don't know what it'll—*no!*"

Roland was turning the dial on the pendant, turning it all the way around.

Vialle quivered and fell to his knees, wracked with a nightmarishly powerful ecstasy. Then his eyes widened and began to bulge from his head. His tongue extended from his mouth . . . and extended more. And more. His neck was swelling; his face was bloating; his body was inflating like a balloon. Bigger, bigger yet . . .

Vialle shrieked in pain and horror.

Roland vaulted over the table, ducked down, rolled away—just in time to stay out of the explosion.

Vialle exploded, splashing blood, body parts, and bits of clothing over half the room. Roland only caught a few splatters.

"New serum, I guess," Roland said, getting up. He found a scalpel, tossed it over to the gurney so it fell next to the Midget's hand. "You can cut yourself loose with that. It'll take a little time. Don't say I never did you a favor."

He put the pendant in his pocket, picked up the shotgun, went to the door—

It burst open, and Fwah was there, a combat rifle in her hands; Smartun was behind her.

"I told you I heard something!" Smartun said, almost dancing with excitement. "Kill him! Kill him fast!"

Fwah was too slow, too clumsy. Swinging the rifle toward Roland, she caught its muzzle on the frame of the door, just for a moment. Long enough. Roland jabbed the shotgun muzzle through Fwah's shield, into her open mouth, and pulled the trigger. The top of her head vanished—the rest of her sagged to the floor.

He looked for Smartun, but he was already rushing out through the front door.

Roland sighed. "Great. Alerting the troops."

He jumped over Fwah's body, then turned back, tossed the shotgun away, and picked up the Cobra combat rifle. He was going to need some effective range.

He looked around, then ran toward the back of the building. A Bruiser Psycho in a vault mask turned the corner, submachine gun propped on his shoulder.

Roland rushed him, smashed the butt of his gun through the Psycho's shield, crunching the shield hardware. The Psycho staggered back, unslinging the submachine gun. He didn't have a chance to use it. Roland stuck the barrel of the Cobra under the Psycho's chin and let loose a long burst of bullets, painting the ceiling with blood and brains.

He was past the Psycho before he had quite fallen dead, running down the hall to the back door. It opened easily enough—but that was the end of easy. First of all, the "special delivery" he'd ordered from Feldsrum wasn't waiting for him out back as planned. Second, a couple of outriders full of Psycho soldiers were roaring up from opposite directions, barely stopping before colliding head-on.

One of them swung a mounted gun toward him, and he threw himself to the left, into the space between the main building and the locked, reinforced storage shed they kept the drug in.

Bullets clanged into the metal of the shed, thudded into the building. Roland jumped to his feet, put the rifle strap over his shoulder, then did a pull-up, till he could get his elbows onto the back of the shed. Grunting, he wormed up onto it, staying flat. It angled up a little, toward the front, giving him some cover if he stayed low. He unslung the rifle—but it occurred to him that he had another weapon. He dug in his pocket, pulled out the pendant, and then got into a hunkering position—lifted up just enough so he could see the Psychos running from the outrunners toward the shed. They'd have him trapped there in a moment.

He waited till they were close—then he turned the dial on the pendant. The pendant chimed, and all six Psycho soldiers fell to their knees, crying out in ecstatic abandon. Roland couldn't keep from laughing. "Ha! They love me! *Man*, it's good to feel loved!"

Then he heard a hissing sound, and a shadow fell over him. He looked up and saw the skimmer he'd requested from Feldsrum, descending to him. It was a silvery delta-shaped flyer, about ten meters long, wingspan of fifteen meters, capable of rapid flight or hovering, with smart missiles attached to the lower side. Roland had been checked out on them—this looked like a new model, but with luck he could fly it.

He noticed that on the underside of the wings, some insignia had been sanded off. Probably the Dahl logo had been removed. Maybe that accounted for the delay.

Repulsors hissing, the skimmer lowered itself to hover just beyond the edge of the roof. It was unoccupied, remote-controlled at the moment from orbit. The cockpit was open and inviting.

Roland grinned and sprinted for it, running along the rooftop, unleashing suppressive fire at an onrushing group of Psycho soldiers. He jumped onto the nearer wing of the small craft; it rocked a little, then adjusted for his weight. He tossed away the rifle, took two more strides, and dropped into the cockpit; settling into the seat, he hurriedly assessed the controls. What did that lever in the corner do? "If you don't know what it is, don't use it," he muttered. He found the external control switch and turned it off. The vessel went instantly to manual, the hissing of its repulsors increasing in volume as if it were impatient to be going.

Something sizzled by just overhead, and he looked to his right to see a smoking rocket launcher in the hands of a Bruiser not more than twenty paces away.

Roland pulled back on the control stick gently, and the skimmer rose straight up about ten meters. He tapped the forward tilt tab and skewed the skimmer over just as the Bruiser raised his reloaded weapon to his shoulder. There was no time to aim; Roland hit the fire button for the right-hand projectile. The missile shot out from under the wing, and the Bruiser vanished in a ball of flame.

He reached up, twisted the pendant one more time, and heard a moan from the Psychos in range. He chuckled and pulled the stick back for quick elevation. His stomach lurched as the vehicle whooshed straight up into the air, so fast and far that before he leveled off he knocked a rakk out of the sky with the tip of his wing.

Humming a half-remembered song, Roland turned the skimmer, tilted it sharply, and fired three missiles at the reinforced storage shed. His aim was good; the projectiles made impact, and the shed spurted flame. He waited, hearing bullets clack into the armored underside of the skimmer—then the smoke cleared, and he saw that the storage shed was largely intact. There was a big hole in it, though. He reduced elevation, spiraling slowly down. About ten meters over the storage shed, he stabilized the skimmer, aimed, and fired the forward machine gun at the drug casks visible through the smoking hole in the storage unit. The bullets pocked the casks. Not much other effect. He looked over the skimmer's armaments—there was just one more, marked "Flame Charge."

He switched to flame charge and fired—and the entire shed rose into the air on a column of fire, spinning, so that Roland had to back quickly away, to avoid flying metal debris. The storage unit had broken open, spilling more than a ton of drug fluid across the ground.

"That works," he murmured, turning the vehicle around just in time to see a rocket spinning toward him.

He veered sharp left, and the rocket flew through the spot he'd occupied a split second before. He aimed the flame charge at the Psycho with the launcher. The Psycho turned and ran, but he ran right into the missile. Roland would have missed him if he'd stayed in place.

"Cooperation," Roland said. "I like it."

More bullets clanged into the skimmer; he turned a hard right, and the skimmer veered—right into a rocket that would've missed him completely otherwise.

The irony wasn't lost on Roland, as the skimmer bucked under him with the rocket's impact, whipping him in his seat, the vessel wobbling, smoking, but not losing elevation. Not yet. He turned it around, fired three flame-charge projectiles over the top of the headquarters building, at the Psychos rushing onto the parade ground, Gynella's soldiers reacting to the general emergency with generalized chaos.

Three fire-charge rounds struck in their midst—men flew spinning through three balls of fire.

There were a lot more of them over there. But more bullets were hitting his skimmer—he didn't dare go low enough to try to affect them all with the pendant. There were too many of them, too much firepower down there. He punched for horizontal motion and skimmed out of the range of fire, beyond the edge of the butte, the wind roaring in his ears. He shook his head, checking out the view. It was a long way down from up there. And the skimmer was still smoking, starting to wobble . . . and slowing down.

"Hellfire," Roland growled. He banked and put the skimmer into a slow downward spiral, fighting for stability. Out of the corner of his eye he saw flames licking up from under the wings. And the repulsor engines whined, beginning to lose power.

TWENTY-THREE

"Roland used me—and betrayed me!" Gynella fumed, shaking with fury, as Smartun trotted up beside her.

They stood on the edge of the Devil's Footstool, looking at the skimmer descending, rather sharply, down toward the rugged plains below.

"I did try to warn you, my General Goddess," Smartun observed.

She turned with a snarl and viciously back-handed him, knocking him off his feet. He lay on his back for a stunned moment, tasting blood.

"I . . . I deserved that," he said, sitting up.

"You deserve *worse*! I gave you a chance, and you let him destroy half a division with a truck and a handful of men! You and the others—I trusted you to keep him contained!" She glared down at him, fingering the meat-cutter knife on her hip.

Smartun decided not to point out that she had

set up the imprisonment protocol for Roland in the headquarters building; she had trusted Fwah and Spung with the job, not him. She knew how Smartun felt about her, of course—she'd probably feared he might try to kill Roland in his sleep. And she was right about that.

He got to his feet, about to beg her to punish him—and then saw that Roland's skimmer was going down faster, really out of control now. "Look, my Goddess! He's going down!"

She turned and gasped. "No! I didn't . . ."

That stabbed Smartun through the heart. Even now she didn't want Roland dead.

Gynella closed her eyes. Tears trickled from the corners. Then she threw back her head and roared with fury, shaking her fists. "Smartun! Take thirty men! Get down the ramp, find the crash site! Make sure he doesn't go anywhere! I will come . . . and kill him myself!"

Roland had just managed to get a jolt more of lift out of the repulsors—seconds before the crash. It slowed him enough, gave him a little forward motion, so that the skimmer struck a sand dune diagonally, cutting off the top of the dune, spuming sand, then skidding across the ground—stopping on the edge of a creekbed in a cloud of smoke.

Coughing, he scrambled out and sprinted away—as the skimmer exploded. A shock wave caught him, throwing him onto his face. He skidded painfully, coming to a stop against a hummock. "Fuck!"

He coughed, spat out dust and sand, and got to his hands and knees. At least he was alive. But so was Gynella. And he wouldn't be safe as long as she was walking around.

Roland got to his feet—and found himself face-to-face with a good-sized skag, opening its tripartite jaws wide to snarl and so it could unreel its long, *long* tongue, which was a kind of lash, almost a club, that could knock a man down, whip around his neck, and drag him close for feeding.

"Forget it, skag!" Roland bellowed, grabbing the tongue as it flashed toward him. He twisted it around his fist and pulled hard.

The skag squealed and tried to wrest free.

He pulled it to him, hand over hand, his adrenaline high after the fight, the crash, another day of near-death . . .

"I've had *enough*! I'm not taking crap from a skag too, dammit!"

Holding the tongue with his right hand, he slammed his left down into its open mouth, down its throat, and grabbed a big handful of entrails. The skag writhed around his arm. Roland wrenched hard, with all his strength, and ripped out the skag's lungs.

He threw the spasming animal and its offal

aside and wiped blood off his hands onto its hide, then straightened up to look around.

And saw a line of red outriders coming at him from the base of the Devil's Footstool about half a kilometer away.

"Son of a *bitch*!"

He was unarmed, and there must be at least four of them coming. One of them would have a cannon turret too.

He looked at the burning skimmer. If there were any weapons in it, they were frying now. And the smoke from the wreck was marking his position. He checked his pocket—and found he'd lost the pendant in the crash.

He could run, hide, or stand and fight. Or . . .

Roland dug the contact box from his pocket and tapped it. It only went to one place: Feldsrum's orbiter.

"You there, Feldsrum? Yo! I destroyed the drug supply. You hearing me up there?"

A crackle, and then the man's voice. "I hear you. Good job. What about Gynella?"

"I took out a lot of her men, both her body-guards, but last I knew she was still kicking. I'm going to need help. I've got no weapons. They shot down the skimmer . . ."

"Yes, we can see that. We've got a good visual fix on you."

"Then . . . either come and get me or nail these

guys. They'll be here in like two minutes. Or less. I've got no gun, no knife, no shield. Just get me the weapons or a little breathing room—and I'll do the job for you!"

"Ahhh, no can do, Roland. We cannot get there soon enough. You see, we're watching, and . . . they're already there. Sorry."

Feldsrum was right. A big outcropping of rock stuck up about thirty meters east of him—and around it, on both sides, came the outriders. Roland knew they were only the advance guard. Others would be coming, in other kinds of vehicles.

This wasn't looking good. But if he could get onto one of those outriders . . .

The nearest outrider fired, its machine gun tearing up the ground in a line of little sand geysers, coming right at him. Roland turned, vaulted over the hummock, threw himself down. The mound of dirt and rock absorbed the gunfire—and then blew up as a cannon shell hit it.

Pieces of dirt and rock rained down on him. Coughing in the dust, he rolled to his left, got his feet under him, and ran for a low boulder between him and one of the oncoming outriders.

The outrider fired a cannon shell at him, and he felt it cut the air close to his right shoulder, missing him by a centimeter. If it had hit him, he'd be jelly now.

The outrider was roaring past him on the left;

a Psycho Midget on its nearest running board was holding on to a rung, firing a submachine gun at him. But it was awkward to shoot from a bumping, speeding outrider, and the bullets went wide.

Roland leapt, jumping onto the back of the passing outrider, hitting it with tremendous impact—the outrider hitting him, as it raced along, more than he was hitting it—so that the air was knocked out of him. He scrabbled at the back of the outrider's seats, got a grip on one, looked up to see a Midget pointing a submachine gun at his head, the Psycho Midget giggling as he prepared to kill him.

Then the outrider hit a rock in the rugged terrain, jolted hard, and Roland was flung into the air, the bullets cutting past just under him. He fell heavily, tumbling, gasping for breath, ending up on his back in a cloud of dust and exhaust smoke.

Dazed, he lay there coughing, wiping dust from his eyes. He heard the outriders rolling up, one to the left, one to the right, skidding to a stop.

This is it . . .

He sat up, breathing hard, aching, and forced himself to his feet. He was going to die fighting, standing up, anyway. Might take a few of these bastards with him.

"Hold your fire!" A woman's voice. Gynella.

The smoke and dust drifted away, and he saw her climbing out of a newly arriving outrider. She wore her finery this time; breastplate, bodice, metallic microskirt, high boots, red cape. She stalked toward him, that "special meat cutter" in her right hand, her eyes burning. He could see the romance was over. She had every intention of killing him.

Trying to sweet-talk her would be too much like begging. And he knew it wouldn't work.

Roland shrugged. Today was a good day to die—as good as any.

Behind her came the compact little guy with the epaulets, Smartun, carrying a large shotgun. This time Smartun looked almost happy.

Gynella raised the serrated knife, its micro-motion edge blurring.

"First thing I'm going to cut off," she said, "is your—"

She broke off, staring past him.

Roland turned and saw Brick, standing all alone, on top of a ten-meter-high, pyramid-shaped outcropping of rock. Brick had a rocket launcher in his hands. And he was grinning. "Brick's here, bitch—bringing the pain!"

And he fired the rocket launcher at Gynella.

Shit, Roland thought, throwing himself flat and almost getting nailed by the rocket, *would it have killed him to say, "Look out, Roland"?*

Gynella and Smartun leapt to the side as the rocket slashed the air overhead and exploded on the outrider to Roland's left. The fireball singed off his eyebrows and seared the back of his neck.

Roland didn't wait for the smoke to clear—he jumped to his feet and ran through the smoke, jumped over the burning scrap metal of the outrider, landed on a dead Psycho, kept going, pounding to the left as fast as he could run, to try to get behind that outcropping.

"Gimme a damn gun!" he yelled at Mordecai, who was waiting on the other side of the outcropping with two guns in his hand. Mordecai had the sniper rifle in one hand, a Hyperion combat rifle in the other. He tossed the rifle at Roland, who caught it and checked the load. Ready to fire.

"Look what I took off some bandits, about three klicks back," Mordecai said, and he kicked a box of grenades on the ground between them.

Brick was firing another round at the outriders, but he was being pounded by rifle fire and knocked back off the rock, to fall heavily onto his back. "Ouch!"

His shield had held up under the gunfire, but it was flickering now. Not much left in it.

Roland had the rifle slung over one shoulder and was filling his hands with grenades as an outrider came roaring up to the outcropping, firing its machine gun. The bullets glanced off a boulder as Roland pitched a grenade with adrenaline-sharpened precision right into the lap of the outrider's driver. The Psycho yelled hoarsely—then the grenade blew, and the outrider spun out, overturned, crushing its outriding Psycho Midgets.

Something fell at Roland's feet—the driver's smoking vault mask, blown through the air to him.

Roland put the vault mask on, turned to Mordecai. "Don't shoot me—it's me behind this thing!" Mordecai was up on a boulder firing over a shoulder of the outcropping, picking off Psychos with his sniper rifle.

Roland was tossing grenades over the top of the outcropping. Grenades exploded; Psychos screamed.

Brick was up, dusting himself off, ignoring the blood coming out of his nose, and walking over to a boulder about three times the size of his head. He picked it up, hefted it, and waited till an outrider swung into view, the bandit racing toward him. He tossed the big rock from hand to hand, then sent it flying, underhand, right toward the cannon turret on the outrider, striking its muzzle just as it fired. The cannon blew the boulder up at point-blank range, turning it into shrapnel and turning the blast back on the outrider, which spun, crunching into the side of the outcropping, the sudden stop sending a Midget flying from it as if propelled from one of their catapults. The Midget flew straight at the surprised Brick, smashing into him so that he was knocked onto his rear. The bloodied Midget scratched at Brick's face. Swelling with rage, Brick twisted the small Psycho's head, snapping its neck. He tossed the body angrily aside. He was trembling, Roland saw, going into his berserker state.

Brick stood up, howled like a rabid beast, and ran thunderingly around the outcropping, out of Roland's line of sight. Almost immediately, Gynellan soldiers began to shriek in fear.

Roland shook his head, unslung the rifle, and fired it at an approaching outrider; he blew off a wheel so that it spun out and stopped against a thicket of the cactus-like growths. Then the three Psychos jumped out of the immobilized outrider and charged toward Roland, howling the usual threats. "You gonna squeal before we cook ya? Nobody shoots my buddies but me!"

Two of them were waving hatchets over their head; one was readying hand grenades.

Roland dropped to one knee, aimed carefully, and fired, hitting the hand grenades in the Psycho's hand. They exploded, and so did the Psycho; the other two went down, one popped by a head shot from Roland, the other shot by Mordecai from his perch on the rock.

Roland decided he'd better back Brick up. Crouching, gun in hand, he jogged around the big outcropping—and stopped dead. Brick was standing up to his waist in a pile of crimson-splashed dead men, frowning. The dead Psychos were twisted like wrung-out rags; some had their faces punched in all the way to the backs of their skulls. And Brick's arms were red, past the elbows, with gore.

"Is that all there is?" Brick muttered, disappointed. "All done?"

Roland looked around. "Seems like. Might be more coming down from the—wait, where's Gynella?" He removed the vault mask—a failed disguise anyway.

"Here!" She stepped out from behind the burning wreckage of an overturned outrider. She had a shotgun in her hands. "You still don't have a shield, Roland," she said, smiling nastily, raising the gun.

Brick started toward her—and tripped on cadavers, falling on his face in the ravaged bodies, cursing, badly entangled.

Last Roland knew, Mordecai was on the other side of the outcropping of rock, without a shot at Gynella. Roland was wondering which way to jump, when an outrider gunned into the clearing, pulled up, and Daphne climbed out.

Gynella stared at her. "You!"

Daphne kept the outrider between her and Gynella. "You put down that shotgun, I'll take you on blade-to-blade, you megalomaniacal skank! I'm tired of looking over my shoulder for you."

Smartun stepped into view, behind Gynella. "Don't do it, my Goddess. Please . . ."

"Shut up," Gynella said harshly. She dropped the shotgun and her shield. "You drop your weapon, Smartun. I don't want you interfering. I want to slice this bitch apart."

She flourished her "meat cutter"; it hummed hungrily.

Daphne had no shield. She drew a long dagger from her boot and flicked it between her fingers, from one to the next and back, so it twinkled in the sunlight. Then she smiled crookedly and said, "Bring it!"

Brick was up now, watching. Roland moved a little closer, thinking to take out Smartun if he had to. From there he could see Mordecai up on the rock. But Mordecai had lowered his gun. He knew Daphne wouldn't forgive him if he interfered.

The instant Daphne came around to the other side of the outrider, Gynella rushed her—head down, arms extended, blade gleaming. The woman was fast, all right, Roland thought; her arm was a blur as she whipped the knife at Daphne's face.

Daphne just ducked, and her body seemed to ripple, in a move Roland had never seen before, as if she were sidling to her right in a dance move, but faster than the eye could follow, and as she went she drew her blade across Gynella's left jawbone, cutting it deeply.

She could have cut her throat if she'd wanted to, Roland realized.

Gynella yelled in hurt and fury, spun around, her knife flashing toward Daphne—but Daphne wasn't there, making that rippling motion with her body again, the blade cutting a bit of her leather jacket but not reaching the skin.

She stepped back, grinned mockingly, and crooked her finger at Gynella.

The General Goddess's eyes narrowed. She put one shaking hand to her face and drew it back, looked at the blood on her fingertips. "You bitch. You fucking *bitch*!"

And Gynella charged her. Daphne ducked easily under the knife slash and body-slammed Gynella's legs. She rolled clear as Gynella fell heavily facedown and made a gasping sound. Blood trickled from the corner of her mouth. She'd fallen on her own knife, which protruded from her back. It had bisected her spine.

Roland heard someone give a heartfelt, piteous cry, and he looked at Smartun, saw him covering his eyes, weeping.

"No . . . no . . ." Smartun sobbed.

Gynella rolled over and pulled the knife free—it had cut right through her breastbone, cut deep. She tried to get up, but her legs didn't work anymore.

She coughed. Blood spattered over her lips.

Roland had to look away. His feelings were more mixed than he'd thought. He had been kissing those lips just last night.

"Finish her!" Mordecai shouted. "Get it done, Daphne!"

Daphne was shaking her head. "I didn't know whose old man I was killing that night. If I had, I might have said no to the job. You deserve respect. You're crazy as any one of your soldiers. But you deserve respect."

"No . . . a loser . . ." Gynella coughed blood. "Gets no . . ." She choked.

Smartun stumbled over to her, weeping, fell to the ground beside her. "I've been saving something for us, my darling," he said huskily, taking a large red grenade from his coat. A Marcus-brand fire greanade. "In case. So that we could be together. My love . . ."

Roland stepped back, out of the blast zone.

Smartun pulled the pin. The grenade exploded, splashing them both in liquid fire, creating a pyre, where they burned, writhing, dying, Smartun clutching at his Goddess . . .

TWENTY-FOUR

They had just reached the road that led west, to the mountains. Roland in the outrunner with Brick and Mordecai and Daphne in the outrider turned onto the road, and then Brick signaled for a stop. Roland pulled up, and the outrider pulled up beside them.

"What's going on now?" Daphne asked impatiently.

Brick climbed down from the turret. "There's a truck coming," he said, pointing to the west. "I'm going to see if I can make 'em give me a ride. I'm going back to Jawbone. All this time, talk of riches, nothing turns up—lotta bullshit. I'm sick of you pussies. Going my own way."

He turned toward the oncoming truck, then turned suddenly back to Roland. "Wait—I just remembered. I haven't killed you yet. You screwed up my fight. Took away my kill."

Roland sighed. "Oh, yeah, right. True, you haven't. You overlooked that. Um, look, you sure you have to do it now? I'm going to come back to Jawbone on the way to Fyrestone. Or . . . someplace. You'll see me. Can't you kill me then? I mean, Daphne here's your friend, right? You want her to be able to get rich with me, right? I've got to take her there."

Brick rubbed his chin. "Well . . . I guess I can kill you later. Sure. Okay. But remind me when I see you, okay?"

"Hm? Oh, sure, sure. I'll do that."

The truck rumbled up and slowed, because the outrunner and outrider were in its way. Roland squinted at it, rubbed his eyes, and looked closer. Was it?

It was. The wizened little man sitting in the passenger side of the self-driving truck was Skelton Dabbits.

"Who's that?" Mordecai asked.

"The guy who sold me the map to the crystalisks."

The truck pulled up. "Please remove the obstructing vehicles from the road," said the robotic truck in a pleasant male voice.

"Hold on, truck," Roland said, walking around to the passenger side of the truck cab. "Dabbits! What the hell? You said you were going off-planet. What're you doing here?"

Roland already had a suspicion.

"Oh, well, fancy meeting you here!" said Dabbits reedily. "Ah, are you on your way to . . . ?"

"I was! What's in the back of that truck?"

"Oh, that truck? Back there? Well. Crystalisks. And Eridium crystals. I gotta couple of live crystalisks. They roll in a ball, see, and if you know what to do, with a steel-mesh net, why then . . . Is something wrong?"

"You little weasel. You sold me the map, and then you went ahead of me to get the stuff yourself!"

"It's not my fault you dawdled all over the planet. I heard stories. I figured Gynella would kill you. And, uh, I met a partner in Fyrestone, had a truck it fixed up itself from a junk pile—"

"*Itself?*"

"Yeah, it's a Claptrap. It's riding in the back. Anyway, I heard that Gynella had some kinda bad reversal in a canyon, withdrew her forces to the Footstool, so we figured we'd head on out to the mountains, since the way was clear."

"Cleared by me!"

"Ah, yes. And thank you for that! Well. Word was you were a goner, so off we went, and there's an old mining road, goes real smooth to the caves. Once you know the trick, not that hard to catch crystalisks . . ."

Roland shook his head. "How many are left up there?"

"There? Well. Not many. That is to say . . . none. There. That I know of. We got a ton of Eridium out of their den and more from the dead ones I blasted with my—Say, have a look, see for yourself!"

Roland walked glumly to the back of the truck, climbed up onto the open trailer, and lifted the canvas covering. Inside he saw at least a ton of piled-up Eridium and two crystalisks, strange tripod creatures, on three legs, semireptilian things covered in crystals, rolled up into balls within steel mesh. Between them, humming to itself, was a Claptrap.

"Hi!" said the Claptrap. "Wanna buy some Eridium? Give you a good price!"

"Shut the hell up," Roland told it. He jumped down off the back and walked up to the trucks's cab. "What about the money I paid you, Dabbits?"

"That map was good! You can't blame me if you ran all over the west, getting involved in ridiculous fights that had nothing to do with your mission!"

"He's got a point!" Daphne called.

Roland winced. He really ought to kill the little guy, take the booty. But . . . he couldn't bring himself to do it. "Oh, just get the hell out of here. I got another payday coming anyhow."

"Please remove the obstructing vehicles."

"All right, truck, all right, you shut the hell up too."

He stalked over to the outrunner, and the

vehicles were soon moved out of the way. "You may as well ride with us, Brick," Roland said, as the truck rumbled away and down the road to the west. "If you want to. We'll get there faster. And you can kill me faster."

"No hurry on that," Brick said, yawning. "You drive, I'm gonna take a nap."

"Something else I gotta do."

He hadn't wanted to contact Feldsrum—he didn't trust him. He preferred finishing his mission. But now there was no mission, and this was the only payday he was going to get this trip.

He took the contact box from his pocket and pressed the stud. "Feldsrum, you there?"

A crackling hesitation, and then, "Have you got it done?"

"She's dead. Maybe two hours ago. You didn't see it?"

"Hard to see what was going on, so much smoke. But we had a report that she was dead. The army's disbanding, I heard, now that she's dead. Couple of them survived, called it in to somebody named Skenk. I guess they're fighting for the headquarters up there, or wandering off . . ."

"So, there's your proof. You want to go down and look at her body, have at it. But there's not much left. Burned to a crisp."

"That fits with the call we intercepted. And Vialle?"

"Dead. Really, thoroughly dead."

"Good job! You're a reliable man. Stay where you are . . . we're coming to you."

"That's the Dahl Corporation, coming down here?" Daphne asked. "If they recognize me . . ."

"Even if they don't," Mordecai said, "I don't trust them, Roland. Feldsrum was trying to keep this whole thing quiet. When Dahl security wants to keep something quiet, you know how they do it, right?"

Roland nodded. "Yeah. It's . . . risky. But he owes us money. I'll share with all of you. Brick too. Maybe with the four of us they won't make a move."

Daphne shook her head. "Their security orbiters have a big cannon, comes out of the underside. Wait—give me that contact box. I know that model. I've got an idea . . ."

It took a good forty-five minutes, but at last the orbiter descended on a cushion of pulsing energy, landing struts extended, columnar body throwing off the afternoon light.

It landed on the road, thirty meters from them. Soon the hatch opened, the ramp was extruded, and Roland and Mordecai strode up to meet Feldsrum and his armored specialists.

Feldsrum and his bodyguards descended the ramp. They looked at the three men, seeing Brick on the turret gun of the outrunner. Brick gave them a look, with that weapon under his hands, that spoke clearly enough: *Don't try anything.*

They didn't look at Daphne—because she was nowhere to be seen.

Feldsrum was carrying a metal suitcase in his right hand. He walked calmly up to Roland and set the suitcase down.

"There it is. You can count it."

Roland knelt, opened the case. It was filled with Pandoran money.

"We have a great deal of Pandoran money on the ship," Feldsrum said. "We don't really have a lot of use for it. Glad to get rid of it. You can always change it in Fyrestone on your way off-planet."

Roland nodded. "Good enough."

He closed the suitcase, and though he noticed movement behind the specialists, Daphne slipping into their orbiter with the expert stealth of an assassin, he was careful not to look directly at her.

He stood up and handed the suitcase to Mordecai.

"Here's my question for you," Roland said, stalling. "Can we trust you?"

Feldsrum raised his eyebrows. "What do you mean? I've just paid you."

"I hear you have a big fat weapon on that orbiter. And I hear you don't like to leave witnesses when you make a mess."

Feldsrum laughed dismissively. "Please! What

absurd paranoia. You're perfectly safe. I'm sure we may want to employ you again. Why waste a valuable resource?"

Roland snorted. "You sure of that?"

"Don't worry. We must be going now. Do tell your big friend on the turret not to get nervous with that gun. I'd hate for my men to have to kill him."

"I'd hate to see them try. Anyway—" He had noted Daphne slipping out of the orbiter's hatch and dropping to the ground.

One of the specialists turned, hearing a sound, to look toward the orbiter. Seeing nothing, he turned to watch Roland.

"Anyway," Roland went on, "have a good trip."

Feldsrum smiled coldly. "Ah. You too."

He turned, and with his bodyguards backing up, not taking their eyes off the three mercenaries, they returned to the orbiter.

Roland and Mordecai moved back, away from the orbiter, and it lifted off on a tail of shimmer.

It rose and continued to rise . . .

Daphne stepped from the brush, a small remote control in her hand. "I knew I'd find one of these on board. They hook up with those contact boxes beautifully." She smiled. "Professional expertise."

"Look!" Mordecai said, pointing.

The orbiter had stopped rising. Something was extruding from the bottom of the vehicle. The unmistakable snout of a rupture cannon. The shell would blow up everything for a quarter-kilometer around, once it hit the ground.

It was pointed at Roland and his friends.

Daphne pointed the remote control at the or-biter—and it exploded in a violent and blinding purple flash, almost vaporized. Only bits of it fell to the ground, like hail.

"Wow," Mordecai said admiringly. "What a girl. Just . . . the best."

Daphne shrugged modestly. "Easy enough to wire the box to a grenade, attach the grenade to one of the rupture shells. Once I had the transmission code for the box . . . easy enough to activate it. It's nothing really. Can we count the money now?"

SUNSET THE NEXT DAY . . .

Outside of Jawbone, they prepared to go their separate ways. Brick had stuffed his vest with cash and had let the others have the vehicles. Daphne and Mordecai would take the outrider, Roland the outrunner. "I'm gonna walk into town from here," Brick said. "I'm sick of being on those machines. Want to use some muscles."

The money was pretty good. Not enough yet, though, Roland thought, to make a new start on some other planet.

Or maybe that was just an excuse. Maybe he

knew, somehow . . . he could never leave this planet. He was damaged by the Pandora; poisoned by it. Probably, he thought gloomily, it wasn't safe for people on a civilized planet, with him around.

Maybe someday he'd make it to Xanthus. Or maybe he'd die right here. On Pandora.

That seemed more likely somehow.

Since the planet was one big cemetery, it was almost as if he was already buried.

As Roland was checking the weapons on the outrunner, he noticed Brick giving him a peculiar squint-eyed look. "Wait," Brick said. "Wasn't there something I asked you to remind me about, Roland? What was it?"

"Oh . . . that. Actually—I forget."

"Well, when you remember, hunt me up."

"Sure, I'll do that." He didn't believe for a moment that Brick had really forgotten, any more than he had.

Brick nodded to him and turned, walked up the dusty road, past the cemetery, into the town.

"So . . ." Mordecai was saying, putting his arms around Daphne. "You going with me?"

Bloodwing, perched on Mordecai's shoulder, seemed to roll its eyes at this.

Daphne nodded. "Thought I would. Might stick with you for a while. Until you screw up."

"And then?"

"Then . . ." She shrugged. "Might have to kill you."

Mordecai sighed. "You hear that, Roland? What a babe. I'm crazy about her."

They waved at Roland, got into the outrider, and drove off—Bloodwing jumping up to flap overhead—toward New Haven.

Roland chuckled and shook his head. *Mordecai*.

He got into the outrunner and drove into Jawbone. He saw Brick arguing with a gun dealer at a hut.

He didn't wave.

He went to the other side of town, where the Bloodrust settlers were. Might as well help them retake their town. Hell, it was something to do.

A man didn't feel right without a mission.

EPILOGUE

Marcus Finishes a Tale

The woman in the back of the stranded bus was laughing.

"What's so funny?" Marcus asked.

It was almost dawn outside.

"The part about that little rat stealing the Eridium under Roland's nose. And he lets him go. Hard on the outside, soft on the inside."

Marcus smiled. "Maybe."

"He go back to Bloodrust Corners?"

"He and the settlers headed back there. They found only a dozen Psychos occupying the place, the imbeciles fighting among themselves anyway, what with their General Goddess dead. Roland led the charge, and they killed the lot in half an hour."

She shook her head. "What a chump he is."

"That's one way to think of it."

"Look!" She had ducked her head to peer out the window.

There were two Psychos charging toward the bus.

"Okay, this is it, what we've been waiting all night for. Let's do this."

They picked up their weapons, and with Marcus leading the way, crouching as they went to avoid bullets from the window, they made their way to the front and out the door—just as the Psychos came rushing around the corner, one of them aiming a rocket launcher . . .

Which exploded in his hands—struck by a shell that sped in from the road.

Four outrunners were charging up, all of them firing their turrets at the Psychos. In the lead vehicle was Scooter, hooting and waving.

"Catch a ride!" he shouted, pulling up.

Marcus looked at the blasted wreckage of the two Psychos, the dead bodies steaming in the dawn coolness. "Yeah, Scooter, we could use a ride."

Marcus turned to the woman he'd spent the night with . . . spent all too chastely.

"Looks like your ride's here. I'm staying to repair my bus."

She nodded and went to get her luggage. When she came back out, she walked over to Marcus and said, "You're pretty good in a fight, for an old, fat guy."

"Thanks—I think."

"And thanks for the story. All that stuff true? I mean, how could it be, really?"

"Of course it's true. Hey, Scooter!"

Scooter came beaming over to them. "Hoo-ee, who's this pretty lady!"

"None of your business," she said mildly,

"Everything's my business, pretty lady! I'll find out sooner or later. Now if you'd take off those goggles . . ."

The woman shrugged and pushed her goggles back on her head.

And Marcus knew her. "Lilith!"

"Oh, yeah. I think we have met before, haven't we?"

"Scooter," Marcus said, "you remember how Roland and Mordecai and Daphne and Brick took on the General Goddess and stopped her taking over the planet?"

"Sure I do! Well, I know they were involved in that. But everything else I know about it, why . . . it came from you!"

Lilith snorted. "So it might be true. Or it might not. For instance . . ." She looked at Marcus. "The part about that Smartun guy using your brand of fire grenade to incinerate him and his lady love. Was that true or just product placement?"

"Oh, well, a little of both. I've got some fine fire grenades to sell you, and other weapons. Just come by the shop and—"

"Never mind. I'll see you later."

He watched her walk away. Which was a pleasant thing to do.

"Hey, Lilith!" he called after her, on impulse. "Where you going now?"

"Now? To find Roland. I've got something to settle with him."

Lilith smiled secretively.

And then she vanished from sight. She'd gone invisible—one of her many talents—just for a moment . . .

. . . She reappeared, grinning. "But chances are," she said as she turned to walk away again, "he won't see me coming."

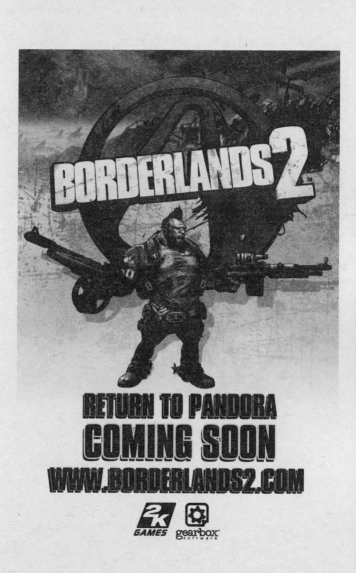